Books By
Misha McKenzie

Burke Witches
Aria's Law
Anna's Knight
Evan's Pride
Ethan's Honor

The Magic of the Heart Series
Magic Found
Magic Hidden
Magic Lost
Magic Revealed

Single Titles
RavenStorm Witches

ETHAN'S HONOR
BURKE WITCHES

MISHA MCKENZIE

ICASM PRESS
SAVANNAH

Published by Icasm Publishing LLC
5710 Ogeechee Rd. Suite 200 #278, Savannah, GA 31405
www.icasmpress.com

Library of Congress Cataloging-in-Publication Data

McKenzie, Misha
Ethan's Honor / Misha McKenzie
     p. cm.

ISBN-13:978-1-942318-41-5 (Trade Print)
ISBN-13:978-1-942318-42-2 (eBook)
I. Title

Printed and bound in the United States of America

10 9 8 7 6 5 4 3 2 1

BURKE'S PROPHECY

"Witches born—two light, two dark

Each possessing an element's mark

Air and Water by the brightness of day

Earth and Fire by the moon's subtle ray

These signs will one day come to bear

And evil kept caged will wake and prepare

As every year passes the bindings grow weak

While the force within strengthens and seeks

Four babies born as foretold by this seer

They'll have until their twenty-fifth year

To mature, to learn, to find their right path

For it's up to them to end its wrath

Their destined arrival is the key

Personal sacrifice will set them free

On the anniversary of their birth

Four into one defeats the devil unearthed."

1

Ethan sat on the soft green lawn—his long legs folded in front of him. He idly picked at the freshly mowed grass. Taking a deep breath, he got on with what he'd come here to do.

"I'm sorry I haven't come." His dark eyes slowly lifted to settle on the granite headstone before him. His gaze landed on the name etched there, *Honor Lee Andrews.* "I haven't been as strong as I should have been," he admitted to her, "and I couldn't face you."

Reaching out, Ethan pulled at the longer blades the groundskeeper had missed around the base. "I tried to go on like you would have wanted…and I think I was actually doing it." His attention switched to the debris in his hands. "Until…" he laughed derisively. "Yeah, until. Until I fucked up. Until Edrick Noor used my love for you to manipulate me. Until I almost cost my family everything. Until I hated myself and knew you'd hate me too if you knew what I'd done.

"Ugh. God, sweetheart, it's been impossible without you." Ethan dropped the clippings, scrubbed his hands over his face and down his bristly cheeks. Feeling the scruffy stubble, he remembered how Honor had always run her hands over it, loving how it tickled her palms.

"Four years. It seems a lifetime since I last saw you, last touched you. Last kissed you." Ethan's heart gave a painful thump. "Everywhere I go, I'm reminded of you. I think I see you or hear you, but when I turn, you're not there. You'll never be there again."

His eyes burned but he blinked the tears away. "When this is all over, when Noor is defeated—and he will be, there's no doubt about that—maybe I'll take off for a while. Get out of here. Away from all the memories."

Movement caught Ethan's attention. He turned his head to see a young couple getting out of their car. Probably going to visit a loved one.

"And far away from all the new love floating around. All my siblings have someone now. They're building lives together, making families. Aria and Seth. Anna and Joe with little Jacob." He laughed again, but this time he meant it. "You'd like Jacob. He's a great little kid. And he's going to have company soon. Evan and Kyra are having a baby. Probably next June. They're sure it's going to be a girl. They're all so happy. So in love. I remember what that feels like. It hurts to know I'll never have it again."

He lifted a hand as if to stop her from arguing. "And before you say I will, even if I do find someone, it won't come half as close to what I felt with you. What I *still* feel for you. You were my one, Honor. The person I was supposed to spend the rest of my life with. But I can't. You were ripped away from me in the worst way." Ethan shook his head and took a breath to ease some of the pain.

"I'm so sorry I wasn't able to get to you that night. I tried. I just hope you didn't feel anything. I hope the smoke took you before the rest ever touched you. I hope wherever you are, you and your parents are happy."

Ethan looked around and noticed how late in the afternoon it had gotten. "I'd better go. I won't stay away so long next time." He gained his feet, kissed his fingers, and laid them over her name. "I love you, sweetheart."

He turned and walked away from the only woman he'd ever

loved. Once in his car, he sat to gather himself again. It was always hard coming here, but once he'd been, he always felt better for having come.

Starting the engine, Ethan pulled out and drove for home. The apartment he'd found near downtown Daytona was small and cheap. It worked great for him. He could cover the rent with the odd jobs he took.

He liked to work with his hands and had learned how to do just about anything. If he didn't know, he'd just look it up online. There were videos out there for everything. Most of the work he did was by word-of-mouth. And most of his clients were single women and the elderly.

Ethan guessed over time he'd become one of those rent-a-husbands—doing whatever needed doing for people who couldn't do it themselves. It usually kept him pretty busy, but with all this Noor crap going on over the last few months, he'd taken kind of a hiatus. He really needed to get back to it. Between that and the workout regimen Joe had him on, he shouldn't have too much time to think about how much he missed Honor.

As he turned onto his street, he glanced up and thought he saw a quick flash of fiery auburn hair. It always caught him off guard to see that particular color. Honor's hair had been that exact shade. He'd kidded her that while he may wield fire, she was the one who'd tamed it. Her hair had been amazing and he'd loved it. Long and thick and soft as silk.

As he maneuvered through traffic, Ethan kept an eye on the woman. Her back was to him as she walked along the sidewalk in the same direction he was driving. The nearer he drew to her, the harder his heart beat.

Everything about her made him think of Honor. He almost wished he'd never caught sight of her as the pain of losing her washed over him anew. But now that he had, he couldn't take his eyes off of her. He knew in his head it couldn't be her.

But in his heart, he needed to see her face—just to be sure. One quick glance would put it all to rest again.

As he passed her, Ethan craned his neck around.

And the breath stopped in his lungs. That face. It was hers. It was Honor.

So as not to roll past her, he slowed even more. Almost to the point that he'd come to a complete stop in the middle of the road.

At the same time Ethan turned to keep her in sight, the vehicle behind him blasted their horn. His gaze shot up to the mirror to see some guy's angry face yelling at him. The implication was clear even if he couldn't hear the words. *Get your head out of your ass and move it!*

With no other choice, Ethan accelerated. But he wasn't going far. The lot to his building was just off Main Street up ahead, so he'd pull in there and pursue her on foot. He had to find her. After four years without her, he needed to see her up close, to touch her face, to feel with his own hands that she was real.

One last look to track her movements, and he turned and swung into his usual spot. Within moments he was hurrying back out to the sidewalk. His dark gaze searched the faces coming at him, but none of them were hers. He spun around, thinking she'd moved faster than he'd anticipated and she'd already bypassed him.

But he didn't see that blazing hair anywhere.

As the crowd flowed around him, Ethan turned in circles looking for where she could have gone.

At a run, he checked all the neighboring shops and buildings, but she was nowhere to be found.

She'd disappeared.

~~~

It was after midnight when Ethan walked into his apartment.
~~~

He hadn't been able to tear himself away from where he'd last seen her. No matter how many times he'd told himself that her being there was impossible, he'd stayed and searched. He'd walked from one end of town to the other, and blocks in every direction checking every store, every restaurant, every alley.

Even after all the shops had closed, he'd stayed, searching desperately for just one more glimpse of her. Something, *anything*, to prove he wasn't crazy.

But of course, he'd found nothing.

Going to the fridge, he grabbed a beer and twisted off the cap. He drank it as he walked back into the living area. He sat on the well-worn second- or third-hand couch and tried to figure out what the hell had happened.

Had he imagined her? Had she even been there at all? Had it only been a woman who resembled her, and he'd filled in the rest? He'd just come from her grave—could his mind have played a trick on him?

Or was Noor fucking with him again?

That option made the most sense. But after the beating they'd put on Noor during their last encounter, Ethan wouldn't have thought he'd be up to messing around in anyone's head just yet. Apparently, he was.

But why this ploy again? Maybe the fact that Ethan was awake and aware made the game more interesting. Last time, Noor had only tormented him with Honor in his sleep, showing him what their life could have been if she'd not died in that fire.

Wanting to hoard that time with her for as long as he could, Ethan had kept the dreams from his family. He'd rationalized it by telling himself that none of them had lost anyone they'd loved. They didn't know the ripping agony that never went away. Or the weight on his heart that made it all but impossible to get out of bed in the morning. Or of those few precious heartbeats of time upon waking when, just for a moment, he could forget.

And then the crushing horror of remembering her tragic death all over again. Only to have it repeated the following day.

And the day after that.

That's what he'd lived with for four years. So when he'd started seeing Honor in his dreams, he'd known they were different—so rich and full of bright colors, with sharp, clean edges—an entirely different class of dreams. But he just hadn't cared. He'd welcomed them ardently and had felt alive again. Loved again. Happy again.

It hadn't taken him long to realize who, or what, was behind the illusions. Their big bad—Noor. When Aria had come home at the beginning of all this and asked if they'd been experiencing anything strange, Ethan had only admitted to having dreams. He couldn't tell them what was happening, because by that point, seeing her had become an addiction. And Noor was his dealer. And, as with all things, it hadn't come free. Though he'd never been asked outright, Ethan was fairly certain he was supposed to have looked the other way when Noor had attempted to kidnap Jacob, Anna and Joe's adopted son.

Of course Ethan hadn't, and in ensuring his nephew's escape, he'd been captured in his place. Noor and his men had let him know, in no uncertain terms, that he was going to regret the decision to get in their way. They'd beaten him to within an inch of his life before his family could show up to rescue him.

It was then that Noor had taken great pleasure in telling his siblings what he'd been doing. And of Ethan's willingness to let it continue. When they'd found out about his betrayal, they'd been angry and disappointed in him. As a result, a rift had developed between him and his twin for the first time in their lives. If Ethan hadn't already been in bad shape, he was sure his brother would have torn him apart for what he'd allowed to happen. And for all that he'd risked.

Thankfully, in the following weeks, they'd been able to talk and work through it. They were on solid footing again.

That didn't stop the guilt Ethan still felt at having deceived everyone, though. The loss of their respect and trust, coupled with their silent disapproval, had cut him deeper than if they'd raged at him.

Ethan couldn't really blame them. He should have told them what was going on and shared his pain with those who loved him most. They would have helped him to get through it, just as they'd done the first time. But he'd withdrawn, turning his back on his real life of loss, instead choosing to cling to his fabricated lie with Honor, just to have that extra time with the one he'd always loved.

Is that what was happening now? Was Noor back up to his tricks? Was he trying to put them at odds again? They were getting closer to the day they'd face off against each other for the last time. If Noor could break the bond between the four Burke siblings and negate their power to stop him, his cage door would swing open come February, and he'd be free.

Ethan took another swig of his beer and made the only decision he could.

"Evan?" Ethan used the telepathic link he shared with his quad-mates. But he didn't realize it was almost one in the morning until Evan's sleepy voice answered.

"This had better be an emergency."

"Oh, shit, I'm sorry. I didn't notice the time." He paused. *"I guess it can wait."*

Evan must have sensed the disquiet in Ethan's mind.

"No, it's fine. Tell me what's got you worried."

Ethan closed his eyes and leaned his head back on the couch. He took a breath and let the words fall. *"I thought I saw Honor today."*

"Saw her how?" Evan's question was cautious.

"Not in my dreams. I was wide awake this time," Ethan clarified. *"I'd just come from the cemetery. I was driving home and I saw her walking down the sidewalk in town."*

Evan was silent for a moment. *"Could it be she was on your mind and you caught a glimpse of someone who looked like her?"*

"That's what I thought at first too." Ethan sat forward and rubbed his eyes. *"But it was her face, Evan."* Anxious and unsettled, he had to get up and move. *"It was the same hair, the same nose, the same mouth. The same everything."*

"Did you talk to her?"

"No." Ethan studied the view out the window and slid his hands into his pockets. *"By the time I'd parked and went back to where I'd seen her, she was gone."*

Before Evan could reply, Ethan went on. *"And before you say it, I know she's dead. So, the only logical explanation must be that Noor is trying to get into my head again. Only this time, he's provoking me while I'm awake."*

"And you're sure it wasn't a case of mistaken identity?"

"It was her—I'm sure of it. She was just as I remember." Ethan returned to the couch. With his elbows braced on his knees, he dropped his head into his hands. *"I can't go through this again, Evan. I'm still trying to find my balance from losing her the second time. I can't have her dangled in front of me everywhere I look, just to give that asshole his jollies."*

"You'll get through this, Ethan. We'll figure it out and put a stop to it," Evan promised. *"There has to be a way to block him from your mind. In the meantime, try to get some sleep. We'll talk more tomorrow."*

"Yeah. Okay."

Ethan knew sleep wasn't in his near future, but he stripped out of his clothes and lay down anyway. And, surprisingly enough, fell asleep.

~~~

The next morning, he felt a little better—more rested and
~~~

his mind was clear. So clear in fact, he was able to see the incident from yesterday for what it was.

Noor taking another shot at him.

Well, he wouldn't give the bastard the satisfaction of losing it again and upsetting his family. Honor was dead. As much as that fact killed him, there was nothing he could do to change it. No amount of wishing or dreaming was going to miraculously bring her back.

He needed to get his shit together. Right now. Today.

No more living in the past. Starting at this moment, Ethan would begin a new way of life. First order of business was to shore up his defenses. No more unauthorized access to his mind. And he'd buckle down and train for the fight that was coming in three short months.

Joe had developed a training program for him, but he hadn't been as faithful to working out as he should. That would change today. They had a lot of work to do, and time was moving fast. They were closing in on Thanksgiving already. So that left until the end of February to bring all four of their elements together and send Edrick Noor straight to hell where he would remain for eternity.

Motivated, Ethan rolled out of bed. Dressed in only navy blue boxer-briefs, he padded barefoot to the bathroom.

Once personal business was taken care of, he brushed his teeth before finger-combing his shoulder-length black hair. Pushing it back and away from his striking face, he studied his reflection in the mirror.

A few days of beard growth covered the majority of his jaw. It wasn't full-on mountain-man style, but it wasn't a five o'clock shadow either. Where Evan, his identical twin, usually kept clean-shaven—a concession to his job as a police detective—Ethan sported stubble. He scratched at it now and thought it could probably use a trim.

His gaze traveled on.

Eyes as black as his hair stared back at him. No matter how closely he looked, the pupil just blended into the iris. A little weird to some, but it marked him as one of the four.

The four destined to battle a great evil bent on their complete destruction.

He grimaced slightly. *Lucky us.*

The prophecy that spoke of their arrival had been very specific. 'Witches born. Two light. Two dark.' Their mother had given birth to quadruplets. Two sets of identical twins. Where he and Evan were dark, their sisters Aria and Anna were light. Pale blonde hair, frosty blue eyes, fair skin.

It went on to say that each would possess an elemental mark. Ethan's attention dropped to his bare chest where his birthmark rested. Most that saw it thought it was a tattoo, but Fate had marked each of the quads with a symbol representing one of the four elements.

He was fire. And on his left pec was a perfect circle about four inches in diameter. He traced it with the tip of one finger. Within that ring, flames rose and danced. He'd always marveled at the detail. It was a dark brown now, but when he called to his power, it would glow in reds and golds. Just as Evan's earth would shine in the colors of fall leaves. Aria being air, her mark would light with greens, and Anna's water was blue.

Though the locations of the symbols differed, the magic was theirs all the same to summon and control.

The rest foretold of sacrifice and bringing "four into one." They still had no clue what they'd have to sacrifice for the greater good, but as far as joining their powers, they were well on their way there.

Anna and Aria had merged the water and air they bore. And he and Evan had successfully brought fire and earth into one entity just a few weeks ago. The next step would be to meld those forces into one. Hopefully they could do that, and figure out how to use what it made to end Noor when the time came.

But no pressure.

Ethan took one last look at his six-foot-four frame in the mirror before turning and going back to his bedroom to dress.

He pulled on a pair of baggy gym shorts and a tank that had seen better days. He must have worn it when he painted his bedroom. It had a rather large hole in the side just above the hem, and it bore splotches of brown over the gray cotton. With an unconcerned shrug, he dug in his closet. He came up with a pair of running shoes and tied them on. They were actually the only part of his attire that were still in decent shape, proving just how much he'd used them.

They'd get plenty of use—starting now. Grabbing his wallet and keys, he headed out.

At just shy of seven in the morning, the fifteen-minute drive to Joe's gym was easy. When he pulled into the parking lot, only the cars of those in serious training for upcoming bouts were in the lot. Joe's SUV was also there, which meant that he hadn't left yet to take Anna and Jake to school.

Anna taught a special needs class at the same elementary where Jacob was enrolled. Being an empath gave her a deeper insight into what the kids were feeling, even if they couldn't communicate in the normal sense. She'd done wonders with all of her students and they loved her. No one knew quite how she did it, but parents and co-workers alike marveled at the difference she'd made in the lives of those children.

Her class didn't actually start until later, but since Jacob was now in first grade and started early, Joe dropped both of them off every morning and picked them up after. In the interest of safety, it was easier for Anna to go in early with their son and use that time to prepare for her own students. No one knew when Noor would make a move against them, and none of them could afford to be caught alone.

Especially Jacob.

Unbeknownst to Noor, Jacob was the son of a Burke cousin,

which gave him magical abilities. Unfortunately, he was also a descendant of Noor's, which is how he'd come to be on the psychopath's radar.

Since learning of Jacob's existence and gifts, Noor was bound and determined to add him to his ranks. And to that end, he'd already made several attempts. In one of the more brutal encounters, Jacob's birth mother had been killed, and little Jacob had seen the whole thing.

In an effort to protect him, the state had whisked Jacob away into the witness protection program, and then into foster care. After being moved several times, he'd come into Anna's class, traumatized and scared. Through her empathic powers, she'd sensed his need and had worked her magic to bring him out of his shell and then into their family. She and Joe were making a home together with the boy who'd become their son.

If Noor was active again, the entire family would need to be extra careful. Ethan made a plan to speak with Anna before she left for the day. She'd need to be on guard and vigilant.

Then he'd put it out of his mind, because Edrick Noor wasn't screwing him around again.

2

Coming to Daytona had been a mistake. Paige Harrison walked the beach and tried to figure out what to do next. She'd come with the intent of figuring out her life, but that had yet to happen. And now she could swear she was being followed.

She'd left her home in Crowley, Louisiana over a week ago. Her arrival here had been uneventful, but sometime in the last few days, she'd noticed the same car showing up wherever she went. When she could get a clear look at it, there were always the same two men in it.

Having never been to Daytona before, she had no clue as to why someone would be watching her.

She couldn't imagine that it would be because of the money. Her parents had left behind a sizeable nest-egg when they'd died—it was enough to live off of, but nothing outrageous or excessive. No one would be getting super rich, if that was their plan. Or maybe they were looking to snatch her off the street and ship her to only God-knew-where to be sold as a sex slave.

She'd watched enough videos on the internet to know a woman traveling alone always posed some level of danger. And the possibilities for what could happen were endless.

Should she go to the police? Tell them her suspicions? They probably wouldn't be able to do much about it though, because the men hadn't done anything wrong. There was no law against parking and sitting in your car.

No matter how creepy it was.

She was probably just being paranoid because of all the documentaries she'd inadvertently watched. Damn that recommended pane of videos that always sucked her in! She'd start out watching laughing babies and funny puppies, but inevitably ended up bingeing on truly scary crime stories that had her seeing nefarious acts everywhere she went.

Paige shoved her long hair back away from her face and pulled her purse strap farther up on her shoulder with a sure and determined movement. Marching over the soft sand to the walkway, she decided she wouldn't let this send her running. She'd come here for a purpose—to learn some very important answers about herself.

But she wasn't stupid either. She'd keep a cautious eye out, just in case it wasn't all her imagination.

Scanning the area as she gained the street from the beach, Paige crossed to where she'd left her car. She hadn't seen the other vehicle, but still she watched as she slid behind the wheel and locked the door. Before starting her car, she checked her phone to see that she had a message. It was a text from Gail Bechau.

Gail was her supervisor at the animal shelter where she volunteered three days a week. Since she didn't have to work—thanks to the money from her parents—Paige had decided to do what she loved most and help those less fortunate. Whether it was human or animal, she gave her care and attention to the homeless, the abused, and the forgotten.

She donated money on occasion, but mostly she was just an extra set of hands. Or a smile and a hug for those in need of one.

Gail ran the facility and had for a number of years. She was a tall, curvaceous, beautiful woman of color in her late forties. She also spoke with the heavy accent most associated with southern Louisiana.

And Paige loved her dearly.

When she'd first met Gail, she'd had a hard time understanding anything she'd said. Having been born in the Midwest, it had taken Paige a while to be able to decipher what Gail and most other people were saying. Sometimes it still got by her, but mostly she didn't have a problem anymore.

Smiling, she placed the return call.

"Hello?"

"Hi, Gail, it's me." Paige settled back in her seat.

"Hey there, girlie. How's it goin' over there in the Sunshine State?" She could hear the grin in Gail's voice.

"Not too bad. Lots of sun and sand."

"That's good, that's good. Are you finding what you need?" Gail's voice was tinged with concern.

"Not yet," she sighed. "I know the answers are here—I just don't know where to look, or even what to ask."

Paige recalled the impetus that had set her on this path of self-discovery.

She'd been having dinner with her attorney. Matt Grier not only oversaw her inheritance, but was a close family friend. Around the same age as her parents would have been, he'd stepped in when they'd died. He'd been by her side through it all and had really cared for her. Or so she'd thought.

A week before she'd come, they'd been enjoying a pleasant meal together when she'd excused herself to the ladies' room. Upon returning, she saw that he was on his cell phone. Not wanting to interrupt, Paige hung back a couple of feet behind him. Trying not to eavesdrop, she nevertheless heard him ask for an update on the status of someone named Nick Cabot, and if there were any indication he was making a move. She didn't think anything of it—the name wasn't familiar, and she just assumed he was talking business.

At first.

Until his next words had her ears perking up. "No. Pai—"

Matt stopped abruptly, glancing around before lowering his voice further, "she's still in the dark. She knows nothing of what actually happened to her or why."

The breath caught in Paige's lungs, and her brain went into overdrive. He was talking about her—her oldest and most trusted friend. What had he meant about her being in the dark?

His previous words echoed in her mind. *"She knows nothing of what actually happened to her or why."*

Did that mean Matt was lying about how she'd been injured? Why would he do that? And what else had he lied about? Nick Cabot was obviously involved somehow. Did he have something to do with what had happened to her all those years ago?

Afraid of making a scene and giving away the fact that she'd overheard, Paige spun and ran back to the bathroom. Slamming into one of the stalls, she stood leaning against the door.

Her head throbbed under the weight of betrayal. Who had Matt been talking to? And why were they discussing her? What did he know about her that he'd been keeping secret?

There were so many questions, and Paige had nowhere to turn for the answers. There was no point in asking him about it—he'd only lie his way out of it, and then she'd never get the truth.

In that moment, she came to a sobering realization. She could no longer trust Matt Grier.

It took another ten minutes to calm herself and come up with a plan.

Taking one more bracing breath, Paige ventured out. Matt was drinking his coffee this time. He looked up with a smile as she stood next to the table.

"Thought I was going to have to send in a search party." He grinned up at her good-naturedly.

She couldn't take another minute with him. "The shelter called while I was in the bathroom. They need me to come in." She pasted on what she hoped was an apologetic smile. "I'm going to have to cut our dinner short."

"Is everything okay?" There was genuine worry behind his eyes.

"Yeah, it's fine." Was her voice too high? Was she speaking too fast? "I just need to go."

She hadn't seen or spoken to him since then.

When she'd gotten home, she'd debated about what to do. How could she find out what was going on? How did she learn more about the man that Matt had mentioned? Paige glanced over at her laptop. Maybe a little internet research of one Nick Cabot would turn up some useful information.

After clicking through several links and pages, she didn't find anything that looked particularly sinister, but it pointed her in the direction of Daytona Beach, Florida.

She'd never been to the east coast before, so did that mean Cabot had been in Louisiana at some point? How else could their paths have crossed? As she shut down her computer, she vowed to look into it more. She had to find out what Matt was hiding from her.

That same night, the disturbing dreams had started. She never remembered them once she'd pulled herself out, but they unnerved her enough that she had to do something. It had all begun with hearing Nick Cabot's name, and with no other clues to go on, she'd have to start with him.

He was in Daytona Beach, so she'd started making travel arrangements, and within a couple of days, had set out to get her answers.

"I have faith." Gail's words brought her out of her thoughts. "You'll discover the truth."

"Let's hope so." Paige needed to change the subject and talk about something that didn't add to the cluttered mess in her mind. "So, how's everything there?"

"The usual. Got some good news. That blue-brindle pup got adopted. Family came in with their little girl. She took one look and fell instantly in love with him.”

"Oh, that’s wonderful.” She smiled. That was the best part about what they did there. When Paige got to see the love and happiness in both the people and the pets, it made all the poop-cleaning worth it.

“That child all but floated right out of her sandals when we put that baby in her arms.” Gail chuckled. “And if her grip on him was any indication, his paws won’t touch the ground for weeks.”

Paige’s heart swelled. “Aw, that’s so sweet.”

“And that’s as it should be. Every girl needs herself someone to love like that.”

Uh-oh. Paige narrowed her eyes, knowing what was coming next. “Don’t even start, missy. You know I’m never home. I would feel awful leaving a pet alone all day.”

“Well, I’m just thinkin’, since you have no man in your life, you need someone to share all that lovin’ with.”

Paige shook her head, even though Gail couldn’t see her. “I’ll just spread what I have around to all the animals there.”

Gail had been on her for years about finding a man. But Paige didn’t date. And hadn’t since moving to Crowley. Her excuse was that no one had caught her eye, but the truth was that she just didn’t think she had those kinds of feelings in her.

She had no problem caring about the people she worked with or the animals she helped. But when it came to men, one-on-one, it just wasn’t there. No one had ever caused her heart to stutter or her breath to catch.

Her girlfriends often whispered about how this guy or that made butterflies take flight in her stomach or caused her pulse to race. But Paige had no idea what that felt like and doubted she ever would.

“All right. You just go and enjoy the sunshine while it lasts. You’ll be gettin’ some rain soon.”

“The news didn’t say anything about rain,” Paige countered

with a frown, looking to the clear blue sky.

"They don't know nothin' about nothin'. You listen to me, and you'll stay dry."

Paige laughed. "I'm sorry. I forgot who I was talking to." She was getting ready to end the call when Gail said her name.

"You be careful now, girl."

The levity Paige had felt moments before slipped. That wasn't just her friend's casual farewell. There was something underneath it, and Paige had been around Gail long enough to know not to disregard it.

With her heart pounding, Paige answered, "I will. I promise."

She hung up with a vague feeling of unease. Was it the reason she was here? Or had Gail sensed something about the men she thought were following her? She purposely hadn't said anything to her friend about her concerns. She didn't want to worry her, and there was no reason to if her overactive imagination was just running rampant again.

But the disquiet lingered for the rest of the day, and the rain Gail had predicted fell in sheets and added to the gloom she felt.

Needing some solace, Paige drove back to the fully furnished condo she'd rented for the time she'd be here. It overlooked the beach and afforded her more privacy than a hotel would have. It was more like a small apartment with a living area, kitchenette, and separate bedroom and bath.

Returning there now, the first thing she did was kick off her shoes and pour herself a glass of wine. Carrying it with her, she walked through the doorway and into the bedroom. On the bedside table sat a universal docking station. Plugging her phone into it, she set it to shuffle through her favorite playlist.

While soft music played from the speakers, she went into the bathroom to draw a bath. She hoped it would loosen some of the tension that had gathered in her neck and shoulders.

Balancing the stemware on the edge of the tub, she reached

out and cranked on the faucet before dropping in her favorite bath-bomb. As the steamy, scented water level rose, she bundled her long, thick hair on top of her head into a messy knot and stripped out of her clothes.

Carefully she stepped in and sank down into the warmth awaiting her. She reclined back and scooted down until the water lapped just beneath her chin.

For the next forty minutes, she sipped and soaked her worries away.

Paige felt better when she crawled into bed and turned on the TV. And it wasn't long before she was dozing as a result of the wine and hot bath. But as she slept, she began to toss and tangle herself in the sheets. As it had been since that day with Matt, elusive scenes flitted through her mind. They were gone as soon as they appeared, but they left her with a gut-wrenching fear.

When she awoke in the pre-dawn hours, Paige lay shaking and scared. Throwing the covers aside, she stumbled to the bathroom sink to bathe away the clammy sweat that had coated her face and neck.

She looked into the mirror and flinched at what she saw there. Her hair was in disarray and hanging mostly down around her shoulders. And even in the shadows of the darkened room, she could see the shock and alarm in her eyes.

This is what had ultimately pushed her to come to Daytona. She had no idea what frightened her so much. She just hoped she could find the answers she needed to end this constant torment.

3

Ethan had stood by his commitment to get his life back on track. Every day for the last week, he'd started his day at Joe's to work out for a good hour. After that, he'd head home to shower and begin his work day.

Today was Mrs. Green. The elderly woman had called and asked if he could help her reattach her kitchen cupboard door. She explained that it had come off in her hand as she was trying to get her extra tea bags down and had nearly yanked her arm out of the socket.

When Ethan arrived to make the repair, he found that all of the cabinets in her kitchen were just as dangerous. He knew he wouldn't make anything from his time here, but he couldn't just leave her like this. If one of the heavy pieces fell on her and she was injured, he would never forgive himself.

So, with her chattering in his ear the entire time, Ethan did what he could to shore up her cabinets.

As he was packing up his tools a few hours later, she approached him with a wrapped dish.

"Young man, don't think I don't know what you did here." Her cloudy green eyes stared up at him through the lenses of her ancient tortoiseshell glasses. "You went above and beyond, and I want you to know how very much I appreciate that." She held out the casserole. "That envelope there on top has the payment we agreed on, but I also want you to take this."

"Mrs. Green, ma'am, I couldn't possibly—"

"Don't argue with an old woman, son. I can't pay you for the extra work you did, but I can damned well make it worth your time."

She thrust the dish at him so he'd take it. "This is a wild rice and chicken casserole that my Liam loved until the day he died. And don't worry about getting that dish back to me—it's one of those foil ones, so just toss it when you're done."

Ethan smiled and accepted the frozen package. "Well, in that case, thank you very much. This'll be one night I don't have to mooch off my family." He sent her a charming grin.

"No woman in your life?"

He shook his head. "No, ma'am."

"That's just too bad." She eyed him. "If I were fifty years younger, I might have given you a run."

He laughed. "Oh, I bet you would." Then he bent nearly in half to whisper to her, "And I just might have let you catch me."

Mrs. Green threw her head back and cackled in delight.

Ethan was still grinning as he stowed his toolbox in the back of his SUV a few minutes later. As he got behind the wheel, he realized he hadn't felt this free and happy in a long time. Smiling down at the casserole on the seat beside him, he pulled out of the driveway.

He made quick work of his next appointment and was home by late afternoon. He took the food Mrs. Green had given him and put it on the counter next to the stove. Reaching up, he set the oven to preheat while he showered and changed his clothes.

An hour later, he was sitting down in front of the television with a heaping plate of diced chicken, rice, and some kind of little red bits.

His first bite was tentative, but he soon discovered how delicious it was. Rich and creamy, it was seasoned perfectly and the chicken was tender and juicy. The crunchy part every now and then worried him at first, but upon closer inspection, those turned out to be slivered almonds. He still didn't know what the red bits were—maybe bell or roasted pepper—but at this point, he didn't really care. He just enjoyed his dinner and watched some TV, wondering if there was anything else Mrs. Green needed done around the house.

He went to bed that night feeling pretty damned good.

That didn't last long though, as dreams of the fire that had killed Honor floated up to haunt him.

Ethan ran. He ran faster than he had ever run before. His lungs and his legs burned as he pushed past his endurance to get to her. He could hear her calling for him. Screaming, begging him to help her, to save her.

The road beneath his feet seemed to stretch out, putting more and more distance between them. He pushed harder, but he couldn't reach her. She was suffering and there was nothing he could do to stop it. He could see the flames licking at the night sky, but no matter how hard he ran, he couldn't get any closer. The fear and pain in her screams ripped his heart out.

He stumbled and fell to his knees in the middle of the road. Try as he might, the further he went, the longer the road became. He couldn't save her. Sitting back on his heels, he cried out in anguish and despair.

Ethan wrenched himself awake and rubbed his hands over his face. Looking over at the clock, he saw that it was three-thirty in the morning.

Fuck.

He knew it hadn't happened that way. By the time he'd learned of the fire and gotten there, the structure had already begun to collapse in on itself. There was no way he could have heard her voice. Even though he'd still fought to help bring the raging inferno under control, she'd been long gone by that time.

And he blamed himself for that. That's where these nightmares stemmed from. The sounds he heard and images he saw were all of his own creation. Noor had nothing to do with these particular horrors. His subconscious never needed any help punishing him in this way.

He was a fire element, for God's sake. *And* a hereditary witch. He should have been able to do *something*. He should have been able to rescue her. But he hadn't been able to. His magic just hadn't been strong enough yet to contain a blaze that size.

And that was the guilt he'd lived with for the last four years. That's what ate at him every day, no matter how many times friends and family told him otherwise.

He was responsible for her death. It had been his job to protect her, and he'd failed.

She had been his to keep safe from the moment he'd seen her. The day he'd first set eyes on her, he'd known.

~~~

Day one of seventh grade, he and a buddy walked into second period Science class, laughing and horsing around. But all that stopped when he saw her. He couldn't believe what he was seeing. Perfection in faded jeans and a blue t-shirt with a popular brand name printed on it.

Her long auburn hair was pulled back in a ponytail, but he could see the red highlights shining through in spite of the harsh fluorescent lights. Even at first glance, he saw the fire in her. And it called to him.

"Gentlemen, please take your seats." Mr. Crawford's command pulled him out of his daze.

"Dude, come on," Scott said when Ethan still hadn't moved. "What's your deal?"

There was no way Ethan could share that he'd just seen the girl he was going to marry. He didn't know how he knew with such certainty, but it was there. Deep inside of him. The knowledge that this girl, one whose name he didn't even know
~~~

yet, was going to be a major part of his life.

At Scott's urging, Ethan finally walked to his seat and sat down. Under the guise of putting his bookbag on the floor, he bent and let his gaze track one row over and two seats back.

When she caught him covertly staring at her, she gave him a withering glare. One that clearly said, *What is your problem?*

"Class," Mr. Crawford called their attention, "we have a new student. Her name is Honor Andrews, and I know all of you are going to make her feel welcome and help her with whatever she needs while she gets accustomed to our school."

Twenty-eight heads turned to look at her and she gave them all a small smile.

"All right. Let's pick up where we left off yesterday..."

Ethan barely heard anything his teacher said for the rest of class. All of his thoughts were on how to get close to Honor.

When the bell rang forty-five minutes later, Ethan had a plan. He told his friend to go on ahead and that he'd catch up. Picking up his backpack, he walked up to Mr. Crawford's desk.

"Mr. Crawford?"

He looked up from the papers he was grading. "Yes, Mr. Burke, what can I do for you?"

"If the new girl needs some help getting caught up to where we are in the book, I'll do it."

His teacher studied him for a minute. "That's very nice of you. I'm sure she would appreciate it."

He looked towards the back of the room. "Miss Andrews?"

Ethan didn't have to turn to see she was coming near. He could feel her.

"Yes, Mr. Crawford?"

Her voice was soft and light and had an instant effect on Ethan. A little embarrassed, he shifted his bag to hold it in front of him, hoping no one would notice.

He motioned to Ethan. "This is Ethan Burke. He's offered to assist you if you think you might need it."

"Oh, well, that's very kind of him." She cast a sideways glance up at Ethan. As a result of a growth spurt over the summer, he stood close to six feet tall and was head and shoulders above her. He smiled gently at her and saw that her eyes were a shocking shade of gray. The exact same color as the smoke that billowed up when he lit something with his fire.

"But I think I'm good right now. My old school wasn't too far off from where you are here. I think I'll be okay."

Ethan felt his heart pang at her rejection. His mind whirled for something, anything else.

"I could, ah, show you around? Walk you to where your classes are?"

She paused and just stared at him. "Yeah, sure, I guess."

"You'd both better get to it," Mr. Crawford told them, "or you're going to be late."

Honor followed him out into the hall. Ethan stopped. "What's your next class?"

"History." She must have memorized her schedule, because she didn't have to refer to it.

"Mrs. Wright?"

She nodded. "Yeah."

"Me too." Ethan heaved out a silent breath at the news that he wouldn't have to leave her so soon.

By the end of the day, they were fast friends. They talked every chance they got, and the more he learned of her, the better he liked her. She was funny, smart, beautiful, and she didn't take anything from anyone.

It had to be hard to be the new kid, but she didn't let that hold her back. She made friends easily and was nice to everyone. She'd told him that her dad had gotten a big promotion at work and had been transferred to Daytona Beach. They hadn't had any beaches where they'd lived before, so she was looking forward to checking it out.

She thought it was pretty cool that he was one in a set of

quads. She met his sisters at lunch and then Evan in fifth period, as his brother shared the same class with her. Unfortunately Ethan didn't, but they'd agreed to meet up again by her locker later.

They became inseparable after that, becoming best friends. One night while they were watching TV, he got up his nerve and told her what he and his family were. She was skeptical at first, but when he showed her the dancing ball of flame on his palm, she accepted him completely. That's just the way she was.

By eighth grade they were a couple, and neither looked back. They were each other's firsts in everything—first date, first dance, first kiss, first love.

And two years later, first lover.

Ethan was nervous. They'd waited so long for this. They'd been tempted so many times to take it further, but both had wanted to wait for the right moment. They wouldn't rush into it in the heat of passion. This was the biggest step they'd take in their relationship, and they wanted it to mean something.

When they finally decided the time had come, Ethan braved the embarrassment and went to his dad. Among all the things they talked about, protection was one of the top priorities for Ethan. He wanted to be responsible and take the precautions needed to prevent any surprises. There were still a lot of things he and Honor wanted to accomplish before they started a family.

Small paper bag in hand, Ethan drove to Honor's house. Her parents were out of town for the weekend at her mother's class reunion, and they weren't due back until sometime on Sunday. He and Honor had the entire weekend.

He'd hung out at her house almost as much as his own, but tonight would be different. Tonight, they'd finally take their love to the next level.

She met him at the door and gave him an anxious smile.

"Hi."

Ethan smiled back. "Hi," he said, leaning over to drop a soft kiss on her lips, just before walking through the door and watching as Honor closed it behind him.

~~~

The night had been everything Ethan could have hoped for. They'd been so happy and so in love. They'd had seven years together, and then it had all been gone. Much too soon.

Ethan threw the covers back and rose, his footfalls silent on the carpeted floor as he went to the kitchen for a glass of water. He emptied it once, refilled it, and then carried it with him into the living room. Crossing directly to the front window, Ethan looked out over the deserted street.

Honor and his love for her had been a big part of his life. To this day, he didn't know how to fill the void that her passing had left in him.

He scrubbed his hand over his face and up through his hair. There would be no going back to sleep for him tonight. He'd had enough nights like this to know it was useless to even try. He'd just lay, staring at the ceiling.

His heart breaking all over again.

In his experience, physical activity was the only thing that would get him past the memories. Setting his glass aside, he retraced his steps to the bedroom and dressed for an early morning run.

He'd been jogging for about ten minutes and just hitting his stride when he decided to take it down to the beach. It was still dark, but the moon shining off the water would light his way.

Lost in the sound of the waves and his own breathing, Ethan barely noticed the woman up ahead. She was standing at the water's edge, arms wrapped around her middle. As he neared her, he saw her long hair blowing in the breeze coming in off
~~~

the water.

A sick feeling settled in the pit of his stomach as her profile revealed itself.

Fucking Noor! Always up to the same goddamned bullshit!

Ethan bore down on his need to stop, to see her, to know for sure. He continued on by without another glance at her. He refused to give that bastard the pleasure of even acknowledging that he'd seen her.

But because of that incident, he ended up running longer and harder than he normally would have. He'd evidently needed the extra time and exertion to burn off the anger and pain pulsing through him. By the time he returned to his apartment, he was winded and sweaty.

Since he'd done more than enough cardio already, Ethan skipped his usual morning workout and jumped right into his day. At a little after six, it would be an early start, but that was good, because he had a full schedule. He'd been packing as many projects in as he could to keep his mind occupied.

And it worked. He didn't have a moment to think until seven that evening when he finally finished with his client list. By then, he'd gotten enough distance from it that he could fill his family in and not have it rip his soul apart.

Going to bed that night exhausted, Ethan fell into a deep and dreamless sleep.

The following days seemed to meld one into another. If he wasn't training, he was working. He kept so busy, he got into bed each night completely drained.

On one such night, he'd just crawled into bed when the scanner across the room sounded a tone he was all too familiar with.

Somewhere in the night, something was on fire.

Ethan jumped out of bed, threw on the first clothes at hand, and ran from the house. Since that awful night he'd lost Honor, he'd done everything he could so that no one else would suffer the way he had.

Working without the knowledge of the fire crews, Ethan used his abilities to take control of the infernos. The men battling the flames never knew it wasn't their efforts alone that beat back the destruction. They just knew that they gained control quickly and extinguished them in record time.

He arrived at the scene minutes behind the trucks and watched as the men and women set up. As they directed their hoses into the empty convenience store, Ethan tapped into his element. The mark on his chest came to life, and soon he had the wild force tearing through the interior of the store within his grasp.

Standing out of the way to remain unseen, Ethan poured all of his focus into what he was doing. Only when he felt the fire was gasping its last breath did he pull back enough to notice the gathering of people who had come out of the surrounding homes and hotels to watch.

Knowing that the fire department had this one well in hand now, he turned and walked away. A short drive had him back home, and a few minutes later, he was stripping out of his clothes again.

Between the demanding work and the concentrated use of his magic, Ethan was asleep almost before his head hit the pillow.

4

Paige was trying to catch her breath and calm her skittering nerves.

Sirens and flashing lights had awoken her from another restless night. Rising, she'd gone to the window of her bedroom and looked out. At the rear of the building, she had a direct view of the street. On the other side of it, the party store she'd visited only a few hours before to grab snacks and soda was up in flames.

She tried to remember but couldn't recall if she'd seen what hours they were open. Was it an all-night store? Had there been people inside? Almost against her will, Paige was pulled out her front door and around the building to the sidewalk. Others had done the same, and they all stood watching the fire crew battle the blaze.

Paige stayed well back. But as uneasy as the scene was making her, she couldn't force herself to leave. And for many minutes, she found herself staring straight into the flames. Lost to the deadly destruction going on before her.

When she was able to break the mesmerizing hold it had on her, she found that her heart was pounding in her chest and she was shaking all over. Needing the solace and peace of her own space, Paige turned to leave. As she did, she caught sight of an excessively tall, dark-haired man standing off to the side. He was alone and stared into the fire as if transfixed.

And something about him heightened her anxiety and fear.

He wasn't doing anything inappropriate. He was probably curious like everyone else. But somewhere deep inside of her, there was a primal and base aversion to this man.

As he watched what was happening in front of them, Paige's gaze was locked on him. And the longer it was, the more her blood raced. Sweat that had nothing to do with the heat coming from the fire beaded her on skin. She began to tremble harder.

She had to get away. Away from the man who seemed to elicit her fight or flight instinct.

Paige slowly backed away lest he turn and see her fleeing wildly. When she reached the parking lot of her complex, she spun and took off running. She made it to her door unscathed, but her hand was quaking so bad, it took four tries to get the keycard into the slot. With every minute that passed, she was afraid he'd find her.

It beeped and the light turned green. Wrenching the handle, Paige darted inside and slammed the door behind her. She engaged every lock installed and pulled the chair over in front of the door for good measure.

Stumbling to the couch, she sat and tried to calm her breathing and heart rate.

"What…the hell…is going…on?" she panted out. She'd never reacted this way to a person before, and a complete stranger at that.

Paige was scared beyond anything she'd ever felt. She racked her brain, trying to make sense of what was happening to her. Were her instincts trying to tell her this man was dangerous? Was she afraid he was one of the men who were following her? She didn't recognize him as one from the car, but there could be more than the two she'd seen.

Why else would he set off this terror within her? She could think of no other reason.

Had he been watching her condo? Waiting for her to become

accessible only to get distracted by the burning building nearby?

Paige rose and paced. What had she started by coming here? What could she have to do with these men? Or was she making more of this than there was? Was she blowing it out of proportion? Was she letting her paranoia run wild? She had no actual evidence anyone was following her or watching her. Was she seeing trouble where there was none?

So, she hadn't liked the man on sight. Big deal. It didn't mean he meant her, or anyone else, any ill will.

Bolstered and calm, Paige decided she'd just finish what she'd come here to do and get back home to Louisiana. Then she wouldn't have to worry about him, or anyone, ever again.

She started to crawl back into bed when she realized how clammy she and her pajamas felt. Walking into the bathroom, Paige peeled off her sleepwear and took a quick shower just to remove the panic sweat.

Not bothering to redress, she settled under the covers, and within a few minutes, was asleep.

~~~

Morning came with a renewed determination. Ready for the day, Paige grabbed her keys and purse and headed out. First stop would be the pancake restaurant a block down. As she stepped out into the early sunshine, she decided to walk instead of drive.

Starting off down the sidewalk, she glanced across the street. Studying the charred structure, she realized that not as much damage had been done as she would have imagined. The fire department must have gotten there fast enough to save it.

Official-looking men were milling around the building. Cops, she would think. They probably wanted to determine if it had been deliberately set. As she watched, a large broad-shouldered
~~~

man stepped out of the doorway.

He was about as wide as a football player, pads on. He was tall and had dark hair that was trimmed short. His features were chiseled and rough-looking, giving him a hard edge. But he was actually a very handsome man. As usual, he didn't flip any switches for Paige. She sighed and mentally shrugged at the lacking in her as she turned back in the direction of the restaurant. Out of the corner of her eye, she saw another man, an even taller one with black hair, walk out behind the first.

The sight of him stopped her in her tracks. It was the same one from last night.

She waited for the apprehension and terror to hit her as it had the night before. But it never came. Curious, Paige studied him a little closer.

There was something different about him. And it wasn't just that he was clean-shaven this morning. No. It was something else. Subtle differences that upon first glimpse hadn't stood out to her. But the longer she stared, the more convinced she was that he *wasn't* the same man.

Brothers, maybe? Definitely family, as the similarities were impossible to ignore.

The sun glinted off something at his belt and it drew her notice. Shifting her position just a little to cut the glare, she saw that it was a badge. They *were* cops.

The beefy one must have felt her scrutiny, because he looked up and over at her. Paige sent him an automatic smile before she resumed walking.

By the time she finished her mushroom and Swiss omelet and made the return trek, they were gone. Which was just as well. She had too much to do to get caught up with the black-haired men and the curious way they affected her. She needed to see what more she could learn about Nick Cabot and how he was involved in her life.

What she knew so far was that he worked at a local bank. A

branch manager who'd been there for about ten years, he was in his late sixties, married, with three kids. Seemed to be a fine and upstanding citizen.

But there had to be more to it. Something about him worried Matt enough that he kept tabs on his movements. And whatever that was, Paige surmised, had something to do with her. Was he somehow responsible for her waking up in a hospital bed?

Her first stop was the library, her destination the newspaper archives to search for any mention of Cabot. She also wanted to know if he had any interests in Louisiana, since that's where she'd been living when she'd been hurt.

Hours later, Paige was beyond frustrated. She'd found nothing more than she already knew. She was pretty adept at computers and searches, but it didn't appear that Cabot had any connection to Louisiana. And if he was dirty or into something, she was finding no sign of it.

Paige wasn't sure where to turn to next. She was halfway tempted to just show up at the bank and see what kind of reaction she could get out of Cabot. But logic kicked in and told her that really wasn't a good idea at this point. She didn't know enough yet. And if he were somehow involved, she'd didn't need to announce her presence.

But she'd hold that option in reserve. Just in case.

Glancing down at her phone, she saw that it was well past lunch and she was starving. Leaving the library, Paige decided to grab a pizza and take it back to her condo. She wanted to go over everything she had again on the off-chance she'd missed something.

Half an hour later, she was trying to get into her room juggling the box, papers she'd printed out, and her key card, when her phone rang.

"Crap. Hold on, hold on." Finally through the door, she dropped everything on the chair in the living room and grabbed her cell. When she looked at the screen, she saw that it was

Matt.

She'd dodged his calls since that fateful day but knew she'd better answer, or he might get too curious.

"Hey, Matt." She hoped she sounded normal.

"Paige. I've been trying to reach you. Are you okay? It was brought to my attention that there was a rather large cash withdrawal made on your account. I just wanted to make sure no one had gotten access to your numbers."

She'd taken the cash just for this reason. Matt oversaw her money and invested it for her. She knew if she used any credit cards for this trip, he could find out exactly where she'd gone. With the large sum she'd acquired prior to leaving, she could pay cash for everything and he would have no clue.

And she'd already worked out her alibi. "Don't worry, Matt. I took the money out. I was speaking with a woman at the abuse shelter, and we got to talking about flea markets. She started telling me about a huge one just over the border into Texas." The complete opposite direction from where she'd gone. "I decided to take some time and check it out and see what I could find."

"Oh, okay." Relief was evident in his voice. "I just wish you would have told me beforehand."

"Yeah, sorry about that. It was kind of a spur of the moment idea."

"No problem," he laughed. "I'll let you get back to shopping."

"Thanks, Matt. Talk to you soon."

Paige hung up and threw the phone on the coffee table.

<center>~~~</center>

Everyone was gathered in the back yard of the family home. Tonight, Ethan and his siblings would work on taking that final step in merging all four elements into one.

Seth, Joe, Jacob, Kyra, and their parents all looked on as the four of them took up their positions. They stood, twins facing each other, and called to their powers.

Aria began.

"Still and calm or a raging storm
We are as one, from the day I was born
I am Air and Air is me
As I will, so mote it be."

The air around her came to life, swirling and dancing so that it lifted her soft golden hair and made it fly about her head. Ethan knew the exhilaration she was feeling as the magic took hold.

Anna went next.

"From the heavens above to the ground below
Always on the move as you ebb and flow
I am Water and Water is me
As I will, so mote it be."

As her hands rose, water gathered from everywhere to surge and undulate around her. Her pale blue eyes, much like water in its frozen form, closed and her head fell back in joy.

Following birth order, Evan called to his element.

"Sand and soil, dirt and stone
Neither you nor I will stand alone
I am Earth and Earth is me
As I will, so mote it be."

The ground beneath their feet rumbled and shook. Small rocks and soil floated up to become a twirling, spinning mass that encompassed his brother.

Anxious to feel his own element rush through him, Ethan

spoke the words that had been a part of him since the moment of his beginning.

"Smoke, spark, ember, flame
You and I forever the same.
I am Fire and Fire is me
As I will, so mote it be."

Ethan sucked in a breath as the force of his gift hit. His vision was obscured momentarily by the blazing tempest engulfing him. He let it wash over him and basked in the pleasure of it.

He'd grown so much stronger in the last year—they all had. They'd never been able to manifest their abilities into storms of energy like this before. Small displays sure, but nothing of the magnitude they now wielded.

And they'd advance further the closer they got to the day of their twenty-fifth birthdays. On the flip side of that coin though, was the fact that Edrick Noor's powers also grew.

But he wouldn't think about that tonight. That dark energy had no place here.

The four of them savored the power washing through and around them. Ethan's fire filled him to bursting and he gloried in it, but there was still a part of him deep inside that remained empty. He wished with all he had that Honor would have been able to see him reach his full potential with his gifts.

To see what they all could do now. What they were capable of. She would have loved it.

"We'd better get on with it," Anna spoke into their minds. He could hear the reluctance in her tone, but they still had a lot of work to do. So, banking the magic to a more controllable level, each of the four readied themselves.

Ethan immediately felt the probing of his twin's mind. He freely opened his own and they merged their earth, fire, souls, and magic into one. Across from them, their sisters were doing the same.

And then four became two.

They worked at it over and over, but there was still nothing to show them how to finish the merging—his sisters' air and water with he and his brother's fire and earth.

"Anyone have any suggestions to where to go from here?" Aria and Anna spoke in unison, and the words blended into one voice. Humor and frustration laced their tone, because they'd all been at this point several times and still hadn't been able to finish that final step.

"What if we ask the one with a little inside knowledge?" Ethan and Evan threw a glance at Jacob. *"He's the one who got us this far."*

His Burke gift was to see a person's true inner self, and that was how he'd helped them before. While they'd been struggling with the initial joining, Jacob had seen that Anna and Aria— being identical—were, deep down, the same. Running with that, the girls alone had attempted it and had been successful, allowing them to take that first large leap towards their goal.

The road block they ran into now was that, though they were quadruplets, the two sets of twins were as opposite as they could get. They'd not been able to surmount that obstacle yet.

They hadn't asked him before now, because they'd thought they could find the key on their own. But time was winding down and they needed to get this done. With Jacob's help, maybe they could.

"It's worth a shot," Anna and Aria agreed.

The guys let their sisters broach the subject with Anna's son.

"Jake, honey," they called to him. "Would you want to help us out?"

He grinned broadly, jumped off Joe's lap, and ran over to join their group. Their combined persona didn't bother him in the least. "Sure, Momma. What can I do?"

"Just do like you did before, sweetie, and look. Use your

magic and see if you can see a way for us and your uncles to bring our powers together."

He stepped back away from them and concentrated. His gaze went back and forth multiple times before his head shook back and forth.

"I'm sorry, Momma. I can't see it. You're just too different."

Anna and Aria let the link between them slip away, and he and Evan followed suit. Once themselves again, they recited the words that would close their circle of protection.

"A circle cast for a favor asked
Closed now that the need has passed
Our thanks and blessings be to thee
As we will so mote it be."

Anna went to lift her son into her arms. "That's all right, sweetie. Thanks for helping, though." She kissed his cheek. "What do you say we go eat? I'm sure I heard Nana say she made a chocolate cake."

"She did." Jake nodded so enthusiastically he bobbed up and down in her arms. "I saw it. It's on the kitchen counter."

Anna smiled. "Well, we'd better get to eating before the big guys beat us to it."

They all knew time was running out. But until that final solution revealed itself, they could only do as they were doing. Living and coming together as often as possible to try.

When Ethan stepped into his apartment a few hours later, he felt relaxed and content. Maybe this new lease on life was working and he was finally moving on. And it helped that he hadn't seen Noor's projection of Honor in a while. Maybe he'd given up since he wasn't getting the reaction he'd wanted.

The next morning dawned so bright and sunny, Ethan opted for a run again instead of the gym. Strapping his phone to his bicep, he set out on his usual route. Music pumping through his earbuds, he set a good pace.

Following the curve of the two-lane road, Ethan jogged along the shoulder. Being a sharper turn, he kept a careful eye out for cars that might not expect for someone to be there. And sure enough, two vehicles were coming towards him at a high rate of speed.

As they neared, Ethan heard the rev of an engine and watched as the mid-sized sedan rammed the small compact car from behind. The weight of the larger vehicle sent the smaller, lighter one into a skid. The driver of the car fought the wheel and got it back under control. Only to be hit again.

What the hell were they thinking? Road rage? Just people being assholes?

Ethan ripped the speakers from his ears. He didn't want any distractions if he had to take evasive maneuvers himself as they barreled down on him.

The sedan gunned it again as they entered the sharp bend. It struck the rear bumper of its target hard enough to lift the rear wheels off the ground. As it landed, the rubber caught at an awkward angle on the pavement and sent it tumbling.

It rolled a few times before falling off the roadway and coming to a jarring stop against a tree. Ethan gasped and ducked behind a nearby boulder when the other vehicle pulled up briefly beside it.

At first, Ethan though they might stop to render aid, but then it sped off. Had they noticed he'd witnessed the whole thing and just didn't want to be identified?

As soon as he saw that they weren't sticking around, Ethan ran for the little car. He reached it in seconds and tried wrenching on the driver's door, but the mangled metal held it fast. His gaze peered through the window and saw that it was a woman in there. Her head was turned away and hanging down. The curtain of her hair hid her face and part of her chest. He couldn't see how badly she was hurt—he just knew he needed to get in.

Grasping the door handle again, he tugged and heaved but to no avail. Stepping back a few paces, Ethan used his telekinesis to rip the opening wide.

Unhindered now, Ethan reached in. He knew better than to move her, but he needed to assess how bad her injuries might be and see what he could do for her. That was when he noticed the color of her hair.

Flaming auburn.

He braced himself and reached out to gently pull her long hair back away from her face.

5

That was when all breath and movement stopped. And the world as he knew it spun away from him.

"No. No. No." Ethan's hand began to shake uncontrollably. "This isn't possible." His heart was pounding so hard in his ears, it blocked out all other sound.

This was Honor. She was real. She was alive. But how…?

Suddenly, he remembered the times he thought he'd seen her recently. Not manifestations made by Noor, but the very woman he'd loved all of his life. Ethan felt sick as he remembered running by her on the beach, ignoring her. If he'd only known.

How is this possible? How is she not dead? Where has she been? Why did she leave? Oh, Honor, what happened to you?

Ethan's mind whirled. His emotions hit all new highs and deeper lows as questions and uncertainties nearly drowned him. He slumped to his knees beside the wrecked car, overwhelmed.

"Ethan?" Anna's sweet voice reached out to him through the turmoil. *"What's wrong? Are you hurt? We're catching bits and pieces of whatever you're going through by our telepathic link, and it has us all very worried. Please tell us what's wrong."*

Ethan hadn't known he was broadcasting his distress to his siblings. But it was just as well. He couldn't deal with this on his own. It was too big. It was too life-altering.

"I'm not hurt. I witnessed a car accident. She's…It's…" He

couldn't say the words, and his voice trailed off as he studied the woman he'd thought dead for so long. "*You have to come. I need you.*"

"*Hold on, sweetie,*" Aria told him. "*We're leaving now. Where are you?*"

He managed to get out his location before a soft, pain-filled moan drew him back to Honor. His mind was reeling, but he knew he needed to get her some help. He could find out where she'd been and why she'd left him *after* she woke up. Right now, he needed her to be okay.

"It's going to be all right, baby," he spoke softly to her. "You're safe now. I've got you. I'm here."

Reluctantly releasing her tresses, Ethan found his earbud again and slipped it into his ear. A quick tap and the hands-free option of his phone was activated.

"Call 911."

A few seconds later, Ethan had relayed what he'd seen happen and the condition of the driver.

While he waited for EMS to arrive, he whispered soothingly to Honor. "Help is on the way, baby. You're going to be okay. Just hang on."

He had yet to hear the sirens when two cars screeched to a stop not too far away. Anna and Aria jumped from one as Evan and Seth piled out of the other. They all approached where he still sat on the ground, still holding her hand. He knew there were tears in his eyes, but he didn't care.

"Ethan," Anna squatted beside him, "what's going on?"

He glanced back into the car. "It's Honor."

"What?" Anna took a step back and glanced around at the rest of them before returning her gaze to him. "What do you mean, it's Honor?"

"It's her," he said as his voice broke, looking from the unconscious woman to his siblings.

"Ethan, what the hell—" Evan started, but Ethan stopped

him.

"Please." He begged for understanding. "Just look at her."

Not letting go of Honor's limp hand, he shifted to the side to make room for them to see her.

Evan reached in and swept the auburn hair aside, just as Ethan had done.

Gasps echoed, and as Evan retreated, his face pale with shock, Ethan looked to his sisters. Tears were already streaking down Aria's face, and Anna had her hands clasped to her mouth, her eyes wide and disbelieving.

Only Seth spoke. "I've seen her before."

Ethan blinked at him, surprised. "What? Where?"

"We were called in to investigate a fire the other day. A convenience store on—"

"I know the one," Ethan revealed. "I was there. I helped them put it out."

Since Seth probably didn't know about his little sideline, he went on to explain. "I listen to the scanner," he said. "When there's a fire somewhere, I go help. They never even know I'm there."

Seth inclined his head and seemed to approve. "Well, we were there the following morning. As we were leaving, I happened to see a woman staring at us from across the street. I met her gaze, she smiled briefly, and then she moved on. That was it."

It suddenly occurred to Ethan where that store was. And it was very close to the stretch of sand where he'd seen her standing in the surf.

He looked at Evan. "That's near where I told you I saw her on the beach. I thought it was Noor's doing, so I ignored her completely. But now that I know she's real, she must be staying somewhere near there." He paused as that sank in. "She was so close. Why didn't she come to me, Evan?" His heart thumped painfully as he turned back to look at the still-unconscious woman. "Why didn't she tell me that she was okay? Explain what happened and where she's been?"

Evan shook his head. "I don't know." His gaze traveled over the damaged car and he looked back to Ethan. "What happened to her car, and how did you find her?"

Ethan relayed the events leading up to the crash, and his brother's expression hardened. "Well, seeing as this is now officially a crime scene, I plan on asking her a few questions myself."

Evan's eyes softened and he clapped a hand on his shoulder. "We'll figure this out, Ethan. Somehow, Honor is alive. The rest you can work out as you go."

Sirens rang in the distance, telling him that help was near. As EMS arrived and the crew got to work on her, Ethan and the others had to back away to give them some room.

Ethan didn't know exactly what they were doing, but before long, they were lifting her from the wreckage.

"I have to go with her." Ethan wasn't looking for approval— he was just giving his family a heads-up of his plans. "I need to be there when she wakes up."

"Of course you do." Anna laid her palm on his cheek. "How about Ari and I run you home real quick so you can shower and change? Then we'll take you to her."

Ethan hated to be away from her for even that long, but Anna was right. "Yeah. Okay."

Evan nodded his agreement. "You go do what you need to do. We'll join you there as soon as we finish up here."

Ethan's jaw set. "I don't know what the hell is going on, but she's obviously in trouble. If this has anything to do with the reason why her death was faked, I'm not leaving her alone. I have to know where she's been and why this was done to us."

Evan breathed out a sigh. "I know. And we'll figure all that out. Just watch yourself in the meantime, in case those assholes come back to finish the job. We'll meet you there in a bit. Hopefully, with some answers."

Ethan nodded and stuck around long enough to see Honor loaded into the ambulance and then climbed into his sister's car.

Taking the fastest shower in history, he threw on some clothes and was ready to head back out again.

The three of them arrived at the hospital twenty minutes later. They didn't bother with the front entrance, but instead went in through the ER. His sisters hung back as he approached the information desk.

Having a face that looked exactly like a local cop made inquiring into Honor's status a little easier.

"A woman was just brought in by ambulance. A car accident."

The nurse checked the computer. "Yes. Paige Harrison. She's still here in the ER, but they have her listed as stable. It says there are no life-threatening injuries, but doctors are worried about the head wound. She's remaining unconscious longer than they'd like."

At first, Ethan thought they must be talking about two different people. But then another thought occurred to him. Could she be traveling under another name? Was she hiding from someone? Maybe the people who were after her.

"Did anyone check her purse? Did she have a next of kin listed in her phone or anything?" Maybe that would give him a hint as to where she could have been all these years.

The nurse tapped a few keys and checked the screen again. "No." She shook her head. "I don't see a next of kin, but her license said she's from Crowley, Louisiana." She looked up at Ethan. "She could have family there."

The city didn't hold any significance to Ethan. "Would you mind if I looked in on her?"

"I can't let you stay long." Ethan could see that allowing this was against her better judgment.

"I won't bother her. I'll only be a moment."

The nurse nodded. "Cubicle nine."

"Thank you."

When she was called away to deal with another question, Ethan sent the girls a look, and they quickly followed him through the doors and into the bustling hum of the emergency room.

They found Honor easily enough and Ethan's heart did a slow heavy beat in his chest as he held the curtain aside for Aria and Anna to enter. Once through, he let it fall closed behind them. On silent steps, they crossed to her bedside.

"She looks just the same," Anna whispered as she got a good clear view of her old friend.

"Do we know anything about why she disappeared yet?" Aria glanced up at Ethan. "Or why she's back now?"

"No. But with Evan and Seth checking it out, hopefully they'll find something soon."

Ethan couldn't take his eyes off her. He couldn't believe she was here. For four long years he'd mourned her, dreamed of her, missed her. What did all of this mean?

He studied the freckles marching across her cheeks and nose, remembering the placement of every single one. He couldn't wait to see those smoky, mysterious eyes of hers again. To have them look at him and see the love shining in them.

He'd always felt like she'd been made especially for him. She was the very embodiment of fire—glowing auburn hair, eyes the color of smoke, body that made him burn.

As he stood there staring down at her, her lids began to flutter. Her head twisted in small movements on the white pillow.

"Shhh, baby." Ethan was there instantly. "You're okay. I'm here. You were hurt, but you're going to be all right.

Dark, sooty lashes finally lifted to reveal the eyes he'd longed to see again. Ethan held his breath and waited for her to realize he was there.

He saw the moment she could see him clearly.

And then he watched as the sleepy disorientation faded, replaced by wide-eyed alarm and then full-on terror.

"No, no, no!" she wailed. "Get away from me!" She scrambled backwards away from him, climbing the raised mattress as if he were physically threatening her.

He held up his hands. "Honor? Calm down, baby. You're safe. No one is going to hurt you."

She wasn't listening. She was still trying to put distance between them, and given her most recent ordeal, he began to worry it was a detriment to her health.

"Ethan," Anna laid a hand on his arm, "we need to go. *Now*."

He looked at his sister, not understanding. "What do you mean go? I can't go. I just found her again."

"I can feel her distress. She's not recognizing you, and she's scared out of her mind. We have to get you out of here."

The last thing he wanted was to cause Honor any suffering. He hated it, but he did as Anna suggested and backed out of the curtained-off cubicle. The girls were right behind him. As he stood there with his sisters, trying to wrap his head around what had just happened, Evan and Seth arrived.

Evan indicated to the closed drape. "How is she?"

"Doctors think she'll be okay," Ethan told him numbly. "She just woke up."

"Good. Maybe she can answer some questions."

Evan made a move to enter, but Anna called him back. "I think it should just be Seth that goes in." She glanced at Ethan before continuing. "When she woke up and saw Ethan, she freaked out. She'll probably have the same reaction to you, and you won't be able to talk to her."

"Why did she freak out?"

"Her feelings were all hazy and confused." Anna shrugged. "Maybe from the knock on her head. But I sensed genuine, bone-deep fear when she looked at Ethan." She sent him an apologetic look.

"From me?" It was like the words didn't compute. "Why?"

"I'm not sure yet."

Evan looked between him and Anna before glancing back in Honor's direction. "I'll have to chance it. We didn't learn much from the condo she's renting. We need to know more about what happened to her, and why she chose now to come back." Evan turned and marched away before anyone could argue further.

Ethan and his sisters waited a couple of minutes. Then a couple more. But nothing happened. No screams. No shouts. Had she fallen into unconsciousness again? Worried, Ethan slid the screen aside just a fraction to see into the room. She seemed to be talking calmly to Evan and Seth. Maybe Anna had been wrong. She may have just been mixed up when she woke to find him standing over her.

Pushing the fabric open enough to enter, he saw her eyes widen and fill with panic.

"Ethan, don't." Anna drew him back. "I don't know why, but she's okay as long as she can't see you."

Ethan's heart plummeted as a hard truth assailed him.

There was no way this could be his Honor after all.

The girl he'd known would never have reacted to him this way. They'd had a bond that went down deep into their souls, stronger than time or distance. If any part of her had been the woman he'd loved, she would have felt that connection. Not trembled in fear at the mere sight of him.

Needing air suddenly, he flung the drape back into place and stormed out to the parking lot, leaving his family to wonder. As he paced the sidewalk that bordered the lot, he thought about a great many things. If this woman wasn't Honor, then who was she? Why did she look so much like her? And who was out to hurt her? Another mystery that struck him was why she hadn't reacted to Evan the way she had him. Most people who met them couldn't tell them apart.

More and more questions bombarded him, and he had

answers for none. He wandered for another ten minutes before his siblings and Seth found him.

Ethan pointed at the building. "That's not Honor. I don't know who she is, but there is no way in hell Honor would have reacted to me that way. That woman in there may look like my Honor, but it's not her."

Ethan's insides felt like they were being shredded into confetti. This was worse than Noor's manipulations. He thought he'd gotten a miracle, only to have it torn from his grasp by a cruel twist of fate.

"You may be right," Evan surprised them all by saying.

Aria turned to him. "What did she say when you spoke with her?"

"When I called her Honor, she told me I had the wrong person—that her name is Paige Harrison. I asked her what happened, but she was reluctant to answer our questions at first. She finally admitted that since coming to town a little over a week ago, she'd felt like she was being followed. That the same dark car kept showing up in the same places she was, time and again. She's never traveled by herself before, and she thought she was just being paranoid, so she didn't say anything to anyone."

Evan paused. "She believes everything she's saying. I could sense it."

Everyone was silent as they took in the new information.

"Why does she think someone is following her?" Even though he was stricken by grief at losing her once again, Ethan couldn't hold back his concern. She may not be the person he thought she was, but she was still in trouble.

Seth picked up the explanation. "She didn't know. Or wouldn't say."

"We'll continue our investigation into the accident," Evan promised. "I also want to look into what brought her from Louisiana. But other than an eerie resemblance to Honor, I don't think she has anything to do with us."

"I hate to bring this up," Seth interjected, "but could Noor have had something to do with her being here?" His gaze traveled around the group. "Could he or his men have found this look-a-like by chance and pointed her in this direction? Just to fuck with us?"

As glances passed between the group, Ethan felt himself spiraling. It didn't matter how or why she was here. Dealing with a dream version of Honor was one thing, but having an actual flesh-and-blood woman here who looked exactly like her was going to be a whole lot harder to take.

And Ethan didn't know how he was going to get through it.

~~~

Paige closed her eyes and stayed absolutely still. She concentrated on just breathing through the throbbing in her head. She hurt everywhere, but her head was making the biggest fuss.

It was sad to admit, but this wasn't the first time she'd awoken in a hospital like this. The accident that had changed her life had left her in much the same condition—swimming through pain, fighting to surface from the blackness of unconsciousness.

But at least this time, Paige remembered what had happened. The first time she'd had to piece it all back together. It had been only with the help of her friends filling in the blanks that she'd been able to pick herself up and re-build her life.

She didn't need anyone's help recalling what had happened this time, though. It was all too clear, in bright living color. Someone obviously wanted her dead. There was no way of mistaking the intent of the men in that car. And the brief glimpse she'd gotten of them confirmed they were the same ones that had been following her.
~~~

Were those Cabot's men she'd been seeing? Were they tailing her on his orders? And if so, then what had made them step up their game? Why go from simply watching to running her off the road? The only thing she'd done in the short time she'd been in town was an in-depth search of Nicholas Cabot at the local library.

Could Cabot have gotten wind of what she was doing? Even that didn't seem to add up—her stalkers had been on her almost as soon as she'd hit the city limits, long before her research had started. So how had Cabot known she was in Daytona?

She suddenly remembered the investigation she'd done on him before she'd left home. Had her online digging somehow alerted him? Had he known about her since then and followed her progress across multiple states right to his doorstep?

Her pulse raced, and it dawned on her how much trouble she could be in. If he wanted her out of the way *now*, did that mean he'd wanted her gone *before*? But why? What had put her on his radar in the first place? As far as she knew, she'd never been to Florida, and neither had either of her parents before their deaths. She had to figure out what Matt's interest in him was, and if Cabot was somehow connected to her past.

Paige carefully raised her arms and wiped her hands over her face. Ugh, there were just so many unanswered questions. Did she dare share all this with the cops? That would probably be the smart way to go. But all she had was speculation and a partial conversation she'd overheard.

Her arms fell back to her sides, and she looked over at the card the tall cop had left on her table. As she thought about calling him, her thoughts shifted to the other tall man, and the trembling started. First in her hands. Then it worked its way through her body until she was gasping for breath in a full-blown panic attack. An image filled her mind of him standing over her bed, and she could no longer move.

Paige didn't know why she was having such a severe physical

response to this man. It was so bizarre—so illogical. Two men, practically identical in every way. Yet one of them didn't affect her at all, while the other one... There was just something about that other one that scared her to death. How could one face, on two different people, evoke such an opposite reaction in her?

The only thing she could even remotely compare it to was her fear of fire. For as long as she could remember, any open flame wrought crippling anxiety, much like what she felt around him.

It made no sense to her, but there was something about them both that was dangerous and threatening to her life.

And she planned to avoid them like the plague.

6

Ethan couldn't get her—Paige—out of his mind. As he and his family gathered for Thanksgiving a week after the accident, all he could think about was her sitting alone in her condo. Since leaving the hospital, that's where she'd stayed mostly, sealed away behind her locked door.

He knew this because he'd taken it upon himself to back up the police watching over her. He remained out of sight, naturally—given how she reacted to him—but if those men returned, he'd be there.

His family was less than pleased by what he was doing, voicing their many concerns over the situation. He understood—he got that this wasn't healthy for him. Being close to her, seeing her every day, didn't allow him to heal as he needed to do. Paige's resemblance to Honor made being near her confusing, at the very least. Ethan could fully admit to himself that he should stay miles away from her.

But that just wasn't an option.

Not being able to save the girl he'd loved haunted him every waking minute. Maybe if he could help Paige, it might lessen some of the guilt that weighed so heavily on him over Honor.

Of course, he *knew* the two things were totally unrelated, but he couldn't help the way he felt. And right now, he was itching to get back to his post. The DBPD had stationed a car nearby to protect her if those men returned, but Ethan still thought Paige was safer when he was guarding her too.

He'd hated to do it, but he'd left her in their hands for the few hours he'd be at his parents' house. He didn't know if the bastards who'd run her off the road thought she'd gotten the message and backed off, but he'd seen no sign of anyone casing her place. He hoped the little bit of time he spent with his family would be okay.

Evan hadn't received any calls to the contrary, so Ethan assumed everything was still quiet.

Even knowing that, he was thinking about making his excuses. His mom wouldn't be happy that he was leaving so soon, but he'd smooth it over with her.

Before he could make his move though, Jacob came from the hall carrying a book. Ethan saw that it was one of the family journals the Burke witches had kept for hundreds of years. They were a source of information that had proven invaluable time and again.

"Jake, honey." Anna spotted her son. "What are you doing with that journal?"

"I saw it on the table in the magic room." The brown-haired, brown-eyed imp glanced down at the book in his hands. "It looks just like the ones my first mom had. I wanted to see if this one had some of the same stories as hers."

The entire room went perfectly still.

"Your mother had storybooks like that one?" Anna carefully asked her son.

During their search to investigate Edrick Noor and his past with their family more fully, they'd realized that there was a large gap in the timeline of the records they had. A couple of hundred years' worth of entries were missing. And they happened to encompass the time that Noor was off somewhere gaining the power he now controlled. They'd made inquiries with key family members, but nothing was known of the journals from those years.

And now it seemed they'd been close all along.

Ethan sat forward in his seat and waited for his nephew to respond. Everyone else in the room was similarly poised.

"Uh-huh," Jake nodded. "She read out of them sometimes when my dad wasn't home. She said one day they would be mine, and that I had to take really good care of them to pass on to my kids."

Joe cleared his throat. "Do you have any idea where she kept them, buddy?"

Jacob's head bobbed up and down. "She pulled a board off the bottom of my dresser and hid them in there."

Anna and Joe's gazes collided, and a moment later, they turned to Evan. "When everything was put into storage, was the furniture included?"

Excitement from the pending discovery lit Evan's eyes. "It was. I had them pack up the entire house and move it to the facility."

"Please tell me it has twenty-four-seven access." Anna's glacier-blue eyes drilled into Evan's black ones.

Ethan shared her worry. Being a holiday weekend, there was a possibility the place could be closed until Monday. They couldn't wait that long. They needed to get them as soon as possible.

Evan confirmed it had a keypad entry.

"We have to get to that storage space." Anna smiled. "Now."

Evan pulled out his phone and entered in the route information. "It's roughly a six-and-a-half-hour drive from here to Tucker, Georgia."

Anna looked at Joe. "We can leave first thing in the morning."

"I can't, hon." Joe shook his head. "Tony's fight is only a few days away. I can't leave the gym right now."

"Well, crap." Anna's shoulders slumped but then quickly perked back up. "I'll just go by myself."

"You most certainly will *not*." Their mom put her foot down as only moms can do. "We know these books worry Noor—you saw that yourself. If he catches wind that we've found them, he'll be on you before you can blink."

"I'll go with her," Aria spoke up.

She shook her head. "I'm still not comfortable with that. I know you girls can take care of yourselves, but I'd feel better if there were more of you."

"I'd offer," Kyra sent Evan a narrowed look, "but I already know how that would go."

"You're damned right," Evan stated with a nod. Then the stern look softened as he laid a hand on her still-flat stomach.

He turned his gaze to their sisters. "There's no way Seth and I can get away right now either."

Last man standing, Ethan knew what was coming. All eyes turned to him.

"I can't," he protested. "If you'll remember, I'm a little busy at the moment." He rose to stand. "And I need to get back to it."

"Ethan—" his mom began, but he cut her off.

"I know you don't like what I'm doing, but I have to do this."

She came to him and laid her hands on either side of his face. Love poured from her hazel eyes as she gazed up at him. "We may not like it, but we also understand why you feel the need to protect her. I'm just asking you to take a day and help your sisters. We need what's in those books. She'll be looked after while you're gone."

Mary glanced at the other men and waited for them to nod in agreement.

"Yeah, sure," Evan said. "He knows we already have men in place."

Ethan hated the thought of leaving but knew he didn't have a way out of it. His mom was right. Having those journals could be paramount to stopping Noor.

He looked over at Anna. "What time do you want to leave?"

~~~

At six the next morning, Ethan was fitting his tall frame into the back seat of Anna's car. They'd been on the road about an hour when Aria turned in her seat to look back at him.

"How are you really doing with all of this?"

Ethan knew what she was asking. "It's hard, obviously. I see her and think, how can this *not* be Honor? How can she look exactly like her and not be *her*?"

Aria cocked a blonde brow at him and he grinned.

"You know what I mean."

She laughed lightly. "I do. But you know what they say. Everyone has someone out there who looks just like them."

"Doppelgangers," he nodded. "Yeah, I've heard that too. But do you ever really think you're going to meet one? And for hers to show up *here*, of all places, is just crazy."

"Do you think she's really in danger?" Anna glanced at him in the rear-view mirror.

"She said she thought she was being followed. And I saw that car run her off the road. I'm not taking any chances. I'm going to watch over her until they're either caught or she goes back home."

"We understand, Ethan." Anna sent a quick look to Aria and then back to the road. "But this woman makes you think of Honor every time you see her. That has to be really hard for you, and we just don't want you to suffer any more than you already are."

"Hon, I think of Honor every day of my life anyway. There hasn't been a single moment when she's gone from my thoughts. Some days are better than others, but she's always there."

Ethan saw heartache flash in their blue eyes but went on before they could continue. "I'm not letting myself see her as Honor. She's just a woman who needs help."

He hoped to God he was telling the truth.
~~~

They talked of easier things on the remainder of the drive. Which ended up taking them closer to seven hours, since they ran into construction on the highway.

Arriving at the facility, Anna pulled up to the black box. Leaning out, she entered the code Evan had given her for the main entrance. The steel gate slid open to the tune of clangs and grinding metal. Once she had enough room, she drove through and, reading the numbers on the buildings, found the correct one.

She parked close, and the three of them got out to approach the roll-style door of the unit. The padlock was quick work, and soon Anna was grasping the handle to lift the door up into the ceiling.

Their first look into the interior was a little bit of a shock. For a household-worth of furnishings, there wasn't a lot here. Ethan took a cursory inventory and came up with the bare minimum of what it would take to outfit a home.

A couch, one reclining chair, and a small dining set. Two mattress sets—one twin and one full-sized. Missing were any head- or foot-boards. Two dressers were stacked in the rear corner, the larger on the bottom and a small blue one standing atop that. About a dozen assorted boxes that Ethan assumed contained clothes or other personal effects were stacked along the walls of the unit.

"Samara didn't have it easy, did she?" Anna asked, looking over what little their cousin had left behind.

They hadn't known Jacob's true identity when he'd first come to them. To shield him, the authorities had changed his name and moved him out of the state. It wasn't until Evan had procured the file on his mother's murder that they learned his legal name had been Jacob Hagan.

In reviewing the file further, they'd discovered a shocking surprise.

Jacob's mother had been a distant cousin. The gift Jacob

possessed was one of their own. Burke magic.

The family had lost touch with Samara many years before, after the death of her own mother. According to what they'd learned in that report, Samara had married a man who'd been abusive and controlling of her and their son. So it was no wonder she hadn't been permitted to give Jake her own last name, as was the family custom.

Their line of witches was a long and powerful one, and each generation held to the practice of continuing the Burke name. It carried respect in the Wiccan world and afforded those who bore it a certain amount of protection. But there were those, like Samara's husband, that wouldn't allow it.

Anna and the rest of the family had already fallen in love with the small boy. Learning he was tied to them by blood had only deepened that bond.

In the aftermath of losing his entire family, everything from his previous life had been put into storage. Anna and Joe had known that someday he'd want to have what had belonged to his mom.

"Since there's only one kid-sized dresser, I'm guessing that's the one Samara hid the journals in." Ethan pointed to the piece of furniture sitting high in the corner. With so little to go through, he figured they'd only be here for maybe an hour. He could be home by this evening.

"Let's check it out." Anna started in with Aria and Ethan close behind.

The three of them moved aside anything that was in their way. Soon it was clear, and they stood feet away from what could be the answers to some very important questions.

Anna reached out and pulled the bottom drawer completely out. She set it aside and bent down to look into the opening.

"Shoot." She straightened. "I thought maybe they were just below the drawer. But it's not open underneath it."

"Jake did say she had to take a board off to the get to them,"

Aria reminded her.

"All right, then that's what we'll do." Anna studied the lowest front panel, looking for a gap or loose spot. Finding none, she grasped both sides with her fingers and tugged at the trim piece.

With a screeching squeak of nails releasing their hold, the board popped off in her hands. Dropping it into the discarded drawer, Anna leaned forward to peer inside.

"There's something in there, but it's dark."

Ethan had his phone in his hand and activated the flashlight app. He angled it into the opening, illuminating what rested within.

Anna gasped. "We found them." She grinned, reached into the cubby, and started pulling out leather bound books of differing sizes. Ethan and Aria took them, counting as they went.

It wasn't long before Anna laid the last one in Aria's hand. "Eleven. I can't believe we found them."

"Samara's husband was such an ass, he wouldn't let her acknowledge her Burke heritage." Aria shook her head. "It's no wonder no one knew she had them. She was denied everything that related to her family. Luckily, she'd had enough courage to share what little she did have with Jacob."

"Now that we have them, is there anything else you want to take back for Jake?" Ethan figured as long as they were here, they may as well check.

"I would like to go through a few things. All he has to remember his mother by is that one picture that Evan got for him. I should be able to read which toys or personal effects are most important to him."

They spent the next half hour going through each box and drawer. Anna culled out a few items and set them in a small box next to the door. They had stacked the books close by and Ethan kept a watchful eye on them. No one knew where they were or what they were doing, but he wasn't taking any chances.

A little over an hour after they'd arrived, they were locking the unit back up. Wanting to keep their find safe, Ethan had unearthed a duffle bag and put them all into it. It sat on the seat next to him.

Aria volunteered to drive for the return trip, so Anna set the GPS for home. They were making their way back to the expressway when Aria swore.

"Shit. We've got company."

"What?" Anna spun in her seat to look out the rear window. "It has to be Noor's men. How the hell did they find us?"

Ethan turned to check it out. From what he could see, it looked like there were four men in the vehicle pursuing them. "They must have been watching us all along, waiting for us to make a move that interested them. My question would be if they know what we have, or are they just curious about what we were doing here?"

"They can't find out we have those journals." Aria glanced in the mirror again. "Whatever's in them has Noor quaking in his boots. We can't let them slip through our hands before we know why that is."

Ethan tried to think of their best option. They were hours from home, in another state, with no back-up. They were going to have to take care of these guys on their own.

"Oh, crap."

Ethan snapped his gaze to the front at Aria's muttered words. A car identical to the one behind them bore down on them from the opposite direction.

Make that potentially eight men.

They were on an out-of-the-way country road. Nothing to see, nowhere to go. As they watched, the one coming at them swerved into their lane and came right at them, head-on.

"What the hell are they doing?" Aria gripped the wheel

tightly.

"They're going to force us off the road." He looked at each of his sisters. "We're going to have to fight our way out of this."

Anna and Aria gave each other a quick glance and nodded.

Ethan quickly tugged the bag off the seat and let it drop to the floor.

"Out of sight, out of mind
Invisible now so no one can find
Hidden well and thoroughly
As I will, so mote it be."

The duffle and its contents shimmered out of sight.

"Let's take this fight to them." He had something of a plan. "Ari, pull off up there. I'd rather still be able to drive out of here. If we wait for them to ram us, this car may be too damaged to use."

She did as he suggested.

"As soon as you stop," he continued to explain, "we're going to jump out and head to that field over there. We'll lure them away from the car and take them on. They know who and what we are, so be ready for anything."

The tires skidded to a stop. All three leapt out and ran a short distance away. As Ethan had hoped, the goons' cars followed and came to a halt. Men poured out and advanced on them.

Ethan sent a cursory glance to his sisters but saw that they were ready. Thanks to lifelong training and a more in-depth instruction in hand-to-hand combat from Joe, the Burke quads could handle themselves.

Not to mention the magic they wielded.

As the large group of men made their way to where Ethan and the girls were waiting, three of them stopped to search the car. Ethan's heart beat hard in his chest.

Did they know?

One wrenched open the front passenger door. Dipping his upper body in, he came out with a box. It was the one Anna had used to bring a few things home for Jacob. The thug upended it and let the contents drop to the dirt at his feet. Once it was empty, he threw the box on the ground and gave it a kick.

Another yanked open the rear door and scanned the interior. Ethan knew they wouldn't see anything, but he still held his breath as he watched the rest of the men continue the examination.

Evidently satisfied that nothing else was in the vehicle, the men moved on. The one who must be the leader of the little band spoke.

"What are you three doing so far from home?"

"Some of my son's things are in storage here." Anna used the fact that they'd found the box of kid's things as their cover. "We went through it to bring some stuff back for him."

"Ah, yes," he sneered. "The little heir. We know all about him. We've been told to leave him alone for now. At least until you bring him to his full potential, magic-wise. Once you've done all you can do, Noor will collect him and finish his training."

Anna pulled herself up to her full five-foot-four-inch height. She was in full momma-bear mode. "Over my dead body will that sick fuck ever get his hands on my son."

The leader laughed and a sinister glint lit his eyes. "He'd prefer it that way, actually. He's *really* looking forward to killing you and the rest of the Burkes."

"Noor can fuck himself and go straight to Hell," Aria spat, and then cocked her head. "If you're lucky, maybe he'll take all of you with him. It'd save your sorry asses from the likes of us. You may want to reconsider where your loyalties lie, because there is *no way* he'll live up to whatever promises he's made you."

Ethan pushed it further. "And while you're at it, check out

how many of your loser buddies have ended up dead or in jail. You're nothing more than expendable pawns in his war against us. Why do you think he keeps sending you out to fight for him? He knows you won't win, and he doesn't care. You're just his puppets—toys to play with and throw away when he's finished."

A few of the men at the rear sent covert glances at each other. Ethan knew what they were saying was striking a chord with some of them. Maybe they'd make the right choice and separate themselves from this mess before it was too late.

But there were those who would believe the lies and stick with Noor no matter what anyone said. Those who were already too far gone down the path of evil.

The leader scoffed. "Don't tax yourself worrying about us. We'll come out of this aces. When he's free of that cage, nothing will stop us. Which is more than I can say for you."

Ethan knew there was no reasoning with this guy. "So, what exactly did you stop us for? Just to chat?"

"Had to make sure you weren't up to something boss-man needed to know about." He grinned. "But since we're all here, we may as well have some fun." He turned to the men behind him and nodded towards the car. "Light it up."

Two of them struck a book of matches each and tossed them in. One through the open front door and one in the back.

Anna and Aria both gasped and took a step forward, but Noor's henchman stopped them with a pointed finger. "Ah, ah, ah. Wouldn't want you pretty little ladies getting burned."

The group of men laughed before backing away a few steps to head back to their cars. Most sauntered away congratulating each other on a job well done with slaps on the back and shoves.

Ethan only waited for them to lose interest in the burning car before he called to his power and took control of the flames. He held it contained so it would stay well clear of the prize still hidden away in there. Once the men had driven out of sight, he quickly doused the fire. He and his sisters approached to assess the damage.

Thankfully, only the front and rear seats and dash on the passenger side were singed. Being a fire element, a younger Ethan had made a few mistakes learning to control his power. Early on, he'd come up with a spell to undo whatever he'd inadvertently scorched. Even though it had been years since he'd needed it, the words came easily back to mind.

"Marred by smoke or charred by fire
A rewind spell is what I require
Reverse the damage perfectly
As I will, so mote it be."

As soon as the spell had left his mouth, the car reverted to what it had looked like before.

After picking up Jacob's belongings, Anna got into the back seat while Aria and Ethan took the front.

"What the hell was that little show of force even about?" Aria demanded as Ethan slid behind the wheel and started the engine. "It didn't accomplish anything."

"If I had to guess," he glanced up and down the road before pulling out, "I'd say some of the troops are getting restless. Noor hasn't let them out to play in a while. I think Mr. Chatty is looking for something that will move him up the ranks."

"Good thing you thought to shield the books." Aria turned to look at him.

He met her eyes briefly before watching the road again. "We're just lucky he was too busy fucking with us and crowing about it to wonder why we'd travel all this way for a few toys."

"We'll have to be really careful about what we do from here on out," Aria cautioned. "We're getting close to the end game, and with them watching our every move, we don't want to tip our hand."

Ethan glanced into the mirror at Anna. She was staring out the side window, silent.

"You okay, hon?"

"Yeah." She turned and smiled in reassurance. "I try not to dwell on the fact that Noor wants my son. That he plans to put him through the same trials he went through to gain power. If I let myself think about it too much, I'd never let the poor kid out of my sight."

"At least we know why they haven't made a move on him in a while." Aria twisted in her seat to offer some comfort to her twin. "And it doesn't sound like they will anytime soon."

"So, what do I do, stop his training until after February?" Anna's uncertain gaze searched theirs.

"No," Ethan stated firmly. "You don't do anything differently. Jake needs those abilities to protect himself. We've got security measures in place to shield him if Noor comes. Trust in that."

"I do. But just the thought..."

"Hey," Aria brought Anna's attention back to her. "It's not going to happen. We won't let it."

Anna took a deep breath and let it out, shoring up her certainty. "No, we won't."

"Okay," Aria grinned. "Who else is dying to know what's in those journals? Pass me a couple, sis. It's a long drive."

7

"Hidden away from prying eyes
The need has passed for this disguise
Reveal yourself and let me see
As I will, so mote it be."

After chanting the spell to reverse Ethan's concealment charm, Anna dove into the duffle bag. The girls each took a few to read while Ethan drove them home.

The reading was slow going. Between the old-world language and the extravagant writing styles, whole entries were barely discernable. Not to mention, some of those in charge of chronicling the events of the times hadn't been worried about penmanship, the scrawling writing nothing more than scribbles. What they'd been able to read so far hadn't mentioned anything about the Bringer—the being who had given Noor his powers—or the trials.

As they neared home, they put the books away. The family would have to go over them again in more detail to see if anyone could decipher the illegible writing.

Between their little detour and traffic, they didn't get back into town until nine that evening. Because it was so late, Ethan drove straight to his place, as that's where the girls had picked him up that morning. After he'd parked and gotten out, Aria moved behind the wheel and Anna took shotgun.

Aria rolled her window down. "Hey."

Ethan turned back to her.

"Love you bunches."

Ethan smiled. "Love you bunches too. I'll see you later."

The girls waved as they drove off. He knew there'd be a family meeting soon to review the journals, but for tonight he was free. Instead of going inside to get some sleep, he got into his car and back to his self-appointed guard duty.

He was surprised to see Evan there when he arrived. He sat in his car in an adjoining parking lot to Paige's condo complex. It was the same location Ethan had found gave him the best vantage point to watch the window and door of her room.

Ethan pulled in next to Evan's car and got out. He rounded the hood and opened the passenger door.

"I didn't expect *you* to be out here." Ethan looked over at his twin.

"Yeah, well, I am." Evan took a deep breath. "I can't begin to know what you've gone through since Honor passed. Or how this look-alike must make you feel. But if this is that important to you, then it is to me too."

"Thanks, bro. I appreciate that." Ethan lapsed into silence as he thought about why he felt so compelled to do this. "To tell you the truth, I don't know why I feel the need to protect her." Ethan rubbed his hands over his face to push away some of the fatigue that was creeping in. "I know she's not Honor, and I know I'd be smarter to stay the hell away from her. Shit, she's scared to death of the sight of me." Ethan shook his head. "Which is mind-boggling, because she seems to be just fine around you. We're identical, for fuck's sake."

He inhaled and let it out, calming his churning thoughts. "Have you learned anything new about her?"

"Some," Evan confirmed. "It looks like she's lived in Louisiana for the last twelve years. Her parents were killed in a car crash and left her well enough off that she doesn't have to work—seems to split her time volunteering at different shelters—animal, women's abuse, and homeless."

"So why is she here? I get the feeling it's not a vacation."

"She hasn't shared that with us yet, and what we've found so far hasn't revealed that information. We'll be talking to her again soon, and hopefully she'll fill us in."

~~~

Paige lay in a tangle of sweat-soaked sheets. Her body twitched and jerked as she suffered through the worst fear-inducing nightmare she'd experienced yet. Her head thrashed back and forth while whimpers and moans slipped past her lips as the horrific scene played out.

Everywhere she looked, fire surrounded her. The snapping, crackling flames inched ever closer to lick at her tender flesh and vulnerable clothing, the heat and pain so unbearable it wrenched screams of agony from deep within her as she fought to find her way out of hell. Her eyes wheeled around the room, searching for anything or anyone to make it stop. To save her.

Through the inferno, Paige thought she could see someone. In desperation, she called out. "Help me, please!"

As she watched, the figure started towards her. Slow, measured steps brought them closer and closer. As they approached, she began to discern the shape of a man. A very tall man. She didn't know how he was doing it, but he seemed to be walking right through the middle of the fire. It danced around him and almost caressed him like a lover as he drew nearer.

Instead of being there to save her, Paige began to fear he was the reason she was burning. He was the fire and the fire was him. And he meant to engulf her.

He called her name and she gasped. His voice was so smooth and powerful. Almost hypnotic. She barely stopped herself
~~~

from moving towards him, further into hell. His hands rose then and extended out to her, beckoning her to come to him.

Paige fought the pull that was urging her to step into the flames. To join him.

That, she just couldn't do. This living, breathing entity of pain and destruction was her mortal enemy. The very thing she'd always feared would one day kill her.

And it looked as if that day had come. Out of options and with nowhere to go, Paige was trapped. She could do nothing as the arms of the inferno searched her out and took her into its embrace.

Her screams of terror broke through the hold sleep had on her body, and she erupted into the real world. She bolted upright in her bed just as a crash sounded somewhere in her condo.

With the horror of her dream still lingering in her mind, she screamed anew when a tall man emerged out of the darkness. He bore down on her with menacing strides. Her arms and legs flailed as she fought to free herself from the bedding that had twisted around her like manacles.

He said her name just as he had before. His arms outstretched. The only thing missing were the flames, but her mind was too far lost in absolute panic to know that they weren't still searing her skin.

Mere feet separated them when suddenly her world went black.

~~~

When she became aware sometime later, she was confused. Had it all just been a dream? She lay in the dark trying to make sense of what she remembered. The dream of fire. Of burning. Of dying. Then the man seemed to be in her bedroom. Coming for her.
~~~

It was all a jumble in her head. *Had it been real?*

Reaching out, she clicked on the lamp. Glancing around the room, she saw no sign that anyone but her had been there.

It must all have been part of the terrifying mental images she'd experienced in her sleep. Ready to wash away the fear and sweat, Paige slid to the edge of the bed. She was about to stand when she heard voices coming through her closed bedroom door. Someone was out there. Someone was in her apartment.

Paige reached for her cell to call the police when a light knock sounded on the door.

"Ms. Harrison? This is Detective Burke. Do you remember me? We spoke when you were in the hospital."

She did remember him, but what was he doing here at this hour?

Shakily gaining her feet, Paige crossed the room and opened the door. She slowly looked up into his face. It took her a moment, but thankfully, he didn't seem to pose any threat.

"Why are you here?"

"There was an incident," he told her and then indicated with his arm that she have a seat in the living area. Once they were both settled, he continued.

"As a precaution, we've been surveilling your condo in case those men who ran you off the road decided to come back. Well, during the night, we heard you screaming. We didn't know if someone had gotten in here, so we...forced our way in to get to you. After a quick search, we discovered you were alone. It seems you were in the throes of a nightmare. Unfortunately, between that and seeing us appear out of nowhere, it scared you to the point that you fainted."

He looked a little self-conscious over what had happened. "We feel horrible for the misunderstanding, but we didn't want to leave you alone until we were sure you'd be okay. My— The door will be fixed shortly, and then we'll be out of your hair."

Paige remembered the dream—remembered screaming—but she hadn't realized that she'd done it aloud. And evidently at a volume that everyone could hear.

"Well, thank you for looking out..." That's as far as she got when the damaged door opened and in walked...*him*.

Her eyes grew round and her breathing became choppy. She couldn't get oxygen into her lungs. It had been sucked out of the room.

"You," she gasped out. "You were...in...the fire." She was hyperventilating. "Coming for me."

He stopped in his tracks. His black-as-pitch eyes found her and locked on. The dark brows drew in.

"What did you say?"

When he started forward, she let out a whimper, scuttled off the couch, and backed away from him. She was in no way in control of her actions. Her flight instinct had full command of her body. Paige withdrew until her back hit the wall and then she slid down against it to cower on the floor.

The cop rose in a rush and came to her, kneeling in front of her. "Ms. Harrison."

She couldn't answer—her gaze was glued to the other man. Seeing this, the cop glared over his shoulder.

"Ethan! Back off!"

Thankfully, he listened and retreated to the doorway. The detective shifted until he was in her line of sight, blocking her view.

"Ms. Harrison," he tried again.

He didn't touch her; he just waited for her to meet his gaze.

When she did, he gave her a small smile. "It's okay. No one here is going to hurt you."

She tried to look over his shoulder to see where the threat was looming.

"Hey," he said softly, drawing her attention back. "We only want to make sure you're safe. I don't know why you have such a reaction to my brother and not me, but he really doesn't mean you any harm."

Paige didn't know why either, but there was nothing she could do about it.

"As a matter of fact, it was actually him that saw your accident and called for help. He stayed with you until EMS arrived. And it's been him that's kept an eye on you since you got out of the hospital."

That drew a surprised gasp from Paige. She'd had no idea.

"Why?" she strangled out.

"Because that's just the kind of guy he is," he assured her. He moved back a little. "How about we sit where it's more comfortable?" He held his hand out to her and waited for her to take it.

Paige sank into the couch, and the detective sat adjacent to her in the chair.

"I'm Evan, by the way. And my brother is Ethan. Again, we're sorry for the way we barged in on you. Ethan has already worked out the repairs with the manager. He's going to fix the door for you."

She turned her head and looked at him where he stood, statue still, across the room.

Ethan must have taken that as a sign it was okay to speak to her. "What did you mean," he spoke softly, "when you said I was in the fire?"

A shiver went down her spine at the sound of his voice. It was the same smooth, inviting tone he'd used in the dream.

"Ethan," Evan admonished, "now's not the time."

Paige found some nerve and made herself speak up. If Evan were telling the truth—and why wouldn't he?—Ethan had saved her life and taken it upon himself to keep her safe.

"It's okay." She cleared her throat. "Can I have some water, please?"

Evan went into the kitchenette and retrieved a bottle from

the fridge. She drank gratefully, and once the dryness was gone, Paige attempted to explain.

She kept her gaze on the safer brother. "For the last few weeks, I've been having dreams. I never remembered them when I woke up, but they always left me feeling sick and terrified."

Suddenly, the similarities between those dreams and the one she'd just had clicked into place. It was that same steal-your-breath horror that always made her wake up in a cold sweat.

"Ms. Harrison?" Evan tried to gain her attention. "Paige?"

"It's the fire," she said, more to herself than to him. "That's at the center of it all."

"What do you mean, it's the fire?" Evan guided her.

"In my nightmares. The ones I couldn't remember and the one tonight. I didn't make the connection; the fear was just so intense. More than I had ever experienced. But now, I recall it completely, and it brought the same panic as the others."

"What happened in this one?" Evan asked.

"Fire. I was surrounded by it. It was coming for me." Paige went on to describe it in full detail, even the part about seeing the man walking through the midst of it.

She slowly tracked her eyes to Ethan in the hopes it would give her time to prepare for the onslaught of emotions.

It didn't help. But she battled back the need to run screaming. "I don't know why, but there's something about you that elicits the same fears in me as those sinister nightmares."

She couldn't take anymore and switched her focus to the water in her hands. Paige took a breath and tried to settle. "Last night, I guess my mind blended it all together into one big terror-fest, going so far as to add you into the mix."

"Why fire, and why me?" Ethan took a step but stopped when he saw her involuntary withdrawal. He huffed out what sounded like an impatient breath but stayed where he was. "You obviously don't have that same response to my twin."

Paige closed her eyes and tried to calm her erratic heart. She actively struggled against the need to move, to get away. She did a few deep breathing exercises, and when it didn't feel as if her heart would leap right out of her chest, she lifted her lids again, braced, and looked over at Ethan.

"I can't begin to know why my brain associates you with fire. But I do understand why it's had a starring role."

A quick look passed between the brothers. She didn't know what it meant, so she went on. "I know a lot of people say they're afraid of fire, but I've always been *deathly* afraid of it. To the point that any open flame puts me into a state of absolute terror."

"What caused the fear?" Evan's question pulled her attention back to him. "Were you ever burned or injured?"

Paige shook her head. "No. That's why my fear is so odd and irrational. There's no indication I was ever in a fire. I don't have any scars or wounds. I have no idea what initiated it. It's just always been there, a part of me."

The perceptive detective's eyes narrowed. "What do you mean, there's no indication? You don't know for sure?"

She paused. Whatever she said from here would venture into the realm of why she'd come to Daytona. She wasn't sure if she should delve into that just yet. This whole journey was based on feelings and speculation... nothing concrete.

But maybe this police officer could find the answers she hadn't been able to.

Making a decision, she looked up into the detective's dark eyes. "I sustained a pretty bad head injury a few years ago. I've had some problems with my memory ever since. My friends have had to fill me in on my life and what happened. One such friend is our family attorney, and it's because of him that I came to Daytona."

"He told you to come here?" Evan inquired. "For what purpose? Does it have anything to do with those men that ran you off the road?"

"I don't know." That seemed to be her stock answer right now. She inhaled and let it out again. "Matt doesn't know I'm here. And I'd like to keep it that way for the time being."

"Why wouldn't you want him to know where you are?" Ethan was still rooted to the spot near the door. It seemed as close as he could come without her falling into hysteria.

Paige swung her gaze over to him but brought it back to her hands. "I overheard a conversation that implied he's been lying to me."

"About what?" Evan pulled her awareness back to him again.

"What happened to me. How I was hurt."

"Tell us." Evan nodded at her.

Paige gathered herself before she started. "A few weeks ago, we were having dinner out. I'd excused myself to the restroom, and when I came back, he was on his cell. I'm not sure who he was speaking with, but it was clear that whomever it was has been keeping an eye on a man named Nick Cabot. Matt was asking if there'd been any movement from him."

"Who's Nick Cabot?" Evan asked. "Did you recognize the name?"

"I don't know who he is. As far as I know, I've never met him. But it was what he said after, that started to make me suspicious." She wrung her hands in front of her. "Matt practically said my name before catching himself. Then he went on to say, 'She knows nothing of what actually happened to her, or why.'" She sighed. "That was also the night the unsettling dreams began."

"And you think all of this is related." Evan sat forward and braced his forearms on his knees.

"This is where it all gets speculative," Paige warned. "But I think this Nick Cabot had something to do with what happened to me, and Matt has kept it from me—for what reason, I can't possibly guess. When I got home that afternoon, I did a search on Cabot. But as far as I can find, he's never had anything to do with me, my family, or with Louisiana."

Paige didn't know if they'd believe her next supposition. "And that's why I think those men are following me. Somehow, he was able to find out that I'm investigating him. I'm almost positive he put a hit out on me, so I can't cause trouble for him. I just don't know what *kind* of trouble I could cause him."

"This incident you keep referring to..." Paige could tell Ethan was trying to keep his tone easy and non-threatening. But there was a note in it that hinted he was invested in her answer. "What exactly happened?"

"That's one of the things that I've had to rely on other people to tell me. Matt specifically."

Her gaze drifted between the two brothers before landing back on Evan.

"Because I don't actually remember."

8

The first thing she became aware of was pain. Her head. Her arm. Her whole body was a massive, throbbing ache.

She tried to open her eyes, but they wouldn't obey her command. She told her tongue to moisten her dry lips, but it ignored her and lay thick in her mouth.

Why couldn't she move? What was happening? Where was she? She waited, silent, trying to make her sluggish brain work this out.

Rhythmic beeping from somewhere nearby caught her attention. It had a familiar cadence to it. *What was that?* She should know. Suddenly it came to her. It was a heart rate monitor.

Hers?

As her senses came back one by one, she smelled something. It was...medicinal but with a layer of bleach.

Was she in a hospital? Why?

The more questions she asked herself, the more agitated she became when the answers didn't follow. The beeping sound sped up and became erratic. Suddenly, someone was there, speaking to her.

"Miss Harrison, can you hear me?"

It was a woman's voice.

"You're in the hospital." She went on to say in a soothing tone, "You were injured, but you're going to be all right."

How could that be true if she couldn't move?

"I'm sure you're frightened. But everything will be okay. I need to go page your doctor and let him know you're waking up. I'll be right back."

She panicked at being left alone with the pain and the dark. A sound came up out of her throat—a hoarse grunt or groan. And her hand finally moved enough to grasp the woman's fingers.

"Shhh, it's all right." A warm hand came down on top of hers.

The mystery person was her only anchor to this world, so she held on. Swallowing, she tried to speak.

It took her three tries. "Why...here?" It was more of a croak than a question, but the woman understood.

"All I was told is that you were hurt in an accident. You have a broken arm that required surgery to repair, you have several bruises and contusions over your body, and you sustained a pretty serious head injury which resulted in a severe concussion."

"When?" Her voice was getting a little stronger.

"You've been here for a little over a week."

No matter how hard she tried to recall any of what this woman was saying, there was nothing.

"Where am...I?"

"You're in the hosp—"

"No," she interrupted. "Where?"

"Oh, you're in Crowley, Louisiana."

She absorbed that but remembered none of it. Not the accident, not being hurt, not how she'd gotten here. Just nothing. She tried to think back, to see what her last memory was, but she couldn't find it. It was like her mind was absolutely blank.

Completely empty.

She tried to think of something simple like her name, what she looked like. But there were just great big holes. Her breathing increased again at that realization, and the woman tried to calm her.

"Who…who am I?" she finally got out.

"Shhh, getting upset isn't going to help. It's okay, some amnesia is common after the type of trauma your brain has sustained." The woman, a nurse probably, patted her hand. "Your name is Paige Harrison."

Paige Harrison, she thought. Paige. Harrison.

She heard the words. But they were foreign. Alien. There was no hint of familiarity. No connection to it whatsoever.

Alarm swept through her as the sensation of being utterly lost swamped her. Her mind whirled, trying to make sense of the void as she struggled to clutch at any semblance of recognition—anything that would define who and where she was. But it was all gone. The nurse was talking to her, but it didn't cut through the panic and fear of not knowing her own identity.

Gradually, a heaviness washed through her body. Her scattered thoughts slowed and a lethargy settled over her.

"There now. That should calm you and allow you to rest. We don't want you to sleep too deeply, but this should relax you, Miss Harrison. Try not to worry and just concentrate on getting better."

Paige floated away.

The next time she surfaced, she was able to open her eyes and move a little easier. After a moment, she remembered what the nurse had told her before. She'd been involved in some kind of accident, but she would be okay.

After adjusting the head of the bed up slightly, Paige looked around. Basic hospital room. She continued her scan and saw the white Styrofoam cup sitting on the table over her bed.

Please let there be water in there.

Slowly, she reached out with the hand not casted and strapped to her chest and grasped the cup. Because of her weakness, it was heavier than it should have been, but she got it off the table and towards her mouth. Thankfully, the straw was already bent, and she was able to get it to her lips without much difficulty.

The cold liquid moistened her dry mouth and tasted clean and fresh. Its icy coolness slid all the way to her stomach. She wanted nothing more than to suck the whole thing down, but she was cautious about getting sick.

One more sip and she made herself put it back. She lay staring at the ceiling, taking stock of her body.

Her head didn't really hurt at the moment, but it was kind of thick and fuzzy feeling. Her thoughts were sluggish but more clear than last time. With her good hand, she reached over to check out the arm that had been injured.

The hard casing extended from her knuckles all the way up to her shoulder. The nurse had said she'd had surgery on it to repair the damage, so that must mean it had been badly broken.

But no matter how hard she pushed, Paige couldn't remember any details of the mishap that had put her here.

The sound of the door opening drew her attention.

"Wonderful." The doctor who entered smiled brightly. He was a short and round older man. What hair he had left on his head was shockingly white and stuck out in odd directions. The glasses he wore overtook most of his portly, hound-dog face. "You're awake. How are you feeling?"

"Okay, I guess." Her voice was still ragged and hoarse.

He came to her bedside, took a small pen light out of his lab coat pocket, and shined it in one eye. He flicked it back and forth a couple of times before moving on to the other one.

"Good. Good. Both of those pretty eyes are reacting equally and normally." He stepped back to look over her monitors. "Now, I understand you're having some issues with your memory."

"I can't remember anything. Not even my name."

He turned to her and finally engaged with her. "That's to be expected with your type of trauma. In cases of TBI, traumatic brain injury, we'd list yours at moderate. Scary enough, but I don't see why you can't make a full recovery."

"So, my memories will come back?"

"In most cases, yes. Though some never recall the moment of the injury or the time leading up to it, most recover everything else."

"And when will that happen?"

"That varies from patient to patient. There's no set time table—days, weeks, months."

"Years?"

He shrugged. "Possibly."

She absorbed that and asked the next question on her mind. "How long do I have to stay in the hospital?"

"You sustained a fairly substantial concussion and have been in a medically-induced coma for a week to give your brain time to heal and keep you comfortable. We'll want to monitor you for a few more days to track your healing and progress, but if all goes well, you can go home then."

"But to where? I don't remember where I live."

"Yeah, well, that much will probably come back to you. In the meantime, I think the gentleman waiting in the corridor can answer that for you."

Her gaze jumped to the door. "Who's out there?"

"He must be a good friend. He's been here off and on since you arrived."

The doctor spun around and waddled off. Paige heard him speaking to someone briefly, and then in walked a man who, like everything else, she didn't recognize. He was dressed in a dark suit and had brown hair that was cut short. He looked to be in his late-fifties. She studied his face, but there was nothing familiar about him.

"Who are you?"

As he approached, his brown eyes widened just a fraction in surprise. "You really don't remember me?"

Paige shook her head gingerly. "Who are you?" she repeated.

He hesitated briefly. She could see something working behind his eyes but didn't know what to make of it. "A friend."

"From work? Through family? What kind of friend?" she pressed him.

"Actually, I'm your lawyer. But still a friend. I'm Matt Grier."

"Why do I need a lawyer, Matt Grier?"

He smiled at her cautious tone. "To oversee your interests."

"And what interests do I have?"

He paused briefly, searching her face. "It's so strange to be explaining all of this to you." He scratched his head before answering. "You're a wealthy woman, Paige, and it's my job to make sure you stay that way."

"What?" Her voice choked off. His words completely took her by surprise.

"Not Gates or Buffett rich, but you won't have to worry about putting food on the table."

"How?"

"Family money."

"I have family? Why haven't they—"

"Your parents were killed some years ago, and you are an only child. They were both estranged from their own families. I never pried, but I was under the impression neither side was happy with the union of your parents and cut off all ties to them."

"So, I'm rich but have no one."

He nodded sadly. "Unfortunately."

"Do I at least have a house or apartment? The doctor said I could leave here in a few days. Where will I be going?"

He grimaced.

That gave her a bad feeling. "What is it?"

"Your house was destroyed. This area is known for its storms. Tornados, hurricanes, and floods ravage everything. We found you unconscious and seriously injured. Medics were called and they got you stabilized. And then you were brought here."

"Is my house being repaired?"

Matt looked down at his hands. "I'm sorry, but everything is gone. There's nothing left." He met her gaze again. "I've been trying frantically to find you a new place to live. I've narrowed it down to three—you just have to decide which one you prefer and we'll close on it."

He was talking again before she could fully take that in. "I'm having new bank cards, checks, and other legal documents— like your birth certificate and social security card—drawn up. You'll have to get a new driver's license when you're up to it. I'm sorry, but you'll be starting from scratch."

"I guess that's okay," Paige shrugged. "It's not like I remember my old life anyway. It's too bad I don't have any pictures or mementos. One may have triggered something."

They spoke a little longer and after Matt left, she cautiously scooted to the side of the bed. She sat and waited for the swimming in her head to subside before going any further. The last thing she needed was to face-plant on the floor.

But there was something she needed to do.

Slowly, ever so slowly, she shuffled to the bathroom using the IV pole as a balancing aid. Inside the doorway, she reached out and turned the light on. She moved in front of the sink but kept her gaze downcast. Taking a deep breath, she looked up and into the mirror mounted on the wall.

The woman she saw there was a stranger. She had chestnut-colored hair that fell to beneath her shoulders. Under the bright lights, it lit with a deep red that seemed to make it glow. It was thick and wavy and appeared to have a life of its own.

Not bad.

Switching her attention to the face, she noted the pale

skin, some of that probably due to nearly being killed, but she thought mostly it was just her natural tones. Leaning forward, she noticed a faint line of freckles that extended across her cheeks and over the bridge of her nose.

Great. Freckles. Hello, sunburns.

Raising her focus, the eyes staring back at her were an ordinary and dull gray. Large and wide, they could almost be a little big for her face. Paige shrugged. She could work with that, though. Her nose was small and straight. Mouth seemed fine—not overly big although her lips were a little on the full side.

Overall, she didn't see anything that would scare small children. Stepping back, she surveyed her body.

Not short, that was good. And not excessively tall. It was hard to judge her shape under the gown, so Paige bunched it into her good hand until it hugged her form.

Pretty lean, maybe a little thick at the hips. Flat stomach, nice-sized breasts.

Okay. Decent.

Just the little she'd done had exhausted her, so Paige made the return journey back to her bed. Once she was settled, she fell asleep quickly.

Four days later, Paige was finally discharged, and Matt drove her to her new home. She'd decided, through pictures he'd shown her, to go with a modest bungalow-style home. It had hardwood floors throughout and great old woodwork.

Some furniture had been provided, he told her. And if there was anything she didn't like, she could have it replaced with whatever she wanted. He just didn't want her walking into an empty house. But seeing it now, she liked the light homey feel of the furnishings.

Over the next few weeks, with Matt's help, Paige put her life back together. Or started a new one, since anything prior to the hospital had yet to return.

She established herself in her new home with only one change. The stove, she discovered, was gas. And just the thought of having an open flame anywhere near her scared her to the point she couldn't function. Matt hadn't said anything about a fire when her house was destroyed, so she had to assume she'd always had the phobia.

But all the same, she called Matt. He assured her he'd get a contractor out there to cap off the lines and install a new electric range.

It was done quickly, and Paige felt better for having made the change.

Months went by, and still nothing of her previous life came back. She became resigned to never knowing what she'd been like from birth to twenty years old. Like Matt had said, she was starting fresh. Clean slate.

She met some new friends and got reacquainted with old ones. The ones who knew her from before were great in answering whatever questions she had, helping to fill in everything she was missing. She occupied her time with things she liked—helping those less fortunate than she. She volunteered her time to shelters—whether it was for the homeless, the abused, or the four-legged variety. Anywhere she thought she could make a difference, that's where she focused her efforts.

And before she knew it, years had passed.

9

By the time she'd finished talking, Ethan's heart was pounding in his chest and his hands were shaking. He'd remained silent throughout her telling, but something—a feeling, a magical tap on the shoulder—was warning him that there was more to this.

A hard lump grew in the pit of his stomach. He felt sick. Too many things were pointing in a direction that would bring him not only hope, but heartache. How had this happened? How had she survived? Who had taken her out of the state? Who'd re-written her entire life under a false name? And why?

The silence grew after her words trailed off. Ethan swallowed and fought to find his voice. There was one thing he needed to know. One thing that could substantiate the thoughts jumping around in his head.

"When were you hurt?" It came out sounding gruff. He had to clear his throat. "How long ago was it?"

Paige turned to him, a little startled. "Um… It's been a little over four years now."

All breath left Ethan's body as if a massive fist had plowed right into his gut. His head went light from the lack of oxygen, and his hands gripped the desk behind him with destructive force.

His black eyes flew to the matching pair across the room.

"Four years, Evan. That's a big fucking coincidence. Her fear

of fire could stem from being close to or in her parents' house when it blew. Her reaction to me would make more sense if somewhere deep down, she knows what I am. But how would she have ended up over seven hundred miles away? Who—"

"Slow down," his brother cautioned. *"Let's not get ahead of ourselves. I can see the similarities, and there's a lot in her story that begs a few questions. Just let me handle this. I'll get you the answers. I promise."*

To Paige, Evan said, "You don't think it went like that?"

She rose up to pace around. "Why else would Matt tell someone that I was still in the dark about what had actually happened to me? Why would Matt need to know if this guy had made any moves?"

Ethan remained locked in place where he lounged against the desk when her movements brought her close enough that he could smell the soap she'd used on her skin. She seemed to be so lost in her own speculations, she didn't realize she'd come within just a few feet of him.

She spun back and headed towards Evan when he spoke.

"Who is this Nick Cabot? You said you'd done some research on him. What did you find?"

Paige stopped and inhaled deeply before letting it out and getting her thoughts in order. "He's the branch manager for The Quality Bank and Trust here in Daytona. From what I could gather, he's been in that position for the last ten years. He has a wife and kids and seems like an upstanding citizen."

She sat down onto the couch, sighing as she sunk back into the cushions. "I just don't know how he and I intersect."

Ethan's attention snapped to his brother again. *"Evan. Honor's father used to work for that bank. He took a promotion and was transferred here when we were in the seventh grade. This Cabot was probably his co-worker or boss. What the hell is going on?"*

"I don't know, brother, but we'll get to the bottom of it. If

Paige Harrison really is Honor Andrews, someone has a lot of fucking explaining to do."

Ethan saw Evan's gaze turn to the woman on the sofa. Her eyes were closed.

"Miss Harrison." Her eyes slowly opened at Evan's prompting. "It's quite late, and we've disturbed you enough. We'll go and let you get some sleep but, if it's all right, I'd like to speak with you again tomorrow. We can go over more of what happened and try to find the answers for you."

She sat up. "Yeah, I'd like that. I really need to know the truth."

Evan looked to Ethan. "Is the door secure enough for the rest of the night?"

"Yeah." Ethan nodded, standing upright. "It should be fine. I'll come back in the morning and finish it."

Anticipating her trepidation at having him near, Ethan tried to assuage her fears. "I'll make sure to stay out of your way."

The reality was, he wanted to plaster himself to her side and never let her out of his sight again. If this woman was who he thought she was, he wouldn't squander whatever miracle it was that had brought her back to him. He would be the happiest man on the planet if it weren't for the fact that she was so damned frightened of him.

As he and Evan exited her condo and returned to their cars, Ethan was still trying to wrap his head around what had happened in the last few hours. He stopped before getting in and looked over at his brother.

"Evan. Please tell me that this isn't a dream or a hallucination. Please tell me that woman in there is real." His throat tightened until he could barely speak and his eyes burned. He didn't even try to hide the searing agony that gripped him. "I don't think I could survive..."

"What this is, is a fucked-up mess. But it's a very *real* fucked-up mess. Ethan, I promise you—if that *is* Honor in there, we'll find out what the hell happened four years ago. We'll find out where she's been and who took her. And what this whole cluster-fuck has to do with Nick Cabot."

Ethan felt lost. Kind of in limbo. "I don't know what to do now." He scrubbed his hands over his face and back through his hair, gripping it in tight fists before letting his arms drop. His gaze was pulled up to the room where his life had just been turned upside down. When he brought his attention back to his brother, Evan was watching him silently. "But I *do* know that I'm staying here. I have to protect her, Evan."

"No. What you're going to do is go home. Get some sleep. We've had guards on her since the accident, but I'll relieve them tonight. I'll watch over her for you. We'll figure this out, Ethan. You'll get your girl back."

"How? She has no clue who I am or what we meant to each other. She freaks out any time I get anywhere near her. How does that bode well for a happily-ever-after?"

Sympathy and compassion swirled in Evan's black eyes. "Give her time, Ethan. If everything she was told about her life in Louisiana is indeed a lie, then maybe the *real* truth will bring her back to you."

~~~

Ethan didn't know how he could possibly be patient at a time like this. Not when it was entirely probable that the woman he'd loved since junior high was here, only a few miles away. What he wanted to do was go to her, hold her, love her.

But that wasn't going to happen.

There'd been no sleep for him, and as he lay wide-eyed in bed staring up at the ceiling, he warned himself over and over not to let his heart override his brain. He needed to hold something of himself back in case he was wrong and this was all just a huge mistake and a cruel coincidence.
~~~

When he couldn't stand his own circling thoughts any longer, Ethan rolled out of bed and dressed for a run. As he picked up his phone, he absently noticed the time. Just shortly after four in the morning. He shrugged and headed out the door.

Making a point of going in the opposite direction of Paige's condo, he set out at a punishing pace. Sweat rolled down his face and torso after the first three miles. But still he ran, breath sawing in and out of his taxed lungs. His mind was in such turmoil, he didn't know if he were running towards something, or away.

Despite all his best efforts to keep his distance, Ethan was helpless to stop it when his feet carried him down the path that would take him to the beach.

As he neared where he hoped she was now sleeping peacefully, he slowed. Staring up at the building, he absently wiped at the sweat dripping down his face. He couldn't see the parking lot from his vantage point, but he knew that Evan was there. Keeping her safe.

Ethan remained, unable to move, until he became aware of a shift in the air disturbing the early morning quiet. He turned slowly to find Edrick Noor.

Their respite was over.

During their last encounter, Ethan and his twin had ripped away Noor's ability to manifest into the beast form he'd preferred, the trauma of that separation leaving him weak and out of commission for quite some time. But if he were back now, it meant he had enough energy and power to start fucking with them again.

Through sheer will alone, Ethan shook off the rage that wanted to spew out of him for everything this sick bastard had done. Instead, he adopted an attitude of mocking disgust.

"Back for more?" Ethan crossed his muscled arms over his chest in an air of indifference.

Noor's demented gaze bit into Ethan. "So cocky without your

backup. Don't forget I've been deep into your mind. I know you and what you crave."

"You don't know jack shit about me."

Noor smiled evilly. "Oh, really?"

Before Ethan could blink, an image of Honor materialized in front of him. She stood in the space between him and Noor, and looked just as she had four years ago. A ghost straight out of his past. Seeing her like this though, he was able to note the differences time had had on her. She still looked just as beautiful, but also subtly changed.

This was just a hallucination made by a sick, twisted mind. Not the actual woman who was tucked away in the building behind him. He quickly blocked that thought from his mind to keep Noor from learning of her existence. If he knew she was here, in the flesh, he'd stop at nothing to use her against Ethan.

Still, the likeness cut into his heart a little for the girl she'd once been. The girl whom he had loved so deeply. Which is what Noor had aimed to do.

When Ethan saw his eyes flare with unholy glee, he knew something else was about to happen.

The breath left his lungs when she suddenly burst into flames, screaming for him, crying out to be saved.

"Do you think she begged for you like that when she died?" Noor's pleasure in Ethan's pain was crystal clear. "Would she love you now, knowing how you failed her?"

Ethan suddenly realized he *hadn't* failed her. Not in the way he'd always thought. Forces beyond his understanding and control had been in play that night. Even if he'd been able to get there, she still would have been whisked away from him. There was nothing he could have done.

He felt a crushing weight lift from his soul. And because of that, he could look at what Noor was doing and not have it rip his heart in two. Ethan made sure to hide that from him though, choosing instead to play into the anguish, the heartache, the devastating loss. Noor thought he was scoring a major blow with this display. And Ethan let him believe it.

He dropped his hands to his sides and fisted them as if he were holding back the grief caused by the horror in front of him. But instead, he was gathering his elemental power close and kept it carefully banked so the glow of his mark didn't give away his plan. In his closed fist, the heat of his fire rose.

Before Noor knew what he intended, Ethan let loose the ball of flames. It struck him mid-chest and engulfed his entire body. Noor screamed and flailed wildly, trying to pat down the fire before howling his fury and winking out of existence.

Ethan waited and watched for any sign he'd return for retaliation. He saw nothing, but in the silence that followed, he heard a sound behind him. He spun on his heel, ready for anything except what he actually saw.

Paige, as he still made himself think of her, stood behind him. She looked at him with utter horror stamped across her beautiful face, her hands clapped over her mouth as if muffling a scream.

Fuck! She'd seen him use his elemental magic. As far as he knew, she wouldn't have seen Noor or what he'd conjured, but she'd seen enough from Ethan to freak her the hell out. And confirm her deepest suspicions of him. That he was the fire she so desperately feared.

He had to try and calm her before she came out of her shock and ran away screaming.

"Paige." Ethan started to raise his hands to reach out to her, but the action made her gasp and recoil.

After seeing what he'd done, she was scared of what those hands could do. And rightly so.

Shit. What a goddamned time for her to show up.

With no other recourse, he shoved his hands into the pockets of his running shorts.

"Please don't be afraid," he tried to soothe. "I would never hurt you."

Her shimmering gray eyes tracked to his face. Her arm came up, and she shakily pointed to the spot on the beach where his fireball had exploded.

"You...you...how?"

Ethan glanced up and down the shoreline. He hoped Noor had been too focused on him to notice the woman who was supposed to be dead. But he didn't want to take any chances.

His black gaze came back to her smoky one. "Can we take this inside, please? I'd rather not discuss it in the open."

Her auburn hair swung around her shoulders as her head shook. "No."

Ethan couldn't blame her for not wanting to be in a closed-in space with him alone. So, even with the danger of being spotted or overheard, he took a breath and plowed ahead.

"I'm a witch. I'm also linked to the element of fire. I think that's why you react the way you do around me. You must sense the fire in me. And taking into account your fear of it, it would explain your aversion to me."

One foot slid back, telling him she was on the verge of fleeing.

"Please don't run," Ethan implored. "I would never hurt you. I swear that on my life."

She stopped, but still she was poised to bolt if he made one wrong move.

"Why did you do that? There was nothing there."

How to explain this? Ethan's hand itched to run through his hair, but he held off the urge, knowing it might spook her into panicked flight.

"There was, actually."

"No, there wasn't. I saw. You threw that...at nothing. Why?"

Ethan tried for patience. "There is a man...a being that is out for my family's blood."

"A...a being?" she stuttered. Her gray eyes were round, filled with fear and confusion. "What does that mean?"

"He used to be a man. An evil, abusive, horrible man. He acquired power and became something else. He was there, on the beach with me."

When she opened her mouth to speak, he went on.

"I know you couldn't see him. There are only a few of us who can. But he was there, and he wants everyone in my family dead. He enjoys torturing us. He was here to hurt me, so I struck out at him before he could."

Her head tilted as she took that in and seemed to be weighing whether he was crazy or telling the truth. As she came to some decision, her body straightened. Those mesmerizing eyes dropped to where his hands were still stuffed inside his pockets.

"Show me."

Ethan wasn't sure he'd heard her right. The words were spoken so softly, they were almost swallowed up by the sound of the waves at his back. If she'd been any farther than five feet from him, he wouldn't have heard them at all.

"Are you sure?"

She nodded tightly as if she had her whole body on lockdown to keep from sprinting the other way.

Ethan slowly slid his right hand free and held it palm up in front of him. He did nothing but stare at her though, waiting for her to meet his gaze. Eventually, her determined focus raised to his. But still he only watched her face until she nodded again.

He called to his power and a small flame ignited, dancing in the center of his palm.

Because his attention had never left her face, he saw her pupils grow large with fear. But to her credit, she didn't move.

They stood that way for several moments until she inhaled deeply and let it out in a whoosh. On the heels of that, Paige took a small step forward.

She was forcing herself to face her biggest fear.

"You don't have to do this." Ethan began to close his fingers around the element to snuff it out.

"No." She reached out and took another step. "Wait."

He opened his hand again.

She studied the fire intently. "If this is why I want to run every time I see you, how would I have known? How would I know this was a part of you?"

Did he dare reveal who they thought she was? What they'd been together? To each other? Should he compound her confusion by telling her that she wasn't who she thought she was?

He was saved from answering by more people wandering out onto the beach. The sun had begun its ascent, bringing out the early risers. Ethan doused his fire before anyone else happened to see.

Paige was about to protest, but he stopped her.

"I need to go," Ethan told her. "If you really want to have this conversation, we can do it when I come back to fix your door."

When she didn't move, Ethan made the decision for her. "Go back inside, Paige." He didn't know why her guard hadn't already come to see where she was. Had he fallen asleep? Ethan would have to have a talk with Evan.

Turning his full attention back to Paige, he could see her need to argue, to find the answers to the questions in her mind. But Ethan knew she wasn't ready to hear those answers yet. Not when the sight of him still triggered such terror.

Ethan hated to do it, but she didn't seem inclined to take his advice and go back to her room. Steeling his resolve at causing her more upset, he took a step closer to her. Then another. As he'd known she would, she blanched and ran for safety.

He stood there waiting until he heard a door slam, and then turned and jogged for home.

10

Paige found herself with her back pressed against her locked door. Again. Breaths panted in and out of her lungs, though not solely just from fear this time. Panic still tipped the scales, but there were also bits of wonder and disbelief.

That he had magical abilities didn't strike her as all that odd. Living in Louisiana, she'd learned a long time ago that some people just had a little something extra. No. Him having power didn't scare her. It was *how* that power manifested that shook her to the core.

Fire.

Could she have somehow known that was in him? Had she sensed that her greatest fear was alive and waiting within him? Why else would she have such conflicting reactions to two men who were essentially the same? And what other reason could there be for her dream?

But what of his claim that an evil...*entity* had been on the beach with him? Paige hadn't seen anyone or anything, but she knew better than most that there was more in this world than could be physically seen.

Ethan Burke didn't seem to be the type who would go around tossing his magic in plain sight for no reason. In the few times she'd actually been near him, she'd had no inkling that he possessed abilities at all. Granted, she'd usually been running in the opposite direction, but still.

Paige didn't understand how she could be so sure, but she innately knew that if he'd known someone was there to observe him, he would have chosen an alternate way of dealing with whatever obstacle he'd faced.

She could also admit that, despite the fact he frightened the bejeezus out of her, she didn't want to see him or his family hurt. It wasn't his fault that she flipped out every time he got too close. And it sounded like this—whoever it was—was a real piece of work.

Calmer now, she stood up straight and stiffened her spine. She didn't know how long it would take him to make it home and then back here. But she'd be ready when he showed up. She wouldn't let her fear stop her from getting to the bottom of a whole shitload of questions.

An hour later, there was a knock on her door. When she looked through the spy-hole, he was there, the roiling in her stomach confirming what she already knew.

She took a deep breath and pulled the door open. When she backed up and pulled the door open wide, he silently stepped through, careful to keep his distance. He was carrying a toolbox and a plastic shopping bag with him. When she closed the door behind him, he set both on the floor within easy reach of where he'd be working.

"This shouldn't take long. Normally maintenance would deal with this, but the manager knows me and my brother. When we explained the situation and offered to take care of the damage, she didn't have a problem with it."

He turned and got to work.

Paige didn't know how to react. He was going to go about his business as if their earlier encounter hadn't happened. Had he decided against helping her to understand what was going on? Did she go along? Pretend like she hadn't seen what he'd done? Learned what she'd learned?

Hell no.

She wanted answers to every damned thing that had gone screwy in her life. And he seemed to be the only one willing to give them to her. This irrational terror of hers would just have to hold off long enough for her to get them.

Gathering her nerve, she stomped over to stand right behind him. When her heart thumped and sweat gathered between her breasts, she fought through it and held strong.

"You said you'd explain." Her tone was hard and said she wouldn't take no for an answer. "So, explain."

His hands stopped moving and his head dropped forward as he looked down at the floor. His ink-black hair fell forward to hide his profile. Paige saw his shoulders rise and fall with the breath he dragged in and released. When he stood to his full height and turned around to face her, she took an involuntary step back. Then cursed herself for her weakness.

Ethan's black, bottomless eyes held her in their depths. If she weren't so freaked out by him, she might find him handsome.

She pushed those thoughts aside and tried again.

"Help me, Ethan. Please."

He drew inward like she'd punched him in the gut, and emotions flashed across his face in quick succession. Pain, sorrow, and…was that guilt? Why the hell would her asking for his help elicit that severe of a response? What was going on?

"Ethan?"

He was silent for another beat. "Are you sure you want to get into this? It'll be a lot to take in, and most you probably won't believe."

"Just tell me. Please. I need to know."

He slid his hand into his pocket, and when it emerged, he was holding his phone. A couple of taps later, and he turned the screen towards her.

She saw herself and Ethan holding each other close, laughing and smiling. She gasped in shock and reached out with shaky hands to take the device from him.

"What the hell is this?" Paige's legs wouldn't hold her, so she sank down onto the couch.

He sat down at an angle from her. "That...is my fiancé, Honor."

"Why..." She had to clear her throat. "Why does she look like me?"

"Because I think you *are* her."

Her gaze flew to his, finding solemn sincerity. "What? No. That's not possible. Why would you say that? I don't even know you."

"That picture was taken five years ago. Shortly afterwards, seemingly out of the blue, her parents' home exploded. Everything was destroyed in the fire that followed. As far as we knew, Honor and her parents were killed that night. I grieved and I tried to put it behind me. And after a few setbacks, I was making progress with that. And then you show up here with her face and a story of waking up in a hospital—very near the time of the fire—hurt and with no memories. You had nothing of your previous life—no pictures, no personal effects. People are *telling* you who you are and where you're from. That your mom and dad are already dead."

Paige shook her head, not wanting to believe. If what he were saying was true...

Before she could contemplate that more, he continued. "Honor knew who I was, *what* I was." He smiled sadly and his eyes dropped to the phone she still clutched in her hands. "We used to joke that she'd been made just for me, because of her fiery hair and smoky gray eyes. She was different. Strong, beautiful, confident, funny. I would always tell her that although I may wield the fire, she was the one who'd tamed it." He glanced up to the hair she'd pulled back into a ponytail. Unbidden, she reached up and touched the ends.

Ethan brought himself out of his thoughts and back to the present. "I'm fairly certain your fear of fire stems from that night. Chances are, you were close to it, if not actually in it. Maybe the explosion blew you clear of it, and that's how you hit your head, but I don't know. However, it's obvious your subconscious remembers that trauma, even if your conscious mind doesn't. Which explains your extreme aversion to fire. And to me."

He drew in a breath. "I think, deep down, you know the same destructive force—the one that killed your family and stole your life from you—is inside of me."

There was pain in his eyes, and Paige knew this was hurting him. She could see the love he still carried for this woman. But was *she* that woman? She looked down at the photo again, dragging the corners of the image outward to magnify the woman there, and studied every aspect of the happy, smiling face. Her face. Her gray eyes. Her lips that were just a little too big. Her freckles.

There was no denying that this was her. Every feature matched exactly with the stranger she'd seen in the mirror for the last four years. But why all the subterfuge from people she thought were supposed to be her friends? Why would they tell her she was someone she wasn't?

How many of them had lied to her? Matt, she knew for sure. But how many others?

"Why would they lie to me like this? What would be the point?"

"I don't know. That's something I'd like to get to the bottom of myself. Whatever happened and whoever these people are that took you away, they'll have some very pointed questions to answer."

He watched her for a moment. "There's one other thing you should know."

She was almost afraid to ask. "What?"

"Honor's father worked at the same bank as Nick Cabot."

Paige gasped and then spun towards the door when a loud

knock sounded, startling her.

Before she could move though, Ethan stood. "I'll get it. It's my brother."

So much was swirling around in her head. Ethan's story filled in so many blanks, the tie to Cabot being the biggest. It finally brought to light the connection she'd not been able to find to Paige Harrison. The link was to the person she'd evidently been before.

Angry voices pulled her out of her thoughts.

"What do you mean? What exactly did you tell her?"

She turned to see Ethan and his twin squaring off. There was another large man with them. Evan's partner, Seth Lawson.

"Everything. She saw me fighting Noor early this morning. She saw me use my fire."

"Noor was here this morning?" Black brows drew together. "Why the fuck is this the first I'm hearing of it? How long has he been back?"

"I don't know. I was jogging on the beach and suddenly he was there. We had some words, and then he tried his usual method of torment." A meaningful look passed between the identical men, and Paige wondered what it meant. "That's when I chucked a fireball at him and he took off."

Ethan glanced over at Paige. "I heard someone behind me and turned to see her standing there. She'd seen me use my magic, so I had to tell her what I was. And that, of course, led to more questions. Besides...she has the right to know, Evan."

"For who's benefit, Ethan? Hers? Or *yours*?" Evan drilled his brother with a heated glare.

They stared at one another for a moment before Evan let out a tired sigh. "Look. This is a complicated situation. I just don't want to see you get hurt again. Until we know for sure—"

"I *do* know." Ethan met and held Evan's gaze. "And I'd bet my life that the reason she's being targeted now has everything to do with what happened four years ago. I don't know what sent Cabot over the edge, but if he's behind her parents' deaths, do you honestly think he's going to let anything stop him from finishing the job? He's already tried once that we know of."

Paige watched Ethan's face harden as he glared at his twin.

"But I can tell from your lack of surprise that you knew that already, didn't you? And you didn't see fit to tell me?"

"Fuck." Evan scrubbed his hands back through his hair.

"Guys," Seth drew their attention. "I'm pretty sure this needs to wait." He gestured to Paige.

All three men turned to look at her. She heard Ethan mutter, "Shit."

She wasn't sure what he saw when he looked at her. But if the kaleidoscope of emotions she was going through showed on her face, it was no wonder they were shocked by her appearance. This was so much more than she'd bargained for when she'd set out on this mission.

Murder?

What the hell had she stumbled into? Was this what Matt had been hiding from her all these years? Was someone actually trying to kill her? Had they tried four years ago? Was she the reason others were dead?

"Paige?" Ethan approached, and for once the need to flee from him didn't tear at her. The turmoil in her mind was overriding everything else. "Are you okay?"

"No." She shook her head to emphasize her point. "I don't think so." She lifted her gaze and looked way up his body to finally land on his face as he stood towering over her.

Paige gathered the strewn bits of her intellect back into her life raft to keep them on target. "Do you really think he killed my parents?" It was the first time she'd actively thought of herself as Honor. It didn't feel as weird as she would have thought. "Is that why they're dead? Because he was coming for *me?*"

"I might be able to answer that." Seth stepped forward and

drew her attention. "I got in touch with a few of my contacts at the FBI early this morning after Evan told me some of what happened last night. They couldn't tell me much, because technically, it's still an ongoing investigation, but evidently, they were building a case against Cabot for embezzlement five years ago. It seems he'd been skimming funds and transferring them into offshore bank accounts. They had an eyewitness who'd managed to assemble solid evidence against him, and he was all set to testify. The information he had would have put Cabot away for a very long time."

His chocolate brown eyes flicked to her, and Paige's gut clenched, already knowing what was coming.

"Until that witness and his family died in a house fire."

It just didn't seem real. How could any of this have anything to do with her? Despite all they'd told her, none of it triggered *any* memories. It was more like a plot in some awful movie.

But that movie was turning out to be her life. And someone had ripped up her script, leaving her blind to what part she played in all of it.

Ethan swung around to pin Seth down. "Did they say anything else?"

"No. My contact didn't know any more."

"Well, someone sure as shit knows more." Ethan paced around the seating area, his long legs eating up the small space. "Someone had to have been there that night. Otherwise, how the hell did she get out of there? Who took her all the way to Louisiana? And who was the third body in the fire that everyone thought was Honor?"

Paige swallowed the lump in her throat to know someone had died in her place. A hopeful thought occurred to her.

"Is it possible...since it wasn't me...Could the others...?" She split her gaze between the three men.

Ethan came back to sit near her. He was already shaking his head and she knew.

"I'm sorry. It was confirmed. They were positively identified."

"They obviously made one mistake though," she pushed. "Maybe…"

Evan squatted down in front of her. "I'm sorry, hon." He kept his tone easy. "Both were identified through dental records."

Hopes that Paige had been grasping at plummeted. She didn't remember her parents, but the possibility that they could still be alive, that something of her past self was still out there somewhere, had already taken root.

"How'd they get the last one so wrong then?"

"The third victim was too…" Evan paused, "damaged. But according to what I read in the file, she was your build and your height. Eye-witness accounts had you home that evening." Remorse was clear in his voice. "With no other reason to doubt it was you, they made the call based on the information they had at the time. Procedure would have been to confirm by some other method, but with the corroborating statement that Honor was home, they didn't. So, the ID was made."

She was lost in thought for a moment when Seth spoke. "Who was the first to tell you your name was Paige Harrison?" He joined them. "When you woke up in the hospital in Louisiana?"

Paige rubbed her head as the weight of what was happening settled over her. "Um, the nurse."

Seth continued with his questions. "How had they known? Did you have anything with you that could have had that name on it?"

Paige was about to ask why they were going through this again when she remembered Seth hadn't been there. She'd told all of this to Ethan and Evan during their midnight chat. They obviously hadn't had a chance to fill him in completely from the night before.

"No. All legal documents, ID cards, and bank cards were reissued to me later by Matt Grier. He introduced himself as my family's attorney, and told me that my house and all of its contents had been destroyed in a storm. That when I'd been found lying in the debris, they'd rushed me to the hospital."

"And when you woke up," Evan picked up the baton, "you were in Louisiana and already listed as Paige Harrison."

He was quiet as he thought about something.

"Do you know how much time had passed? Before you woke up?"

"The nurse told me I'd been there for a week."

"Do you remember the exact date?"

Paige thought back. The first time she'd become aware of the date was a few days into her stay. She counted back to the day she woke and shared that with the men.

Ethan spoke to no one in general. "That would make it ten days after the fire. So, if she was in Louisiana seven days— she could have been in a medical facility here for a few days, getting her stabilized before they transferred her."

He switched his gaze to his brother. "The timing fits, Evan."

"Yes, it does." Where before sympathy softened his face, Paige now read anger in the detective's chiseled features. "I'd like to have a word or two with this Matt Grier."

"Why don't we call him?" Seth grinned with anticipation. "See what he has to say?"

This is what she'd come for. To find answers. Paige nodded resolutely. "I'd like to know that as well."

11

She rose and went into the bedroom to retrieve her phone. Resuming her seat on the couch, she pulled up the dialing keypad. Once she heard the call had connected, she set it on the table in front of her and engaged the speaker.

The four of them sat forward, waiting for a voice to come on the other end.

"Hey Paige," Matt greeted in lieu of hello. "How goes the antiquing?"

Paige took a fortifying breath. "I'm not in Texas, Matt."

"You're not? Are you back already?"

"No. I was never in Texas. I'm in Florida."

There was complete silence on the other end for a good fifteen seconds.

"What, ah—What are you doing there?"

"I thought I might have some business in Daytona."

They heard rustling through the phone line. Could he be shifting around in a suddenly hot seat? "What kind of business?" His tone was curious but cautious.

"I'm not sure, Matt. Why don't you tell me? There are some people here who seem to think I'm someone named Honor Andrews."

The three men sat quietly and let her handle the attorney. She knew they were itching to speak with him, but she appreciated they let her have her say first.

"Paige. Why don't you come home and we can talk about this? There's no reason for you to be there."

"I think there is, Matt. And the fact that I'm being followed and was run off the road confirms that."

A sound came through the line that could have been a muttered, *fuck*.

"You need to come back here. *Now*." Evidently, he was done playing games.

She opened her mouth to speak, but Evan waved her off. "Mr. Grier. This is Detective Evan Burke with the Daytona Beach Police Department. Am I right in assuming you recognize my last name?"

He ignored Evan's question. "Put Paige back on. I need to speak with her."

Evan glanced up at her. "Oh, she's here. And so is my partner, Detective Seth Lawson. But the one I'm sure you're really wondering about is my brother, Ethan. Yeah, he's here too. Now, why don't you start explaining what the fuck went down four years ago? We'll see if your version matches what we've already been able to piece together."

"I don't have to explain anything to you. That information is attorney-client privilege. Paige needs to get her ass out of there. She's not s..." His words abruptly cut off.

"She's not safe?" Evan finished for him. "We got that loud and clear a few days ago, when she ended up in the hospital."

"Paige? Are you okay?" There was genuine concern in the lawyer's voice.

"I'm fine, Matt." Paige said, annoyed and dismissive. "Cut the shit, and tell me what's going on. You've been lying to me for the past four years, and I want to know why."

"I can't."

"Well then, let me tell *you* what we've been able to gather so far." Evan went through everything they'd learned and how they suspected it had gone down.

"But what we'd really like to know is why he's still after her."

Matt sighed loudly over the phone. "I'm probably going to be fired anyway for letting her slip by me. I might as well put the nail in it."

He cleared his throat, and his voice took on a tone of resignation.

"We'd been working with Mr. Andrews for a year to get the evidence we needed to put Cabot away. Things were finally coming to a head. But what we didn't realize at the time, was that Cabot had some dark connections. At the last minute, we got word that there had been a hit placed on the family. We rushed in that night to move them and take them into protective custody.

"And it would have gone off without a hitch if Paige... *Honor*," he corrected, "hadn't fought us. She refused to leave without first telling her fiancé what was going on. We'd put a gag order on the family through the whole investigation, and she'd agreed, reluctantly, to keep her mouth shut about the case. But leaving without a word didn't fly with her. Myself and two other agents went in to relocate them, but Honor fled out the back door... I assume to get to your brother. I and another agent, Owen, went in pursuit of her. The last, a young new agent, stayed with her parents to keep them on track as they rounded up a few necessities. We'd just cleared the house when it went up. The three of us were blown out into the yard. Owen was the first to come around. He made it over to me just as I was waking up. Once I was on my feet, we went to check on Honor. She was unconscious. Working quickly, we were able to get Honor out of there before whoever had blown the house sky-high could figure it out."

Paige listened, but none of it seemed real. It was like he was referring to someone else. She glanced over at Ethan and saw pain etched across his face. Matt was casually discussing the night he'd lost the love of his life.

"Honor's amnesia had to have been a real blessing for you." There was more than a little derision in Evan's comment.

And Matt heard it. "I won't lie. It helped matters tremendously. After we got her situated, we kept a close eye on her for a while—had people strategically placed around her, both to keep her safe, as well as to acclimate her into her new life. But as time passed and it looked like the memory loss was going to be permanent, we got lax. Which I see now was our mistake. Did you begin to remember, Paige? Is that what led you to Daytona?"

"No. It's all still gone." Out of the corner of her eye, she caught Ethan's wince. "But I heard you on the phone that night at dinner, discussing me and Nick Cabot. And knew then that you'd been lying to me."

"Shit."

"Who were you talking to?" Paige asked. "Why have you been keeping an eye on Cabot?"

"We wanted to make sure he never caught wind that you'd survived. The evidence your father had gathered is still out there. He stashed it and wouldn't tell us where he put it. We had to keep you safe until we could find it and use it to put Cabot away."

"What evidence?" Evan broke in.

"It's a flash drive with account numbers, transactions—the whole money trail leading back to Cabot."

"How can you be sure it's still out there?" Evan pushed. "It may have gone up with the house."

"Andrews was too smart to keep it with him. And he told us that if something were to ever happen to him, Honor held the key."

Paige gasped. "What? What does that even mean?"

"We don't know. As convenient as your memory loss was when it came to protecting you, it also posed a major problem in closing the case against Cabot."

"Without her knowing who she was, she couldn't give you the evidence you needed to put Cabot down," Evan surmised.

"Exactly. This case has been at a standstill for years. Until we can find that flash drive, he remains free. And Honor remains in danger."

He pushed his next comments at her. "Do you see now why you need to come back to Louisiana? We can protect you."

"No." Ethan spoke for the first time, and his voice was hard and cold. "We'll protect her *here*."

Evan jumped in before Matt could argue. "Even if she were to come back there, Cabot would only follow her. Here, she has an advantage. She's surrounded by people and places that are a part of her true past, and she's more likely to regain her memory here in Daytona than there. Plus, I'm guessing the evidence you've been looking for is here somewhere as well. We'll find it."

"We're the government, for Christ's sake!" Belligerence laced Matt's statement. "What could she possibly have there that she wouldn't have here?"

"She has *us*." Her gaze flew to Ethan, who had a small flame glowing brightly on his palm. "She has the Burkes."

Did that mean...? Her eyes flew to Evan. He understood her wonder and nodded.

He was a witch like Ethan.

"And what makes you think you can do a better job than we can?"

"You'd be surprised what we can do." Ethan reached out, disconnected the call, and then shut the phone off.

Paige startled a little when he rose off the chair in a rush. He started moving back and forth across the small living room.

Evan turned to her and drew her attention. "Did any of that trigger anything? Do you have any idea where your dad could have hidden that evidence?"

She slowly pulled her gaze away from the tall, troubled man

prowling around. "No. There's nothing. There's never been anything in all this time. It's all just…gone."

Paige felt their frustration; she'd lived with it every day since waking up, confused and alone. She'd tried everything she could think of to pull the memories back to the surface. Psychics, hypnosis, word association. But nothing worked.

"I just don't know how I'm going to be of any help."

"You let us worry about that." Evan grinned.

Paige studied him for a moment. "You're like Ethan?"

"Yes and no. Yes, I'm a witch. Everyone in our family is, but my power is different than his."

It should have occurred to her that there would be more than just Ethan. "How many of you are there?"

Evan grinned. "Of Burkes, we are legion. But our immediate family consists of our mother and our sisters. The four of us are quadruplets—two sets of identical twins—two girls and two boys."

"Your sisters. Are they petite and blonde?"

Ethan swung around and pinned her with dark eyes. "You remember them?"

His intense concentration on her made her feel as she had in the nightmare, when the heat and flames had held her within their grasp. She wrapped her arms around herself in protection. "No. But I do remember they were at the hospital with you. After my accident."

His gaze slid away and his shoulders slumped as he slid his hands into his pockets. His body language told her that wasn't the answer he'd been hoping for.

Seth stepped forward. "If you're worried about being around all those witches and magic, don't be."

He needn't have worried. Her urge to safeguard herself had nothing to do with the supernatural in general. "I don't have a problem being around people who have a little something extra. I may not have lived in Louisiana as long as I thought I had, but I was there long enough to know there's more in this world than most even know."

Ethan shifted where he stood. Paige looked up at him and waited for him to speak.

"Since it's just me you seem to have a hard time being around, I'll try to keep my distance. I'm still going to watch over you, but I won't come close enough to trigger your fears. I don't want to cause you any further suffering. Will you be okay with that?"

As far as that went, Paige suddenly realized she hadn't felt the desperate drive to get away from him for the last hour or so. The anxiety he wrought in her was in no way gone, but it was lower on the scale—pushed to the back of her mind by everything else that was happening.

Deep down she didn't think she'd ever be able to be around fire and not tremble and panic. Even with the knowledge of where the fear was based, she didn't think she'd ever get past it.

From the looks Ethan cast her way when he thought she didn't see, she could gather he'd really like to pick up where he and Honor had left off. But Paige just didn't think that would be possible.

Aside from the fact that being near him caused her such terror, she wasn't the girl he remembered anymore. She had no clue who that person was. And with no resurfaced memories after all this time, it didn't look like they would ever come back.

She couldn't be the woman he'd known and loved.

And she had a life in Louisiana. Work she enjoyed, friends, neighbors...

Her thoughts were cut short when she remembered something Matt had said. That they had placed people strategically in her life to watch over her. How many? And who were they? Could she trust anyone? Had they *all* lied to her?

Was Gail one of them? Had she been reporting back to Matt

this whole time?

No, Paige decided. Otherwise, he would have known she wasn't in Texas. Gail hadn't betrayed her. But who else had?

"Paige?" Ethan calling her name pulled her out of her thoughts, bringing her back to the present.

"I would really like to live through this, but more than that, I want to make that bastard pay for stealing my life and killing my parents. Since you all seem to be the only ones who can help me, we'll both just have to deal, won't we?"

He didn't say anything, but he nodded.

Paige turned to the others. "So where do we go from here?"

~~~

As Ethan sat in his car watching over her later that night, he tried to distance his mind from what he wanted. Being around her was killing him. Having her look at and treat him as a stranger hurt worse than living without her ever had. Seeing her and smelling her alluring scent tormented him, because for as close as she was, he couldn't touch her, hold her, or nuzzle that sweet spot on the back of her neck.

The one that never failed to melt her. Whether he brushed it with his lips, tongue, or fingers, she would shudder and moan in need.

Had anyone else found that spot? Had she surrendered to another's touch in the last four years? So as not to drive himself insane with thoughts of someone else kissing her, loving her, he recalled, in every detail, the last weekend they'd made love.

~~~

Ethan and Honor both still lived with their families as they tried to save up some money for their own place. While Honor attended college nearby where she was studying to become a nurse, Ethan worked every minute he could and banked the money.

Between work, school, and their living situation, privacy was always a problem. But a holiday weekend was coming up, and Ethan had splurged and gotten them a room at a little bed and breakfast near the beach.

Honor wouldn't be happy about the cost, but once he put his plan in motion for a romantic weekend, he knew she'd fall under the lure of the time alone.

He thought of the cozy room he'd just left and the preparations he'd finished only a short time ago. Ethan smiled and knew she was going to flip out when she saw it. There may even be some happy tears.

Evan would probably rib him mercilessly for it, but then his twin didn't have a romantic bone in his oversized body. Ethan figured he'd gotten them all when the egg had split, and he had no problem with that.

Rushing home, he wanted to shower, shave, and change his clothes before going to pick up Honor. He'd already dropped off their bags and all the other essentials they would need for the three days they'd be tucked away.

So as not to worry them, he'd spoken with both his mom and hers to let them know what he had planned. Honor's mother had even packed a small overnight bag for her. At twenty years old, he and Honor had been together forever. They both had good heads on their shoulders, so their parents didn't worry about them too much. They knew they had a plan for the future and were working towards it.

Pulling into the Andrews' driveway an hour later, Ethan couldn't contain the excitement coursing through his veins. And he couldn't keep the grin off his face as he drove them to their destination.

And he'd been right. There were definitely happy tears shimmering in Honor's eyes when she saw the room he'd decorated for them. Groupings of candles waited only for the spark of flame. As the sun descended, it would leave everything awash in a golden glow. Lilies—her favorite flower—stood tall in vases, their fragrant blooms filling the room.

The bed had already been adorned in a floral quilt, so Ethan had dropped a few of the petals onto it, setting a tray with an ice bucket and glasses in the middle. Chilling there was a bottle of sparkling white grape juice.

"Oh, Ethan," Honor whispered in awe before turning to him in the doorway. Her face beamed as she looked at him. "It's beautiful. I can't believe you did this for us."

He leaned in and kissed her gently on the lips. "I love you."

Her arms snaked around his neck and she leaned into him. "I love you too."

With her still in his arms, he walked her backward until he could close the door behind them. "We happen to have a full bath in this room." He glanced over her shoulder to the open door. "Why don't you go take a hot bath, and I'll get everything ready out here?"

Pleasure lit her face and she all but bounced into the other room. When she walked into the bathroom, she gasped. He knew what she was seeing. Candles and flowers took up every available space.

Ethan grinned and, with just a thought, he had all the wicks flickering to life.

She turned her head and shot him another dazzling smile before closing herself inside the enchanting room.

Ethan took a breath and set his stage. When she emerged thirty minutes later, dressed in only a short robe, he had two glasses poured and a small table set with the food he'd had the owner of the B&B keeping warm for him.

He stopped and stared at her, drinking in every last detail. From the blazing auburn hair piled loosely on top of her head, to the lovely and perfect features on her flushed face. His eyes tracked to the open V at the front of her robe and saw soft, dewy flesh tinged pink from the warmth of her bath.

Her long, slender legs gave way to delicate feet with toenails painted a deep red that somehow matched her hair.

Heated blood flowed throughout his body, sending a delicious need flooding his system. He wanted nothing more than to untie that sash and taste every inch of her. But he also wanted to give her the romance.

"You look so damned beautiful." His voice was raspy with arousal.

She glided sensuously across the floor. Her gray eyes never left his. "You're not looking so bad yourself." When she drew even with him, she laid her hands on his chest and his heart kicked in response.

Ethan couldn't resist her. He lowered his head into the crook between her shoulder and neck. A sweet spot with her, he licked and bit until she was shuddering.

With a will of iron, he lifted away from her and showed her to her seat.

Her eyes had darkened with arousal and her pert nipples pressed against the silky robe, but she dropped her gaze to the table. "What do we have here?" Her voice sounded sexy and hoarse.

Ethan gingerly took his own seat, his erection pushing painfully into his pants. "Fettuccini Alfredo with grilled chicken."

Honor leaned over and sniffed the delicious aroma of garlic and cream sauce. As she did, the robe parted to reveal more of her creamy skin. "Mmm, my favorite."

He tore his focus away from that tempting sight before he bypassed dinner all together. "I know."

Getting through the next hour was sweet torture. They talked and laughed and teased each other with looks of longing.

Ethan could finally take no more, and he rose to hold out a

hand for hers. When Honor placed her palm in his, he pulled her to her feet and into his hard body. He ground his swollen shaft into her.

"I want you so much." He cupped each side of her face in his large hands and dipped his head to kiss her. Speaking against her lips, he whispered words of love and his promise of forever.

Grasping her beneath the arms, he lifted her as her legs wrapped around his waist. The robe parted to let her hot, slick sex settle over him.

He walked them to the bed and laid her gently on top of the strewn lily petals. She took some into her hands and brought them to her face to breathe in the delicate scent. Watching him with seductive intent, Honor dropped them onto her upper body where the silky fabric had parted to expose smooth skin.

Ethan just stared at her. She looked so gorgeous there, waiting for him. She gazed up at him with desire shining in her eyes.

Careful not to dislodge the blooms, Ethan reached down and untied the bow that lay against her supple stomach. Placing his lips where the knot had been, he licked and nibbled the skin there.

The scent of Honor and lilies nearly sent Ethan over the edge.

Her fingers threaded into his hair and gripped it tight. He loved the feel of her hands on him, and when he began a leisurely, erotic downward path, those hands fisted harder in anticipation.

His tongue found her, and when he ran it from the bottom of her entrance to the top, her hips thrusted upward and she moaned. "Oh God, E."

Ethan wrapped his lips around the swollen bud and sucked gently. Her legs quivered on either side of his head, and her breaths panted in and out. Inserting two fingers, her channel clamped down on them. Bending them at the knuckle, Ethan found the sensitive patch of skin at the top of her sex and stroked over it. At the same time, he sucked her clitoris further into his mouth.

Honor erupted into orgasm, her sheath clenching around his fingers, drawing them further into her.

He continued more slowly until the peak subsided and then rose to remove his own clothes. She watched unabashedly, and that made him even harder. He loved how bold and fearless she was. His erection jerked and she grinned at him, licking her lips.

"I want you inside of me. Now."

Ethan couldn't think of any place he'd rather be. With a practiced hand, he donned a condom quickly. Mounting the bed, he crawled over her and looked down into her stunning face. Her hair had come loose and now lay across the bedding in rolling, sexy waves.

She lifted her hands and ran them around his hips to his ass. As she pulled him down to her, she raised her knees and spread her thighs wider.

He pushed against her slick core and slid slowly into her, savoring every sensation until he was seated deep inside. Her body fit him to perfection, and he groaned with her as their bodies became one. Body to body, their limbs tangled together and her gray eyes scorching, he brought his lips down to hers and knew this is where he wanted to be for the rest of his life.

12

Little did he know, he'd never feel her body surrounding him again. He'd never lose himself completely in her love.

Ethan scrubbed his hands over his face and tried to quell the bulge that was pushing against his fly. It wasn't an easy task, as it had been so long since he'd had release. He'd not been with anyone else since that magical holiday. Until just this minute, he hadn't believed he'd ever get hard again.

Honor was his one and only. No one else could stir him the way she had.

He couldn't expect that things had been the same for her. She hadn't known he even existed. As far as she knew, she'd been free and clear of any attachments. Had she found love since then? Was there someone waiting for her to come back?

Needing to get away from that line of thinking, Ethan got out and walked to the edge of the parking lot. Angling himself to keep her door in sight, he breathed deep and drew in the cool, salted air coming in off the ocean.

He had to put this away. Dwelling on the memories of their past together wasn't helping anyone right now, nor was speculating over Paige's love life. He had to concentrate on keeping her safe, so she could find the answers she was looking for. That *he* was now looking for.

Ethan fell into kind of a routine after that. During the day, he worked and did what he needed to do in the fight against

Noor. At night, he watched over Paige.

He was settled into his usual spot. It was late, probably around two a.m., when he saw the lights in her condo flick on.

Maybe she was getting a drink of water. Ethan watched and waited for them to go off again, but when fifteen minutes had gone by and they remained on, he began to wonder if something was wrong.

Taking his phone from the center console, he dialed her number.

It rang three times before he heard her voice. "Hello?"

"Are you okay?" he asked her in a gentle voice. "Is everything alright?"

"How did you…?"

"The lights."

"Oh. Right." He heard her sigh. "Dreams."

"The same one?" He paused. "Of the fire?" His unspoken question was if her mind was still lumping him in with the cause of her fears. If he were going to star in her dreams, this wasn't the way he wanted.

"No. Just a disjointed mess of unsettling crap." There was frustration clear in her tone.

"Do you want to talk about it? Getting it out and into the open might help."

"No. I don't want to talk about it. It doesn't do any good."

She sounded like she needed to blow off some steam. It had been a few days, and he knew she hadn't been leaving her condo at all. An idea struck Ethan.

"I think I know of something that might help. It's not far." Ethan knew the rental company had provided her with a new vehicle after the accident, so he made the offer. "You can follow me if that would make you more comfortable."

"Right now? It's so late." Paige hesitated, but she sounded reluctantly interested. She had to be tired of staring at the same four walls all the time. "Where would we be going?"

"It's a surprise." He waited for her to come to a decision.

Her voice was tentative. "Do I need anything?"

Ethan released a breath he hadn't known he was holding. "No. Just throw on some sweats. Or something comfortable."

"I'll be right there."

His eyes stayed glued on her door and a few minutes later, she came out and approached where he was parked. He hit the button to unlock the doors and she slid into the passenger seat.

Her actions stunned him. "I thought maybe you'd prefer to follow me."

"I'm tired of this fear ruling my life. I think I can handle a few minutes in a car with you." Paige's body language was stiff despite her words. He admired her will and hoped she could handle it.

They rode through the quiet night not saying anything. When he pulled into Knight's Place ten minutes later, she looked out the windshield at the large block building.

"Where are we?"

"My brother-in-law's gym. He used to be an MMA fighter, and now he trains them."

"It's two-thirty in the morning. Won't he mind us breaking in?"

"Nope." He held up the key. "Come on." Ethan smiled at her and opened his door.

She followed a little more slowly, still not too sure.

Ethan disengaged the bolt. Holding the door wide, she preceded him in and stopped in the darkness.

Reaching out, he flipped a couple of switches and had half the lights humming to life.

"Wow. This is quite a place."

"We've all started working out here since Anna and Joe became a couple. There's even an apartment up those stairs at the back. Kyra stayed there for a little while when Evan first met her."

"Why?"

"That's a long and complicated story for another time. Let's do this."

"What did you have in mind?"

"We'll get you gloved up, and you can take out all that frustration on a heavy bag."

"I don't know." She looked apprehensive. "I've never hit anything in my life."

Ethan stopped and looked back at her. "Actually, you have."

"No, I…" Her words halted. "Well, shit. You?"

"I'm sure you wanted to now and then," Ethan laughed. "But no. It was actually Evan you clobbered."

Her eyes widened in shock. "Why on earth did I do that?"

"All of us had gone to a local theme park. You, me, Evan, the girls. I think we were all about eighteen. We'd been there most of the day and had ridden just about all of the roller coasters, multiple times. We were walking along, trying to decide what to have for dinner, and Evan just kept picking at you—teasing and poking like he usually did with our sisters." Ethan chuckled at the memory. "Suddenly, you'd had enough. You spun around and lit into him."

The chuckles grew to genuine merriment. "Your fists were flying. You could only reach to about his chest and stomach, but it didn't matter. You totally let him have it. I don't know who was more shocked—him or everyone else." Ethan got a hold of himself. "And then, just as calm as could be, you turned back around and stalked off. I loved it."

He could still see a stunned Evan standing there, stupefied, and his grin reappeared. "Oh, the look on his face was priceless." He shook his head. "He's never forgotten, and he never messed with you again."

"Was I a violent person?" she asked.

"No. Not in the slightest. It was a one-off moment, and that's why it was so funny. Though I personally always knew you had it in you. That red in your hair is there for a reason."

Ethan waited as she tried to reconcile the person he described with the person she knew herself to be. It had to be hard to have someone tell you something about yourself and not remember any of it.

"Come on." Ethan motioned her along. "We'll get you suited up."

He led her to the equipment supply cabinet and found the smallest padded gloves. He held them up and said, "It'll be easier if I put them on you."

Paige visibly gathered herself and nodded. Ethan worked quickly and efficiently, knowing the close proximity would bother her whether she admitted it or not. As soon as he tied off the last lace, he backed away.

"You'll start out on the heavy bag." She followed him to where there were several spaced out and hanging from sturdy chains. Ethan circled the bag and braced it from the opposite side.

She positioned herself in front of it and gave it a half-hearted girly punch. He watched for all of three slap-style punches before he had to stop her.

"Seriously?" Incredulousness laced his tone.

"What?" Her hands dropped to her sides and smoky eyes met his.

"That's pitiful." He came out from around the bag to stand next to her. Not too close though. "You need a crash course in the art of not punching like a girl."

That got her ire up. "What do you mean? I was doing what you wanted."

Ethan sighed. "No, you were swatting at flies."

"I was not," she argued, a little indignant.

He grimaced. "Yeah, you really were."

"All right, hot shot. Show me how it's done."

When she forgot to be afraid of him, she gave as good as she got. And pieces of the old Honor came through.

Ethan tucked that away and took up a fighting stance. Legs spread, knees loose, hands raised and guarding his face.

When she just stood there staring at him, he nodded at her. "Come on, Rocky, get 'em up."

She shook her head but copied his posture.

"Now, we're going to throw a right jab." He shot his right arm out, straight from his shoulder as Joe had shown him.

Paige repeated his move.

"Good. Go ahead and strike the bag, and we'll go through a few more."

Soon she was wailing away, and he'd returned to his job of bracing the piece of equipment for her. He watched her face as she finally let loose the hurt and frustration and confusion. He didn't know who exactly became her target, but if the real person were standing here, they'd be laid out.

Thirty minutes later, she was sweating and breathing heavily. Arms that had to be shaking by now hung limply at her sides.

"Feel better?" he inquired, standing upright.

"I do," she panted out. "I feel, I don't know, energized." She swung her arms back and forth, stretching out her muscles. Using a gloved hand, she swiped at the hair stuck to her face but missed it.

Not thinking, Ethan reached out to help.

And she jumped back away from him with a gasp.

"Fuck. I'm so sorry." He backed away too. "I wasn't thinking."

He was mad at himself for causing her even a moment of distress and ruining the progress they'd made. Just before turning and going to the men's room, Ethan told her, "I'll give you a minute."

The farther away he was right now, the better he figured she'd be.

Closing the door firmly behind him, he went to the sink and

grabbed hold of the edge. Leaning hard on it, his head hung down between his shoulders. How the hell was he going to do this? Just when he thought they would make it through, the terror she still felt in his presence struck him straight in the chest and ripped his heart out.

He should just call one of his siblings to come and take her back to her condo. After his careless blunder, she probably didn't want to be anywhere near him. And it was probably for the best, anyway.

But before he could make the telepathic call, there was a knock on the door.

"Ethan?" she called softly.

He went to the door to open it but stayed his hand. He couldn't bear to look into her fear-filled eyes, so he took the coward's way out and spoke through the wooden panel. "I'll call Evan, and he can take you back home. This was a bad idea. I'm sorry."

There was a pause and he assumed she was counting her blessings that she wouldn't be trapped in the car with him again.

When her voice carried through the door a second time, though, it was filled with concern and worry.

"Um, Ethan? I think you need to get out here. Some men just walked in, and they don't look so nice."

Ethan about ripped it from its hinges to get to her. Had Cabot sent his guys after her again? Had they followed them here? As soon as he saw the men, though, he knew this had nothing to do with Cabot and everything to do with Noor.

He stood front and center in the group of five of his human goons.

Son of a bitch.

He stepped in front of Paige, blocking Noor's view of her at the same time he put out the call to his siblings.

"All hands on deck, guys. Hate to drag you all out of bed, but

I need some help here. I'm at the gym with Paige, and Noor just showed up with reinforcements in tow."

"Why is it always the gym?" Anna groused sleepily. *"Joe is going to be pissed when I tell him."*

"Hold them off," Evan told him. *"We'll be there soon."*

"With Paige here, I'm a little stymied with my magic," Ethan returned. *"Just get here, and fast."*

"Who do we have here?" Noor crooned and tried to see around Ethan. Surprise marked his face before an unholy glee took it over. "Isn't this a fortuitous surprise? You've been holding out on me, Ethan. I won't even ask how it's possible that she's here."

"What do you want, Noor?" Ethan's voice was tight, but he had to keep Noor's attention off of Paige and on him. He sent a smirk to his enemy. "And what's with all the backup? You think you need this many men to take me on? What's the matter? Are you still shooting blanks from what Evan and I did to you?"

As if acknowledging them had brought them to life, the men spread out around Ethan and Paige.

Noor grinned and that wasn't good. He looked way too sure of himself, and a trickle of unease crawled up Ethan's spine. "When my men informed me you'd come here, I thought it the perfect opportunity to revisit our prior arrangement. But I see that you have no need of what I can offer. Though," he shrugged, "if she were to come to some kind of harm, just as you got her back..."

His men moved in as if to make a grab for Paige. Ethan sent two of them hurtling backward with just a thought. He heard Paige gasp, but he couldn't let that distract him. Shifting gears, knowing he couldn't take on all five plus Noor, Ethan took every piece of gym equipment that wasn't nailed down, and lifted it. They became his arsenal.

The other three men, and the two he'd tossed, stopped, not sure of how to proceed with so many weapons hovering around them.

"You'll keep your fucking hands off her," Ethan ground out. "Or deal with me. Try it, and I won't need any help sending you scrambling back to your cage."

A malevolent light lit in Noor's eyes. "As I'm sure your nosy siblings are already on their way, we'll take our leave." He eyed Paige menacingly before turning back to Ethan with a sinister smile. "A far better opportunity to exact my revenge has unexpectedly presented itself." Without looking at them, he spoke to his men. "Come, gentlemen."

Turning away from Ethan, they filed out. Ethan waited, fists clenched and vibrating with barely controlled fury and fear. When the last one cleared the doorway, he was able to return the suspended objects back to their rightful places before his limit was reached. He spun and paced, running his hands through his long hair. "Fuck. Fuck. Fuck. *Fuck!*"

After the mess he'd gotten himself into a few months back, Ethan knew exactly who Noor thought Paige was and what she meant to him. He would stop at nothing now to take her from him. Permanently and viciously.

Ethan's stomach pitched. Noor had proven, many times over, just how sadistic and demented he really was. He'd targeted just about everyone who meant anything to the Burke family. Knowing what Noor was capable of and seeing it focused on Paige made Ethan sick.

He'd lost her once. He couldn't go through that again, even if she never remembered who they once were to each other. Ethan was trying to come up with a plan when she spoke from behind him.

"What the hell was that?" Paige demanded. "Why did those men try to attack us? And who were you talking to?"

Ethan swung around to face her, but before he could explain, the front door burst inward. He pivoted back around, ready to fight in case Noor or his minions had decided to come back.

He relaxed when Anna and Joe stormed in. They stopped and stared at the empty gym.

"Where is he?" Joe scanned the space looking for the enemy.

"They left," Ethan relayed.

"What? Just like that?" Anna, hair messy and down around her shoulders, approached. She'd be able to pick up on the turmoil racking him.

Ethan looked deep into her blue eyes. "He saw Paige." It didn't require any further explanation. Anna would know just how fucked he was with that simple statement.

Suddenly the room was filled with the rest of his family. And chaos reigned until everyone figured out the threat was already gone. When they all quieted, Ethan filled them in on the encounter with Noor.

"And he just walked out?" Even Seth had a hard time believing it.

"As he said," Ethan's glance slipped in Paige's direction, "he found a better way to get to me."

Paige suddenly stepped into the middle of them. "Since none of you have seen fit to explain it to me, I'm going to guess and say that something is me?"

Ethan hated to have to share with her what he'd done. But in order for her to understand the danger she was in, she needed to know.

"Noor knows exactly how much Honor meant to me. And he uses that, uses *you*, to torment me. Since the fire, I've always dreamed of you. But then almost a year ago, the dreams changed. It was like you were still here. Like our lives hadn't stopped that night. My dreams were showing me what it would have been like if you hadn't died. We were living the life we'd always wanted."

Ethan took a breath. "I knew deep down Noor was behind them. But by then I didn't care. That time with you became my salvation—my sanctuary from everything else that was going on in our world. It also became my addiction. And Noor happily supplied what I needed. Then payment came due, and Jacob was almost taken. I could have cost this family so much because of my weakness."

Anna stepped forward and laid a hand on his arm. "You protected him. And you paid a weighty price for that."

Ethan held his sister's gaze and admitted a truth that still rested heavy on his heart. "It wasn't enough to make up for what I did." He'd lost his family's respect with his actions, but more than that, he'd lost respect in himself. He didn't know how he'd ever get that back. "It'll never be enough."

"Ethan." Anna's face was awash with shock at his admission.

He turned away and spoke to Evan before his sister could try to ease a burden that was his alone to carry. "We need to get Paige out of town."

But Paige jumped in. "Wait. What? Why?"

Ethan ignored her and told his brother, "He can't be allowed to get anywhere near her. She won't even see him coming. We'll have to think of someplace for her to go—"

"Wait just a damned minute!" Paige shouted to get his attention. "I don't remember putting *you* in charge of my life. I have too much to do here. You know that."

Ethan spun around and pinned her with an unmoving glare. "That will have to wait. Edrick Noor is infinitely more dangerous than Cabot. If he gets his hands on you, your life will be utter hell. He's sadistic and brutal in ways you can't even imagine. He literally gets *off* on hurting people. Especially women."

He shook his head. "No. I won't have you here. It's too dangerous now that Noor knows about you."

She stood firm and got in his face, their noses almost touching. "I don't care who knows what. I'm *not* leaving."

They stared at one another for what seemed like years, and Ethan couldn't help noticing it was the closest they'd been since she'd reappeared back in his life. Before things could escalate further, Aria spoke into the tension-fraught silence. "I think we all need to just take a minute and come back when we have clearer and calmer heads to discuss this. We're all tired and a little on edge right now."

"I think that's a good idea." Anna aligned herself with her twin. "Why don't we just plan on a family meeting tomorrow at Mom and Dad's? Aside from this new development, there's still the journals. We've been working on them—well, Mom mostly—but it's slow going, and we need to get through what's in them."

Ethan still wanted Paige out of harm's way, but he could see the merit in his sisters' plans. Though with the way things now stood, he doubted he'd get any sleep. With two psychos hunting her, there was no fucking way he'd leave her unguarded, even for a minute.

"Fine," Ethan muttered. After all that had happened, he could guess that the last place she wanted to be right now was anywhere near him, so he looked over at his brother. "Will you take Paige back? I'll follow and then watch over her for the remainder of the night."

"No," Anna surprised him by stating firmly, "you won't. You're going to go home and get some rest. I can feel just how overwhelming your exhaustion is, which tells me you're too tired to even attempt to block me out." She rested her hand on his arm. "You're no good to anyone this way, Ethan. One of us will keep her safe."

"I can do it," Seth offered.

Ethan stared at his sister and scowled. He knew that look. She wasn't going to budge on this.

Sending Seth an appreciative nod, he looked back to Paige. She was still fuming, and he couldn't blame her. But that didn't change how he felt.

Turning on his heel, he strode for the door.

13

Paige's head was still reeling as she lay in bed. The last few hours had been more than her mind could handle. First, weird dreams. Then the oddly calming phone call from Ethan just to check on her. Followed by a boxing lesson that had actually helped to clear away more of the stress caused by the mess she was in.

She'd even forgotten for a while that the man with her was the embodiment of her greatest fear. He'd been sweet and funny and gentle. Then one moment of distraction had ruined it. All he'd done was reach a hand out to her, and she'd freaked out. It hadn't been a conscious reaction; her reflexes had just taken over.

From there it had gone downhill faster than she could keep up. She'd been trying to find a way to fix what she'd done when the men had shown up.

It had surprised her how fast Ethan had positioned himself between her and the newcomers. As soon as there was danger, he'd jumped in to protect her.

Still recovering from that, he'd started to carry on a conversation she could only follow half of. He'd speak, she thought to the men, but there'd been no reply. And then he'd answer, like someone had actually said something back to him.

It was just like she'd seen on the beach. The invisible enemy he'd spoken of, one that he could see and hear, but she couldn't.

Even if she hadn't *seen* him, she'd most certainly seen the men staring them down with killing looks. Suddenly, without a command from anyone, all five of them had moved in on her and Ethan. She'd been sure they were going to kill her, and maybe Ethan too. But then two of the men had flown backward and the equipment in the gym had risen to float above the floor. It had all hovered there, threateningly aimed at the men. She hadn't known Ethan could do that, but it'd been enough to hold them off. Until, apparently, their invisible boss had told them to leave.

Paige had still been trying to process what she'd seen when Ethan's family had descended on them. How had they known to come? Maybe Ethan had called them from the bathroom. But then, there really hadn't been time for that, because he'd come out as soon as she'd said the men were there.

Her head was aching with so much swirling around in it. She rubbed her hands over her temples and tried to wipe it away.

For the next hour she attempted to sleep, but slumber proved elusive. Aside from everything else, there was a vague feeling of unease inside her. When she examined it more closely, she found it stemmed from the fact that it wasn't Ethan outside keeping watch. As much as she feared him, he'd proven over and over his commitment to protecting her. Knowing someone else was out there left her unsettled.

She knew Seth. He seemed like a nice guy and a good cop— more than capable of taking care of anyone who came for her. So why couldn't she relax enough to drift off?

Paige tossed and turned a while longer until somewhere around dawn she finally dropped into a restless doze. When she opened her eyes a few hours later, she still felt groggy and her brain was only firing on one or two cylinders. She needed caffeine. Massive amounts of it.

Administered intravenously, preferably.

She took her first cup of coffee into the shower with her and sipped as the hot spray hit the back of her head and slid down her body. The second cup was greedily poured once she was dressed.

Sitting in the living room, Paige savored the hot brew and let it do its thing.

She'd drank about half when there was a knock on the door. Setting the cup aside, she went to answer.

And found both of Ethan's sisters on her doorstep.

They grinned. "We've come to take you to breakfast."

Paige could only stare. They looked fresh and rested. Like nothing at all had occurred during the night. Despite the shower and coffee, she still felt like a train wreck.

"I'm Anna, by the way." She held out a slim hand in greeting.

Paige took it by rote and shook it. "Hi."

Anna finished the introductions. "And this is Aria."

Paige turned to the identical woman beside her. "Good morning."

She studied Ethan's sisters, waiting for something to click. For some memory to surface. But as usual, none did. She should be used to this by now, but it still hurt a little that these people knew her and she not them.

"We thought you were due for some girl time," Anna explained. "As much as we love our brothers, they can be a bit much."

"Come to breakfast with us," Aria cajoled. "We'll talk and get reacquainted."

She didn't have any other pressing business, and she needed something to take her mind off of everything. "Sure. Why not?" Paige stepped back in to grab her purse and she was ready.

They took her to a cute little café not too far from her condo. She'd have to remember it when she got tired of eating at the pancake place.

Once they were seated and they'd placed their orders, Anna leaned forward on the table. "Tell us about your life in

Louisiana. I've never been, but it looks like a place I'd love to visit someday."

For the next two hours, they sat and talked about everything. The twins were careful not to drown her in stories she wouldn't recall anyway. They treated her like someone they'd just met and were getting to know, and she appreciated their efforts.

Anna was full of stories about her son, who Paige learned was adopted. Anna skimmed a little of what had happened to him and how he'd come to be with them.

It was a miracle he'd found his way to people who not only could help him and show him the ways of his gifts, but who were actually blood-related. He sounded like a very lucky boy.

When she asked, they explained about the powers they carried. When she asked about Noor, they hesitated.

"Maybe that should wait until later when we're all at Mom and Dad's," Aria warned. "We've got a lot to discuss, and there's no sense in going through it more than we need to."

Paige could see her point. She'd just hold off with the rest of her questions.

A short while later, they dropped her back off at her condo. She glanced around as she stepped inside and saw a familiar car parked close by.

Ethan.

She waited for Aria and Anna to drive away before walking back out to the parking lot. Before she could talk herself out of it, she strode right up to the passenger side of the car and got in.

"Have you been sitting here the whole time I've been gone?"

"No. The girls let me know you were on your way back."

He looked like he'd gotten about as much rest as she had. "Did you get any sleep?"

A large coffee cup raised to his mouth and then lowered. "Tried. It didn't work out that well."

She laid her head back against the headrest. "Yeah, me

neither." She cast a quick glance at his drink.

"What I wouldn't give for one of those."

Without hesitation, he handed the cup over to her.

"Oh, I couldn't take that. If you feel anything like I do, you need it."

The proffered drink stayed between them. "I've lost count of how many of these I've had already. You'd be doing my stomach a favor by taking it."

"Are you sure?" He nodded and pushed it at her. "Thank you."

She took a careful sip, only to discover that it had gone cold. "Eww, it's cold."

Ethan stared at her as he held out his hand. "I can warm it back up if you want."

It took her a second, but she finally figured it out. He was offering to use his magic to reheat the liquid.

Did she have enough guts to let him? Or would she run screaming?

Her belly wanted to rebel, but she beat it back. Taking her nerves in a tight grip, she passed it back to him.

His black eyes stayed on hers as he held it aloft. She saw something flare in his gaze and then he gestured that she could take it again. He was careful not to touch her as the cup transferred from his hand to hers.

This time when she grasped it, she could feel the warmth radiating through the cardboard sleeve. She took a sip and then decided to push herself further.

"I don't want to be afraid anymore. Show me. Please."

She watched as myriad emotions flicked across his face. When his eyes took on a determined resolve, he turned his hand palm up. A small flame appeared and seemed to dance. At the same time, she caught a glimpse of a faint red glow through his shirt. When her gaze tracked to that, he looked down at his own chest.

Using his other hand, he pulled the collar down. "My birthmark. The one that connects me to the element. Each of us has one."

Paige couldn't take her eyes off of it. It could almost be a tattoo instead of something he'd been born with. The outer circle was perfectly round, and the flames inside it looked real. And now it lit with his power. Power over what she feared most.

As he released his shirt, she tore her gaze from his mark to his hand. As she studied the fire there, he gradually made it larger until it was about six inches tall.

Her heart was pounding in her chest. Everything in her was telling her to run and not look back. Instead, while images of being burned alive flooded her mind, she raised a shaking hand and brought it near the flame.

Waiting for the heat of it to grab her and hold her, to Paige's surprise, there was none. Her breath whooshed out and her gaze jumped to his.

Ethan knew instantly what caused her reaction. "When it's of my own making, I can determine how hot it is. And even when it's not mine, I can control the temperature to a certain extent."

Thinking of her dream, she asked, "Can you really walk through it?"

He nodded. "Since I am fire and fire is me, it doesn't affect me as it does everyone else. It can't hurt me. I've been fully engulfed, and came out without a singe."

There, sitting in the car with him, Paige took the first steps to getting over a fear that had crippled her for as long as she could remember. She knew it wouldn't be an immediate fix, but it was a start to taking her life back.

After he extinguished his power, they sat in silence for a while just staring out the window. She should have felt uncomfortable and looked for something, anything, to fill the quiet. But, to her surprise, she felt calm and peaceful.

"Paige." Ethan's gentle voice pulled her out of her thoughts, and she turned to look over at him.

"Are you going to be okay at my parents' house? I would hate to have you feel overwhelmed. Or to have you think we're pushing you to remember."

She recalled how the breakfast had gone with his sisters. "I appreciate how considerate and patient you and your family are being with me. It can't be any easier to be on your end of this situation. Here I am, the girl you all remember, back from the dead. Yet, not the same person at all. I can't imagine what you're going through whenever you look at me."

She paused and took a slow breath. "As far as pushing me to remember, I don't think that's even possible. I've been here for weeks now, and nothing has even budged that locked door in my brain. I grew up here, for God's sake. Any number of things in this area should have blasted it wide open, but nothing has. Not a single place or person."

Paige needed him to know he wasn't going to get his love back. "I'm afraid my memories are gone for good. I'll never remember who I was before."

A quick wince of pain flickered in his eyes before it faded. "What have your doctors said?"

She couldn't tell if there was still hope lingering behind his question. "They were very optimistic at first and told me that with my kind of head injury, some amount of amnesia was normal. Said I probably wouldn't ever remember the accident, but that the rest should gradually come back. They kept telling me to be patient, to wait, to believe. I could see it in their faces, though. The longer it went on, the less even they thought it would return."

She dropped her gaze to her hands in her lap. "I eventually stopped showing up to my appointments. I just couldn't stand to see the pity in their eyes anymore."

Paige suddenly needed some air. "I think I'm going to walk

on the beach for a bit before we have to leave." She placed her hand on the handle, but he stalled her.

"I don't think it's a good idea for you to wander around by yourself."

"I won't go far—I just need to think and breathe. I don't have a problem with you keeping an eye on me. But I need to be alone for a bit."

She didn't give him a choice at that point. Wrenching the door open, she closed it behind her and started across the parking lot to the beach access. When her feet hit the sand, she stopped and let the sound of wind and waves wash over her.

Picking a direction, she strolled down the sandy shore. Keeping her word, she trekked a little ways down, but then turned and slowly retraced her steps back along the white sands, stopping to watch as a small group of pelicans flew overhead.

Paige closed her eyes and let the breeze coming in off the ocean play through her hair, whipping it back away from her face, the sound of the water breaking over the beach in front of her soothing to her soul.

She'd like nothing better than to stand here for hours, but she knew if she stayed out much longer, Ethan would come for her. She didn't like the limitations on her freedom, but she knew it was only for her protection. Until they found a way to stop two madmen out to destroy her, she had a target painted on her.

Turning away, Paige made her way the few yards back to the gate that would take her onto the condo property.

And then the ground beneath her feet was suddenly gone, and she was falling.

One second, she was walking along the edge of the Atlantic Ocean, and the next, she was being swallowed up. There'd been nothing there to warn her of the vast chasm awaiting her. It had looked just like any other stretch of the shore.

A scream was ripped from her throat as she dropped into the unknown.

As the earth closed over her head, her shrieks of fright were abruptly cut off. Paige opened her mouth to call for help, but nothing emerged. The abyss surrounding her absorbed the sound. No one could hear her.

That's when she noticed the wind and waves she'd taken solace in only moments before were also silent. No sound at all could penetrate this cavernous void. Nor could any light. Paige could see nothing but blackness as she was enveloped. A weight pressed in on her, encasing her body just as water would at great depths.

But this was not anything as innocuous as water. This was oppressive and deadly.

Her whimpering cries echoed inside her own head as she tried to move her arms and legs. To find some way out of whatever this was. Her movements were slow and laborious, the substance that held her thick and heavy, clinging to her like a gelatinous weight. Tears fell down her cheeks as she wondered if anyone would ever find her. Would she be buried forever in this oblivion?

Paige wanted so badly to scream, to rage, but she was afraid to open her mouth as the darkness molded itself to her face. She tried desperately to hold her breath as it pressed in closer to cover her mouth, nose, and eyes. But when her lungs burned from lack of oxygen, she had no choice but to gasp for air.

That's when she realized she wasn't going to suffocate, and a deep terror overtook her. This place would kill her, surely. But it would be a slow, agonizing death.

Oh, God. Please don't let me die here. She sobbed. *Ethan, please help me.*

When she'd gone on her walk, she'd left him sitting in the safety of his car. Had he even seen what had happened to her or where she'd gone? The expanse of beach where she'd been walking was well below the level of the parking lot. Did he know she was missing? Would his protective instincts have made him follow, if only to stand on the edge of the lot and watch over her?

As she struggled against the heaviness pressing in on her, Paige had to pray that's what he'd done and that he'd come for her. But in the meantime, she had to get a grip on herself and fight. She was scared shitless and couldn't stop the tears from falling, but she wasn't about to give up.

Slowly, and with an effort that wore her out, she was able to pull her hand up her body until she thought it was outstretched above her head, her fingers wiggling and reaching, seeking out something, anything to hold on to in the darkness.

Please. Please. Please.

Suddenly, she felt something bump against her hand.

Paige strained to wave her hand back and forth, her movements sluggish and slow, hindered by the crushing weight. She choked on frustrated moans as what could be her salvation brushed by her a couple more times.

No. No. No. Come back.

The next time she felt it, Paige curled her fingers around what she now knew was someone's hand and held on to it for all she was worth.

As soon as she touched it, she knew exactly who it was.

Ethan. He'd come.

Hope flared in her heart and relief washed through her. But those were both overshadowed by the flashes she saw in her mind when her flesh touched his. They weren't full-blown memories, but snapshots of a previous life. A high school hallway, a picnic in a sunny park, driving with the windows down and the breeze in her hair. Laughter, fun, and love. And each one had a common thread.

She and Ethan. Holding hands, just as they were now.

Paige gasped, shaken that after all this time, something from her past had finally emerged. She dearly wanted to examine them down to the last detail, but a tug on her arm reminded her she needed to escape this hell before she could think about anything else.

Tucking those precious scenes away for now, Paige kicked her legs as if swimming upward as Ethan started to pull her from the depths of blackness.

Bright sunlight nearly blinded her as her head breached the surface. More tears rained down as she looked up into his face and begged, "Please, get me out of here."

"I'm trying, baby." His deep, soulful eyes bore into hers and promised her he'd save her. "Give me your other hand."

Paige didn't think he was even aware of the endearment. But she was. And for the first time ever, her stomach fluttered.

Again, now was not the time to figure out what any of this meant, so she pushed it away and concentrated on survival. She struggled to bring her other hand up and out. Once it was free, Ethan grabbed it and heaved.

With better leverage, he hauled her up and out of the pit. When the suction finally gave up its hold with a loud squelching sound, Paige flew forward and landed on top of Ethan. Their bodies aligned from chest to toe, lungs laboring from the exertion.

Paige lay there for a moment, held in his arms, as she tried to calm her rioting emotions.

"Are you okay?" His deep voice rumbled in his chest.

Her cheek rubbed against his shirt as she nodded. "Thank you for saving me. Again."

"You're welcome. I'm just glad I saw where you went in."

Raising her head, she stared down into his dark eyes and saw fear, guilt, and love each taking a turn in his gaze. And quick as a heartbeat, she saw another scene. One very much the same. Her lying on him, and him smiling up at her.

More than she could take right now, she rolled to the side

and sat up, breaking the connection between them.

She took a steadying breath and wiped at the moisture on her cheeks. It was then she noticed her hands and arms were clean. Looking down at her body and legs, they were also clear of any muck. There was nothing to show where she'd been. No residual goo stuck to her, or her clothes.

Her gaze jumped to the sand in front of them and scanned for any signs. It all looked normal. "What the hell was that?"

Ethan had sat up also. Bending his legs, he rested his forearms over his upraised knees.

"I'm not sure what it was, but I'm fairly certain Noor was behind it."

Paige swung her gaze back around to his. Her stomach pitched a little when their eyes met. She wasn't all that sure if it was due to what was inside of him, or what was inside of her.

"That guy from the gym?" she prompted, keeping her mind on track. "The one you were talking to that I couldn't see?"

"Yeah." Ethan nodded. "Edrick Noor. When he saw you last night, I knew he'd try to hurt you, and that's why I wanted you out of his path. But I thought he'd send his men. I never even considered he'd use his abilities on you. It shouldn't have been possible. I don't understand how he was able to trap you like that."

"What do you mean?"

"For the last nine months, the only ones to see or be affected by his games were me and my siblings or those who carry his blood. You're neither of those." His eyes tracked to where he'd pulled her out. "That magical snare shouldn't have had any effect on you. You should have been able to walk right over it."

He paused as he considered something. "His powers grow stronger the closer we get to February. If this is the next level of his power, and he can target anyone he chooses..." He let his thought trail off, and Paige could see that it really worried him.

"Why is he so focused on you and your family?"

Ethan drew in a deep breath and released it. "He's trying to stop us from fulfilling a prophecy."

That had her blinking. "A prophecy?"

Ethan stood and cautiously looked around. "I'd rather not do this here."

When he turned back to her, she could tell his first instinct was to reach out a hand and assist her up. But he held off from touching her further. She was glad for that. Not because she was afraid it would trigger her fear, but that it might cause more flashes.

She should probably tell Ethan about them, but she wanted to take some time and examine them further. This was the first time she'd ever had a recollection from her life before the accident. Until she understood what that meant, she felt strangely protective of her new insight.

And one of the things she'd have to find out was if it was his touch alone that had allowed the door to peek open. Would it happen again if she let their skin meet? She wasn't quite ready to put that to the test. Not yet.

For four years, all she'd wanted was for some knowledge of her life to return. Now that a little snippet of it had, she was scared. And utterly unsure of what to do next.

Until she knew that, she'd keep her memories, and her hands, to herself.

14

As Ethan escorted her back to her condo, he fought with his need to hold her. To comfort her. To make certain she was okay. He knew the last thing she would want right now was any more contact with him. But he couldn't just leave her. She was still shaken up by what had happened.

And so was he. The sight of her being swallowed up by the sand at her feet would haunt him for a long time.

He'd about come unglued when she'd disappeared. After she'd left him in the car he'd followed, but to give her some privacy, he'd stayed up above her on the condo property. He hadn't liked that she was out there by herself, but short of physically restraining her, which he wouldn't do, he'd had no choice but to wait.

There hadn't been another soul in the area—he'd checked to make sure of that—so Ethan had idly observed her. And as he had, he'd let his mind wander.

He hadn't been all that surprised when she'd come to him. She'd always faced her fears, and that was no different now, memory or not. He had so much respect and admiration for her. For her strength and her courage.

Ethan didn't think that fundamental part of her would ever change. She'd been fearless and independent, sometimes wild, but also caring and gentle and compassionate. He recognized those traits in her now, even if she didn't.

He was cautioning himself not to let his heart make too many comparisons between the old Honor and the new when her terrified scream had jerked him out of his thoughts. Ethan was at a full run before he'd realized exactly what was wrong. When he'd seen her drop completely out of sight, down into the beach she'd walked upon, he'd poured on the speed and sprinted towards where he'd last seen her. Since nothing looked out of place and he didn't want to lose track of where she'd been, Ethan never took his eyes off the spot as he ran.

~~~

Getting as close as was safe, he slid to his knees. When the debris flew forward and sprayed over the area, the sand and grass shimmered and waved slightly, telling him this was, indeed, where she'd gone in.

Spreading himself flat on his stomach to evenly distribute his weight and avoid being sucked in, he didn't think twice about shoving his hand and arm down into the unknown. Moving it was harder than he would have thought, but he lowered further until he was in up to his shoulder. He felt around desperately, searching for any sign of her. He was fully prepared to go in after her, but hoped she hadn't yet slipped beyond his reach so quickly.

Straining against the tar-like substance below him, he struggled to find her. Blindly fishing was taking too long, and every second she could be slipping farther and farther away from him.

He had to do something. He couldn't lose her again.

Ethan splayed the hand below ground wide and concentrated on the woman he loved. His telekinetic power usually required him to see the object he affected. But if his power were ever going to expand to the next level as his siblings' had in times of need, it was now.
~~~

He refused to accept that he couldn't save her.

Closing his eyes, Ethan centered all of his focus into pulling Paige back up to him through the muck. He had no clue if it was working, but he wasn't going to stop until he had her.

More time passed before he felt something bump against his hand. But it disappeared just as he tried to grab hold. Had he imagined it? Were his attempts even working? Without being able to see her, he didn't have any idea.

He took a breath, brought her image back to mind, and pictured her hand in his. On the next brush, he felt skin and knew he'd done it. He had her.

Tightening his grip until he was afraid he'd crush her bones, Ethan pulled with every ounce of strength he had.

He could feel he was making progress, but it was taking way too long. Shifting around, he dug his feet into the sand at the edge of the pit and fought against whatever was holding her.

With the added leverage, her hand clutched in his cleared the surface. He locked his other hand around her wrist and pulled. Her arm and then her head emerged from the abyss next, her smoky eyes and gasping breaths pleading with him to save her.

Her other hand broke free, and he let go of her wrist to grab hold of that one too. Once he had a firm grip on both, Ethan heaved with all his might. Even with the aid of his telekinetic abilities, it seemed as if the earth didn't want to give up its prize.

Sluggishly, her torso rose until her waist and then her hips breached the facade. When only her legs remained stuck, Ethan gave one final tug and she popped loose. With no further resistance, Ethan fell onto his back, taking her with him. She ended up laid out completely on top of him. Chest, belly, hips, legs. His arms went, unbidden, around her to hug her to him.

The sudden contact of her body against his after so long had nostalgia coursing through him, and euphoria nearly swamping him.

Except, all too soon, she pushed at him to release her. Being that close to him must have only added more fear to an already traumatic experience, as evidenced by the flash of anxiety in her eyes when she looked down at him.

Ethan had no choice but to reluctantly let her go.

~~~

Ethan shook his head. Even now, several minutes later, he could still feel her weight pressed against him. His skin tingled where hers had been. He hardened just remembering her supple curves on top of him.

Ethan quickly steered his mind back to the present as they neared her door. He hesitated now, not sure if she'd want him to come in. But she looked up at him and just held the door open for him.

Ethan entered her condo and closed the door as she crossed to the sofa and sat. She pulled her legs up and hugged them to her, not looking at him.

Neither had said a word since leaving the beach, and Ethan wondered what she was thinking. Was she completely freaked out? She'd just been the victim of a supernatural booby-trap set by a deranged psychopath. He couldn't begin to imagine what it had been like down there.

"Are you sure you're not hurt?" he began. "Do you need anything?"

She shook her head. "No. I'm fine."

"I'm sorry you've been dropped into the middle of this mess." Ethan slid his hands into his pockets. "You didn't count on any of this when you came here. You're looking for answers to your own life, and you shouldn't have to worry about anything other than that. If you want me to go, I will. I'll call my brother and get someone else over here to watch you."
~~~

Her gray eyes finally met his. Instead of fear or shock though, he saw determination. "What prophecy? Why did I just get sucked into a black pit of nothing? Explain this to me, Ethan."

Resigned, he took the seat adjacent to her. "This is going to take a while. Can I get you some water or something?"

"I just want answers."

And she deserved them. "To fully explain, I need to start at the beginning."

Paige nodded, indicating he should get on with it.

"Back in the fifteen-hundreds..."

Ethan talked through it all and ended with the incident on the beach.

She stared at him, absolutely motionless, and then suddenly rose. "I think I *will* have something to drink." She moved to the kitchen area. "I've got some wine. Do you want some?"

Her next words were muttered under her breath, but Ethan heard them. "I definitely need some wine."

He could understand completely. "Yeah, that would be great."

She came back, handed him a glass, and resumed her seat. He watched her take a few sips before she seemed to gather herself.

"So, this Noor." Paige lowered her glass to her lap and met his gaze. "His goal is to either take one of you out or mess you up so badly you can't work together to stop him."

"Yeah." He dropped his attention down to his goblet. "That about sums it up."

"But you said that only those with his blood, or you four, had any contact with him."

Ethan raised his head and nodded.

"So how did his snare work on me? And how did he know when or where to set that thing to make sure I'd find it?"

"I'm not sure yet why it worked. If it's for the reason I think it is, we could all be in big trouble. The second part of your question isn't too difficult to figure out. He has his stooges watching us all the time. I wouldn't be surprised if they'd already reported that I've been spending a lot of time here. I'd seen you out there myself, before I knew you were real, so it was only a matter of time before you'd take a walk. Somehow, one of his men must have gotten word to him that today was the day."

She sat quietly for a moment. "He'll keep coming. He won't stop, will he?"

"I'm sorry, but no. Don't worry about that, though. We're not going to let him hurt you." Ethan paused and weighed what he was going to say next. "Are you sure I can't talk you into leaving? At least until we deal with him? When that's done, you can come back, finish what you started with Cabot, and find the evidence your dad hid away."

She was already shaking her head. Ethan had known it was a long shot, but he'd had to try.

He glanced at the clock on the cable box and noted the time. "If you think you still want to go to my parents' house, we should probably head out soon."

"Okay. Just let me clean up a little."

~~~

They were the first ones to arrive. They still had half an hour or so before the rest got there, so he could use this time to introduce Paige to his parents without the noise and chaos that followed when all of them got together.

He found both of them in the kitchen. His mom was at the stove preparing the food it would take to feed the lot of them. His dad was at the table reading the paper.

They both turned when he and Paige came into the room. He saw a bit of shocked surprise on their faces when they saw who was with him. They both knew everything that was going on,
~~~

but this was the first time they'd actually seen her in person.

Honor had been a fixture in this house. His parents loved her, and she them. They'd spent countless hours here in this very room laughing and talking.

Ethan walked straight to his mom and gave her a hug and a kiss on the cheek. As was his habit since boyhood, when he released her, he copped a mushroom out of the pan she was sautéing.

She made a move to slap at his hand, but he'd learned a long time ago to be quick when he snitched bites from under her nose.

He sent her a cocky grin as he licked his fingers.

"Mom, Dad, this is Paige." He put a subtle emphasis on her name so they'd remember to call her that instead of Honor.

Mary set the wooden spoon on the counter. She came over and took Paige's hands in hers and greeted her with a loving smile. "Hi, Paige. It's so nice to meet you. I'm Mary, and this is my husband, Paul. Welcome."

His mom turned her gaze up to his and studied him a moment. "Something's happened."

"Yeah." Ethan brought them up to speed on Noor's most recent attempt. "His powers must have advanced again."

"You will all have to be more vigilant." Anger and frustration washed through his mother's hazel eyes. She returned to the stove and stirred what she had cooking there with more force than was necessary. "I *hate* how much he's violated each of your lives. Every single one of you has something hanging over your head, making it impossible for you to be completely happy. He's tormented Aria from the very beginning, and then he took an interest in Seth and tried to recruit him into his ranks." She shook her head. "Anna and Joe are out of their minds worrying about Jacob and when Noor will come for him again. Evan and Kyra have to be so careful to hide her pregnancy from him, or he'll kill that innocent baby just out of spite. And you. He's taken something so miraculous and turned it against you in the worst way possible."

It wasn't hard to hear the tears in her voice. His dad went to her and wrapped his arms around her from behind and held her. Ethan glanced down at Paige and saw moisture gathering in hers as well. He wanted to comfort her as his dad was comforting his mother, but that just wasn't an option.

"I'm sorry," Mary said after pulling herself together. She gave them a small smile. "I try not to let it get to me, but sometimes it just overwhelms me what you kids have had to suffer through. We knew this was going to be a difficult path for you all, and we'd hoped to prepare you for it. But never could we have imagined the havoc he'd be able to cause, even before February came."

Ethan stepped in close to her and took her hands in his. "We've taken some hard knocks, but we're all still here. If it wasn't for what you and Dad taught us, I think I can say with some certainty that none of us would have gotten this far. We're only a few months out from D-day, and we're so close to what we need to end him for good. It doesn't matter what he throws at us. We'll fight back, and we'll make it through. I have no doubt whatsoever that we'll win this battle. Once that's done, we'll have the rest of our lives to live free and happy. And that's all on you and Dad."

Her eyes shimmered again, and she went up on her toes to kiss him. "Thank you, my sweet boy." She released him and took in a deep breath of air. When she let it out, Ethan saw that some of the sadness that had weighed her down was gone.

Commotion behind them indicated the others had begun to arrive. When the sound of small feet running reached them, Ethan braced for the whirlwind that was his nephew.

"Nana! Papa! Guess what?" Jacob barreled into the kitchen. But stopped short when he saw Paige. "Who are you?"

"Jacob," Joe scolded, hearing his son's question. "Manners."

Jacob glanced up at his dad and then turned back to Paige. He stuck his little hand out. "Hi. I'm Jake Burke."

Paige smiled brightly, took it, and gave it a pump. "Hello, Jake Burke. I'm Paige Harrison."

Hand still held in hers, he cocked his head and scrutinized her. Ethan saw the brows over his coffee-brown eyes narrow and knew he was looking deeper into her. "No. That's not right."

Anna rested her hand on his shoulder. "Jake, that's enough. How about you tell Nana and Papa your news."

"No," Paige interrupted and glanced over at Anna, "it's all right." She squatted down in front of the little boy. Her face was serious now. "You're very smart. Paige isn't really my name. But you see, I have a little problem with my memory. I hurt my head a while ago, and that other person went away. No matter how hard I tried, I couldn't remember her. And since I couldn't go around without a name, I had to find a new one to use until I did."

"I can see her in there." Jacob studied her face. "She's waiting."

Paige gave a little start. Ethan knew how perceptive his nephew was and knew it had to be disconcerting for her to be read like that. And to learn her past self was still in there, as Jake had said, waiting.

"Okay, buddy." Joe collected his son. "Didn't you have something exciting to share?"

Ethan thought Jacob was going to ignore Joe's deflection, but whatever he had to tell them was a bigger draw.

Jake looked up at his grandparents and smiled widely. "One of my drawings won a contest!"

"Oh, honey." Mary picked him up and kissed his cheek. "That's wonderful! I bet you're so proud."

Paul reached out and tousled his hair. "Good job, short stuff. Which one was it? I bet it was the one of me, right?" Paul struck a superhero pose like the one Jake had drawn of him a few months before.

When Jacob had first come to them, he'd been withdrawn and wouldn't speak. One of his initial forms of communication had been his drawings. In them, he'd color a person as he saw them with his power. He'd pretty much nailed everyone.

He'd initially drawn Anna as an angel, and then later when she'd saved him from Noor, he'd added armor to go with her wings. And that, in a nutshell, summed up his quiet sister. Soft and loving but with the heart of a champion.

Joe had been Jacob's knight in shining armor from the very beginning. And he'd proven how true that was over and over in defense of his new son. Evan had been drawn as a warrior of old, attired in leather and chainmail. In the picture, he'd even carried a large, heavy sword.

Ethan remembered the portrait Jacob had sketched of him. Looking at it had almost broken his heart, but it had accurately depicted what he'd been at the time. He'd been dressed in the full turn-out gear of a firefighter. Jacob had drawn him down on one knee with his helmet dangling from one hand. His head was bent forward, and where his jacket hung open, there was a white bandage over his heart. For one so young, Ethan was always amazed at how much he really saw.

His thoughts were pulled back as Jacob's laughter subsided and he spoke. "No, silly," he told Paul with a laugh. "It was the one of Daddy in his knight's armor."

"Well, that's okay then. That was a pretty good one too."

Paul took Jacob from his wife's arms. "We need to celebrate this." He turned with Jacob towards Mary. "Ice cream sundaes after dinner?"

Jacob gasped in excitement. "Can we, Nana?"

She grinned at him and cupped his cheek. "I can't think of a better way to honor your accomplishment."

Jake and Paul high-fived.

"Now take your Papa and get out of my kitchen," she jokingly scolded. "Go play." She shooed them out. All of them could still hear Jake whooping it up as the pair of them headed off to the game room.

Mary smiled at Anna. "He's doing so well."

"He really is. He's come so far." Love for her son shone in Anna's light blue eyes.

Just then the rest of his family came in. Evan, Kyra, Aria, and Seth.

As was the norm, his mom took charge. "While I'm finishing up dinner, you all go into the living room. Ethan and Paige can tell you about Noor's latest stunt."

That had everyone's attention, but no one said anything until they were all spread out and seated.

"What did he do now?" Aria asked with a frown from where she sat next to Seth, leaning into his side.

"He set a trap. For Paige." He hated to have to relive those harrowing, endless minutes, but everyone needed to know exactly what had happened and what it might mean. So Ethan went through it, moment by moment, with Paige filling in what she'd experienced.

"I was so sure the threat would come from one of his henchmen. I wasn't even looking for an attack to come from Noor himself. And, because of that, I almost cost Paige her life."

"Have his powers grown?" Aria asked. "Is that how he was able to do this?"

Ethan grimaced. "I hate to say it, but I think we need to prepare ourselves for the possibility that the general public may no longer be safe from him."

By the looks on their faces, the implication wasn't lost on any of them. If Noor's ploys could work on anyone, not just those tied to him or the prophecy, it opened up a whole new world of potential victims.

While everyone was trying to wrap their heads around the ramifications of this new prospect, Anna's caring gaze swung to Paige. "Are you okay?"

"Yeah." She cast a quick glance at Ethan. "It was scary as hell, but there doesn't seem to be any lasting effects. Thankfully, your brother got me out, so I'm good. That's not to say I'd like to go through anything like that again."

Seth, ever the detective, leaned forward in his seat. "Did you notice anything odd? Or see anyone nearby? Were there signs of anything unusual where you fell in?"

Paige shook her head. "Not that I noticed. I was walking, and then I was falling. I didn't see anything or anyone, before or after. Once Ethan saved me, I looked back to see if I could detect what had taken me. There was nothing. Just sand and rocks and grass."

Seth's focus swung to Ethan. "Was there anyone hanging around the area?"

"No," Ethan answered. "While Paige was on the beach, I was keeping watch. Besides us, the whole place was deserted. No one, real or otherwise. I made sure of that. The ground didn't look any different to me either. The only time it showed itself was when I ran over to where I'd seen her go down. I kicked some sand onto it, and it kind of shimmered for a second. Whatever cloak or invisibility spell he used hid it even from me."

"If you're right, and he's able to target anyone now..." Anna looked at Joe. Not being connected to any of this, he'd been spared from the majority of Noor's tricks and magic so far.

Aria glanced in the direction of the kitchen. "Mom and Dad." Her expression of worry was reflected on all their faces.

"If he's gained this much strength, we need to know more about his powers." Evan glanced around at each of them. "We have to find out if there's any way to ward against them."

"I say we hit those journals—see what's in there that he's so afraid of." Kyra absently rubbed her hands over her small baby bump. "I, for one, am all for neutering the bastard. The sooner, the better."

When Noor had discovered Kyra, his demented mind had thought she was his wife, Isabel, who had taken their sons and left him back in the late fifteen-hundreds. In an effort to save her two boys, she'd run to their Burke ancestors for help in escaping his brutal and torturous treatment.

Given Kyra's uncanny resemblance to his estranged spouse, they all assumed she was Noor's descendant through the children he and Isabel had borne together, explaining how he had found her in the first place.

Upon seeing Evan and Kyra together, he'd lost it a second time, thinking his *property* had once again fled to the safety of a Burke witch. He'd sworn to exact his revenge on his harlot wife by taking from her any offspring she conceived with another man.

When Evan had realized Kyra was pregnant with his child, he and Mary had worked for days to find a spell that would cloak the baby from Noor. Until they could put an end to him in February, that innocent life was in constant danger.

"It's been difficult getting through the books," Aria said. "Some of the writing is pretty hard to decipher."

"I think it's time for all of us to sit down and see what we can find," Evan declared.

"And we'll do that," Mary announced, coming into the room, "*after* we eat. Food's on."

15

Paige felt so out of place. Here she was, sitting at a large dining table with this group of people who had known the old her. Yet she knew none of them. And not only that, but they were all discussing things that were way out of her league. She'd been exposed to some of the otherworldly living in Louisiana, but this...this was something else altogether.

To add to her discomfort and unease, Ethan's leg had brushed against hers under the table. And just like on the beach, more of her past was revealed. She saw a quick glimpse of a scene very much like this one. She was seated at this same table with Paul and Mary and the quads.

It only lasted for a blink of time and had her wanting more. She wanted to free the person who was inside of her waiting. She wanted to know what she'd been like. Who she'd been. She yearned to finally make peace with her past.

Wondering how these memories had come about, Paige peeked at Anna seated on her right. Shifting in her chair in such a way that brought her nearer Anna's leg, she purposely bumped into it. But nothing happened. Just as nothing had happened when Mary had hugged her, or when she'd shaken Jacob's hand.

Was it only Ethan then? The few times she'd touched him, she'd gotten glimpses. *He* must be the trigger that would break open the door that had locked her previous life away.

As desperately as she wanted those memories back, could she risk her well-being to do it? Her fear of what was inside of him had by no means gone away. She fought it every time they were near each other. Her first instinct was still to run. To flee. To save herself from pain and anguish. It was only by telling herself, over and over again, that he wouldn't hurt her—that he had, in fact, saved her multiple times—that she was able to combat it. Somewhat.

Could she get, and remain, close to him long enough to get her life back? Or would that vicious force within him destroy any chance she had?

While she'd been lost in thought, conversation around the table had begun to wind down, and now they were starting the cleanup. Rising, she automatically gathered the dishes around her. As she carried them into the kitchen, Anna was rinsing some to put into the dishwasher.

As Paige set the plates on the counter and turned to leave, Anna called her back.

"Paige?"

She turned back to the other woman to see her wiping her hands on a towel.

"I don't know if Ethan has told you about us," she started out gently. "About our abilities."

"He has."

"So, you know I'm an empath then."

Paige nodded. Had she picked up on something when she'd brushed against her at dinner?

Anna held her hands up. "I didn't look. I would never do that without permission, but I couldn't help sensing that something is bothering you. And I think it has to do with more than just what Noor did." She stepped forward and took Paige's hands in hers. "I just want you to know if you ever need to talk to someone, I'll be here. You've been put through so much, it might not hurt to get some of it out."

Paige didn't know what to say. "Thank you." She smiled at Anna, drawn to her warmth and sincerity, but still hesitant and wary. "I may take you up on that, but I need to get it straight in my own head first."

"I understand. Whatever you need, I'm here. We're all here." Anna gave her hands a squeeze before releasing them. "I know you don't remember, but we all love you."

Tightness gathered in Paige's chest. "Thank you," she said again.

When she walked back into the dining room, Ethan must have seen the emotion lingering in her eyes. He instantly came to her, though he stopped short of touching her.

"Is everything okay? Did something happen?" His voice was pitched low.

She shook her head. "No. Anna is just really sweet."

His features relaxed and he grinned down at her. "Yeah. She is. But don't tell her I said that."

Paige laughed softly.

Shortly after, everyone gathered again in the living room. Someone had placed a stack of books on the table. Paige knew enough to know that these were a part of the family's written history that had been missing until recently. And they hoped that in them would be the answer of how to divest Noor of his ill-gotten power before he struck at her or one of the others again.

Mary came in from the hall. "Paul's going to keep Jacob distracted while we work on this. I didn't make much headway with them, but I'm hoping between all of us we can find something. There's more than enough to go around, so everybody take one."

Paige hadn't thought she'd participate in reading the Burke family history but, evidently, they didn't feel the same way. She found herself situated between Ethan and Aria with a book in her lap that looked hundreds of years older than the others.

She carefully opened it to the first page and saw what everyone had been talking about. The cursive writing was unlike anything she'd ever seen. Big and fancy and with so many flourishes it was almost impossible to read.

Tuning out everything else around her, she bent to the task of figuring out what the heck it said.

An hour later she had a headache, but she'd been able to decode most of the loopy decorative letters. She'd made out enough to discover the first section was an accounting of what magical supplies had been made and stored. It listed who had made what, on what day, what it would be used for, and where it would be stockpiled.

About halfway through the pages, a new scribe took over. The writing here was a little easier to read. But again, it detailed everyday occurrences.

Someone had had a new baby that needed to be blessed. A young couple wanting to strike out on their own had been given a going-away party. A family that lived outside of the settlement had come to the Burkes asking them to cleanse their farm. It seemed something bad had settled over the property. Whatever it was had taken several sheep, cows, and their best plow horse.

Paige began to develop a picture in her mind of this community, with the Burkes right at the center. It was as if they were thought of as the lords of the settlement. People came to them with problems and asked for their help. It seemed as though they were respected by those they cared for.

Beside her, Ethan groaned and rubbed his eyes. "I need a break. If I have to look at any more of this mess, I'll go cross-eyed."

"Well, at least that would be an improvement to how you usually look," Evan teased, but he was blinking his own lids to alleviate the strain.

"Ha ha," Ethan bit back.

"Did anyone find anything?" Aria closed the journal in her lap. "Any mention of the Bringer, or the trials that Noor went through? Hell, I'd even settle for anything just weird or potentially worrisome."

Paige didn't know if she should say anything about what she'd read. It had all seemed so harmless and mundane. Wolves or coyotes had probably gotten to those animals.

As if reading her mind, Anna turned to her. "Paige? Did you find something?"

"I don't think so. It was just a little entry about a farm. They'd come to the Burkes to ask if they would cleanse their property. They'd had some bad luck and had lost a number of animals. I'm sure it was just predators."

"Lost, as in found dead?" Mary's gaze was intense. "Or gone completely?"

"Just gone without a trace."

"How many?" The others glanced at Mary as she asked Paige questions.

Paige couldn't remember off-hand, so she opened the book she'd been reading and found the entry.

"One plow horse, five cows, and seven sheep."

"Thirteen." Mary's face went white.

"Mom." Anna rose and went to her. "What is it?"

"That's how it starts." She looked at Anna. "Remember we found that website that told of the three trials, the next one more heinous than the last? That was the first," she repeated. "To kill, dismember, and drink the blood of thirteen animals."

"Are you sure?" Ethan asked.

Mary nodded. "I'll never forget the progression of horror he had to commit to become what he is."

When Anna spoke, Paige couldn't help but notice how truly scared and worried she seemed. "Do we want to know what the rest of the trials entail?"

Paige recalled that Noor had plans to send Anna's son

through those same steps, so he could ascend to Noor's right hand. She couldn't blame Anna for being so frightened for what her innocent child may have to suffer if they didn't stop that monster.

"No," Mary told her. "You don't want to know, but I think you all *need* to know so that, going through these journals, you'll understand what to look for." She took a breath to steady herself. "From animals, he would have moved on to people. Inflicting pain and torture. Blood-letting. Mutilation. Dismemberment. Over and over until he *graduated* to the next level. Which was more of the same..."

Mary took a deep breath, eyes downcast, and finished in almost a whisper. "But this time, to children and infants."

"Oh, God," someone gasped. Paige wasn't sure who it was, but it mirrored how they were all feeling. Horrified. Repulsed. She, herself, was sick to her stomach at the thought.

Reaching towards the table, Paige needed a drink of water to wash down the bad taste that had crawled up the back of her throat. As she leaned forward, the book on her lap slid. She caught it before it fell to the floor, but in jostling it, a loose page fluttered out to land on the carpet.

Paige retrieved it and was about to return it to the book when she noticed there was no torn edge. It hadn't come from the journal; someone had just tucked it in for safe keeping.

Curious, she read the words on the old parchment.

16

'My name is Beatrice Wills, and I am dying. I have prayed for these many months that someone would find me and rescue me from this monster, but no one has come.

And now I will die here, by his hand.

I know not his name. In my own head, I call him Demon, for that is surely what he is. His power is like none I have ever seen. It radiates from him in waves. It glows in his unholy eyes like some macabre Hallows Eve talisman.

That power is only rivaled by his depravity and need to inflict pain. I don't know how I have survived what he has done to my female person. I have begged for death so many times…but still it evades me.

Who was to know it would be because I saw him in a moment of weakness that I would finally be spared from this eternal misery?

As I lay chained to the floor, he slept, and dreamed. In those dreams, he called out for someone named Isabel. He shouted for her several times, thrashing and rolling upon the mattress, lost to his own torments.

Suddenly, he awoke. He sat straight up on his bed and looked over at me. And in him, I saw only a man. A vulnerable man. I don't know how or why, but the magic that usually filled him was gone.

And that's where I made my grievous error. I did not look

away. I openly stared at him. And as I did, I watched it happen. As the dream faded away and his wrath returned, so too did his power.

Any weakness he'd shown was now gone, and I saw my fate in those shining eyes. In a fit of killing rage, he descended upon me. He has at last slain me for the simple sin of witnessing his impotence.

But with the last ounce of life I have left inside of me, I shall have my revenge. I am secretly writing this letter with the hope that someone will find it and get it to those who would benefit most from what I have seen. People he has cursed greatly and often for thwarting him. A coven of witches named Burke. I know of them, and they are fair and compassionate people. So, with my last breath, it is my prayer that this missive finds its way to them.'

Paige sat stunned. She didn't know what to think, but she knew the others would need to read this. This could be what they'd been looking for.

When she brought her gaze up, Ethan was watching her. Without a word, she handed him the letter.

As he read Beatrice's last words, his expression went from sadness for her pain and suffering to excitement at her selfless gift.

His dark eyes flew to meet hers and he smiled. Paige's heart did a slow roll in her chest and she felt herself flush.

Before she could recover from that look, he was calling everyone's attention.

"Guys. Paige may have just found the kryptonite we need."

"What is it?" Evan's interest was piqued. And his wasn't the only one. All eyes were on her.

Ethan handed her back the note. "Read it."

She did.

"Isabel is his weakness," Anna summed up when she was

finished.

Paige knew that Isabel had been Edrick Noor's wife. She'd gone to the Burke ancestors for help, and they had gotten her and their sons hidden away. Noor had raged when he'd found out what had been done, and he'd sworn out his vengeance on the entire Burke line.

Soon after, he'd disappeared. When he'd reemerged years later, he'd gained unimaginable power. He'd become so strong, the most powerful of the Burke witches had only been able to trap him.

Which brought her thoughts full circle, as it was Ethan and his siblings who would now have to stop him. Hopefully, for good.

So, knowing what rendered him mortal would go a long way to defeating him.

"He had to have had some kind of genuine feelings for her," Anna surmised. "Only someone important to us can make us that vulnerable. That has to be why dreaming of her affected him the way it did."

"You honestly think Noor is capable of love?" Aria was dumbfounded.

"Not as we know it, no." Anna sighed and shook her head. "But in his own sick and twisted way, maybe."

Seth interrupted. "It doesn't matter what he did or didn't feel. Isabel's dead. Has been for hundreds of years."

Movement pulled Paige's attention. She looked over to see Kyra raising her hand.

"Um, guys? I think you're all forgetting something."

Evan's head spun around towards her. "Absolutely *not!*"

Kyra shifted, turning to fully face her fiancé. "He's already mistaken me for her once, ace. If seeing his dead wife again will make him human, why not use that to our advantage?"

"Because I won't risk you or our baby getting that close to him again." Evan's black eyes were glittering with anger and what Paige could only describe as fear.

She'd heard how Noor had held Kyra captive for over a week, beating her and torturing her in his misguided attempt to break his wife and punish her for leaving him all those years ago. Evan and Seth had found her and saved her, but not before she'd been brutally beaten and whipped until her back was shredded.

In trying to keep her safe from Noor, Evan had ended up falling in love with her. And she with him. Which had pissed Noor off even more because, as he saw it, his wife had run off with a Burke. Again.

"Shouldn't we do whatever we can to take him down?" Kyra asked him.

Evan held his hand up. "No. Not that. It's not up for discussion. You're three months pregnant, for God's sake. I'm not risking you or our daughter getting anywhere near him."

"You want to hear me out, ace? I think I know how it can be done."

"I repeat, *no*."

Before Kyra could blast him as the thunderstorm in her eyes indicated, their mother spoke up.

"It hurts no one to listen to what she has to say."

Evan sent her an incredulous look. "You would endanger them?"

"Don't you take that tone with me, Evan Burke. You know better than that." She sent him a blistering glare before nodding at Kyra.

"Okay," Kyra didn't look at Evan, "I say we put me in period garb—a wig, the clothes, everything. Do me up to look more like her, maybe even accentuate the bump." Her brown eyes finally tracked to the man seated next to her. "Evan can pop me in, I do my thing—talk to him, plead with him for the sake of our baby, remind him of the fun times he had when he beat me senseless. Whatever it takes. As soon as we see that it's working, Evan can pop me right back out, and you guys can ream him a new one while his pants are around his ankles. Not literally, but you know what I mean."

"I still don't like it," Evan told her stubbornly.

"All of you will be right there." She pressed her point. "You'll have complete control over when I come and go." Kyra took his hand in hers. "He won't hurt me or our baby."

"You're damned right, he won't." Evan pulled her in close to his side and kissed her, but Paige could see that he wasn't fully on board yet.

"While that sounds like a good plan," Mary said after a moment, "there's something we all need to take into consideration." She waited until she had everyone's attention. "Noor isn't a corporeal being right now. Even if it worked and you stripped his power temporarily, his physical form is locked away somewhere else. Out of reach. The most you'd be doing right now is pissing him off. And you'll have ruined your element of surprise. I say we wait. You'll only get one shot at this. However you decide to go about it, you need to strike when it'll do the most damage."

The ringing of the phone startled the thoughtful group. Mary rose and went to answer it. The rest of them sat for a moment longer, and then Evan rose and walked a few feet away to look out the window. Kyra followed. She reached up and wrapped her arms around Evan's neck, leaned in, and kissed him. After a moment, they talked quietly.

As Ethan spoke with his sisters and brother-in-law for a moment, Paige wandered over to a set of bookshelves against the living room wall. Framed photos of the family crowded each shelf.

Happy, smiling faces glowed from each picture. She even saw herself in some of them. Most were candid snapshots of joyous times, but there were also some more professional ones of school dances and proms.

Studying each one in turn, Paige saw a timeline of her life with Ethan. After having lost all of her belongings when she was hurt, she didn't ever expect to find anything like this.

She felt Ethan's presence behind her. He indicated to the photos. "We have tons more."

"You do?" Need swelled in her heart.

"Yeah, my mom has always been camera crazy." He bent and started pulling books off the bottom shelf. "I think there may even be some of your parents in here."

Paige gasped and moisture gathered in her eyes. "Can I see?"

"Of course. I'm just sorry I didn't think of these before." Arms laden, he turned back to the couch. Paige was close behind, excitement causing her heart to pound.

She settled next to him, and as Ethan leafed through the albums page by page, he gave her a soft smile. "There's no need to start from the beginning. I'll just fast forward to when we met."

As he found the page he wanted and handed the book over to her, she saw herself as a teenager just in the first throes of innocent love. Playing on the beach with the four of them and other friends. Birthday parties, barbeques, bonfires— every step of her teenaged life had been documented beside the Burke quads.

She could clearly see that this extraordinary group of people had considered her an integral part of their family. And that gave her a sense of belonging that she couldn't remember feeling before.

She was still reveling in that when she turned another page. What she saw there made her breath catch in her throat. She was standing on the lawn in a formal floor-length purple dress with the water shimmering behind her. A man and a woman stood on either side of her.

"Your mom and dad." Ethan lifted the film from the cardboard backing and pulled the picture out. He handed it to her slowly.

Paige studied their faces. Touched them reverently. She could see bits and pieces of herself in each of them. Her dad was tall and stood a full head over her and her mother. He had dark brown hair and her gray eyes. He looked strong and confident, and she could see love and pride shining in his eyes.

She and her mom had been the same height. Delicate features gave her a youthful appearance, and her medium blonde hair was worn shoulder-length and floated around her head in soft waves. Paige noted the shape of her mom's eyes. She saw them every time she looked in the mirror, along with the plump lips and wide smile.

With a fingertip, she traced around each of their faces again, trying to bring memories of them forward. When still nothing came, sadness enveloped her. She put a hand over her eyes and let the tears fall.

Trying to offer comfort, Ethan pulled her close.

Like on the beach, another quick flash of the past assailed her mind, and she gasped. Mistaking her reaction for fear, Ethan abruptly withdrew from her.

"I'm sorry. I hate that this is hurting you. I wish there was something I could do."

But there *was* something he could do. If only she had the guts to act on it. "It's okay." Paige tried to gather herself. "It's not your fault. You didn't take my memories." She looked down at her parents again.

Mary came back just then.

"That was our researcher," she explained, "the one who got us the name of the evil bastard that Noor went through all those trials for. He's still in the process of deciphering the text but said it's looking like he's found something that might help us. I couldn't get him to tell me what it was over the phone. He said he needed a little more time with it to finish the translation—see if he's right about what he found. I asked him how long, and he groused that it couldn't be rushed." Mary glanced around the room at all of them. "I think we need to go to him. Prod him in the ass a little to find whatever answers are there. It's a long drive, so your dad and I will head out first thing in the morning."

Evan came back and crossed to where his mom was standing. "I don't think that's a good idea, Mom. You won't have any protection. What if you're attacked?" When she looked like she might argue, Evan started again. "You didn't want the girls traveling alone. How is this any different?"

"He's not interested in us," Mary told him. "The four of you are the ones he needs to stop."

"And just what do you think would happen if he got his hands on either of you?"

Mary smiled and reached up to cup his cheek. "That's not going to happen. I may be getting old, but I still have a few tricks up my sleeve. Or have you forgotten who taught you everything you needed to know for this fight? Your father and I will be fine. Just hold down the fort until we can get back with whatever it is he has for us."

Paige took in the worried glances they gave their parents. But no one said anything else to try and stop them.

And in that silence, two text tones went off simultaneously. Seth and Evan both reached for their phones, read the message, and looked at each other. Evan then turned to the group.

"We have to go. There's been some kind of disturbance reported out off Highway 1. They don't know what it is, but it sounds big."

They were nearly to the door when Aria called out to them. "Wait!"

The urgency in her voice had all eyes snapping to her.

Paige wasn't sure what was going on, but the others seemed to know as Anna rushed to her sister's side.

"What is it, Ari? What do you see?"

Aria's face was blank as her eyes stared off into space, out of focus. "Panic. Fear. People running, screaming. Trampling each other." Aria suddenly came back to herself, her eyes darting between her siblings. "It's Noor. *He's* causing this."

Ethan glanced down at her before looking around to the others. "I guess that answers our question. His powers have grown. No one is safe."

"These are innocent people." Anna's pale blue eyes shimmered with moisture. "We have to help them."

"I'm going with you." Joe stepped up next to Anna. "You're going to need all the hands you can get."

Evan looked over at Kyra, but she beat him to the punch.

"I know. I'll be staying behind." Paige watched as she placed her hands protectively over her lower belly, obviously thinking of the baby there. Kyra pointed at Evan. "If anything happens to you, ace, you'll have me to answer to. So watch your back."

He nodded with a grin.

Ethan's gaze jerked to Paige as if suddenly remembering she was there.

She thought she knew what concerned him. "You go and don't worry about me. Those people need help."

He made a move to reach out to her but stopped himself. "I'm sorry for leaving you stranded, but I've got to do this." At her nod, he turned to his mother. "Do you mind keeping Paige company until we get back?"

"Of course not, sweetheart. It'll give us a chance to get reacquainted a bit better. Now get out there and kick Noor's ass!"

With that, the four Burkes, Seth, and Joe were gone.

Before Paige could gather her thoughts over the evening's events so far, Mrs. Burke spoke. "Come on, girls. I baked a batch of chocolate fudge brownies earlier. We can stuff ourselves stupid while we wait for the boys to get back."

~~~
~~~

Ethan, Anna, Aria, and Joe were in his car as they followed close behind Evan and Seth.

He cast a quick look at Aria. "Do you know what we're walking into here?"

"No. I just saw people running and screaming. I don't know what Noor is doing to them, but they're very frightened and hurting each other in their efforts to get away from whatever it is."

They sped through the streets of Daytona Beach, each lost in their own thoughts about what they might find.

An endless fifteen minutes later, they all saw the commotion up ahead. Police cars and ambulances with lights flashing were parked haphazardly in the road and on the grass.

Pulling up as close as they could, the two cars parked. They immediately saw this was a roadside park. One where families and groups gathered to cook out and enjoy the warm Florida days.

Suddenly, Aria gasped. "Oh, God. Seth and I met here a couple of times when he was still undercover."

Ethan scanned the area and saw the men and women in uniform guiding the traumatized people to safety. Many were still clearly crying and upset by whatever Noor had subjected them to in the park.

Up ahead, Evan and Seth jumped from their vehicle.

"Let's go." Ethan wrenched his door open.

Everyone else piled out and together they ran. The park was empty now, but the evidence of Noor's trickery was still present. A thick black fog crept over the entire area, billowing through trees and curling around bushes, the insidious haze wafting along the picnic tables where people had been sitting only minutes before.

Within the sinister mist, Ethan thought he heard something. A low, menacing growl, like something deadly awaited anyone unlucky enough to be overcome by the advancing vapors.

"There." At Evan's word, everyone turned to follow his gaze.

Noor stood deep in the shadows of the wooded area beyond the picnic section. He watched them with a sadistic smile on his face, truly reveling in what he'd done here today. And Ethan realized in that moment it was only a preview. Now that Noor knew he could torment whomever he pleased, they were likely to see more of the same.

Seth stepped forward. "I'll wipe that fucking grin right off his face!"

But as he took a second step, Noor began to fade away. Just before he disappeared, he waved his hand with a flourish and took a bow, as if to say, "Thank you, ladies and gentlemen. This has been fun. Until next time."

Without the power of Noor to sustain it, the fog dispersed and finally melted away.

"Son of a bitch!" Evan muttered at the missed opportunity.

They all shared the sentiment.

Turning to the innocents in need, Ethan and his siblings, along with Seth and Joe, did what they could to restore peace and calm.

An hour later, Ethan was driving Paige back to her condo. Neither said anything on the short ride there, but when they finally pulled up into a parking space, she spoke.

"How did it go?"

Ethan relayed the events that had taken place at the roadside park.

"Can you stop him from doing this again?"

"Unfortunately, no." Ethan scrubbed his hands over his face before letting them drop back to his lap. "The only thing we can do is try to contain it. Evan will likely issue a press release through the PD with a plausible reason for what so many people saw tonight. But this is only the beginning of his theatrics. Now that he knows he can get to anyone and everyone, he'll be merciless. The best we can hope for is that these displays will take enough out of him that he'll need a break in between."

They sat in the darkened car, each absorbing what was to come until a jaw-cracking yawn took Paige by surprise. "Oh, God. Sorry."

"Why don't you go on in and get some sleep?"

Paige turned and watched him for a moment. "Will you? Go home and sleep?"

He gave her a quick shake of his head.

"So, you're going to sit out here for another night?"

Ethan waved off her concern. "I'll be fine."

After another moment of staring him down, she opened her door and got out. As she rounded the hood though, she stopped. Turning sharply, she approached the lowered driver's side window.

"I don't think so." She had a determined edge to her voice. "The couch in the living room pulls out into a bed. You can watch over me from there. If you do happen to fall asleep—and I hope you *do*—I'm sure you'll wake up fast enough if you need to."

He studied her for a moment, confused. "You really don't want me that close, Paige. It could trigger your fears, and that'll defeat the purpose of you trying to get some rest."

She cocked a brow at him. "You let me worry about me. Now move your ass, Burke."

He couldn't help the small grin that lifted the corner of his mouth at her command. But he got it under control quickly.

"Are you sure?" Ethan's gaze caught and held hers.

She didn't look sure, but she nodded. "Come on."

He shrugged and hit the button to raise the window. When he shut the car off, she stepped back so he could open the door.

He trailed behind her as she swung around and headed for her door. A swipe of the key card, and they were in.

It wasn't hard to see how nervous she was now that they were inside. Together. Alone. "Okay, well, I'll just get the bedding for you." She fled into the bedroom and closed the door. It seemed to Ethan like she'd been in there a long time. When he started to think she wouldn't be back, the door opened.

"Here you go." She held the sheets and blankets out to him.

"Thank you." He took the pile from her and dropped it on the couch. He didn't like that she was so jumpy with him in her space. "This isn't necessary. It doesn't take an empath to know my being here is making you anxious already. I should just go." He turned to head for the door.

"No!" Paige burst out but caught herself. "I'm good. This'll be fine. We can do this." She gestured behind her. "The bathroom is back through there to the left. You can have it first." She went to the kitchen area to busy herself.

When he walked by her and into her bedroom, he stopped in the doorway. He saw her sag against the counter and shake her head. She had to be second-guessing her decision to invite him in. But Ethan knew she wouldn't change her mind. He promised himself he'd do what he could to make this as easy on her as possible.

~~~

Paige hadn't been sure she'd sleep. Nightmares plagued her on a good night. There was no way to know what would happen with living, breathing fire in the very next room. She'd been worried she wouldn't be able to close her eyes at all without seeing it coming for her.

But in the end, she slept better than she had in weeks. Deep and dreamless, she awoke refreshed and feeling pretty damned good.

Her day got even better when she smelled coffee. And breakfast.

Paige jumped up, brushed her teeth, tamed her hair, and threw some yoga pants on under her sleep shirt. Quietly
~~~

opening the door, she saw Ethan at the little stove, flipping pieces of bacon in the pan.

He'd pulled on his jeans, but that was as far as he'd gotten. His upper half and his feet were bare. She was afforded an unobstructed view of the expanse of his muscled back. Her stomach fluttered. And it had nothing to do with the fear that always plagued her when he was near.

This was a needful type of feeling. One she was completely unfamiliar with. She placed her hand over her belly, but she didn't know if it was to try and stop the dancing butterflies, or to hold them closer.

Still reeling from these new sensations, her gaze found and locked on to the deep groove down the center of his well-defined back. The long, sinewy muscle running along either side bulged and shifted with every movement he made. She'd never known a man's back could make her feel so...*warm*.

Thinking about all the other guys she'd known and tried to date, she realized that none of them had been Ethan Burke. Her mind may not have remembered him, but somewhere deep inside of her, he still held a place of honor.

17

Ethan had a hell of a time remaining still and calm. He'd heard the water running in the bathroom and knew that Paige was awake. When he heard the door behind him open, he'd expected her to say something. But when the silence had grown, he began to feel her study of him.

His entire body heated, but most of it seemed to concentrate on his back. A tingling awareness moved up and down his spine, telling him her eyes were tracking the shape of him.

Ethan recalled vividly how it felt to have her look at him like this. The last time had been the weekend he'd surprised her.

Was she remembering something? Had the love they'd shared before begun to slip back in and override everything else? Could they come together again? Not as they'd been before, but as they were now?

Ethan's heart was torn. Should he continue to keep his distance and wait for his Honor to return? Or accept that it may never happen and try to make a life with Paige?

Or should he just let her go altogether? To live out the life she'd created for herself in Louisiana without him?

He vowed to accept whatever choice she made. Whatever she decided was best for her. Even if that meant living the rest of his life without her.

Ethan took a breath and made sure none of what he was thinking and feeling showed on his face. Once he was sure his expression was casual, he turned to look over his shoulder at her.

"Good morning." He sent her an easy smile. "Coffee's on and breakfast should be done in a minute."

She stood there another moment before starting forward. "Um, yeah, coffee would be great." Skirting around behind him, she made sure to keep a good distance between them in the small kitchen. A feat Ethan hadn't thought would be possible.

As he moved the cooked bacon to a plate lined with paper towels, he watched her out of the corner of his eye. When she saw the coffee mug he'd set out for her, she paused and cast him a quick, cautious glance. Slowly, Paige picked it up and held it in her hand for a second.

He couldn't imagine what she was thinking.

Setting it back on the counter, she reached out for the carafe and poured. Doctoring it the way she liked, she took her first sip standing in front of the brewer.

"Mmm, that's good," she hummed.

Ethan hid the grin that quirked his lips. Honor had never been a morning person. She'd always needed the kick of caffeine to get her moving, and that seemed to hold true now as well. He waited until she'd taken a few drinks before broaching something he'd been thinking about.

"If you don't have anything else in mind for today, what do you say we try to poke at that memory of yours a bit? There's not a whole hell of a lot we can do about Noor right now other than stay aware, but Cabot is another matter. Since I'm at your disposal for the duration, we may as well team up and try to deal with him. But in order to do that, we need your memories."

Paige thought it over for a minute. "Yeah. That's fine. But don't get your hopes up," she warned. "I've already driven around some, and no place I've been to has brought anything back."

"You weren't trying to remember then. Now you know there's a tie between you and this area."

"That's true." She raised her coffee cup. "Well, here's to hoping."

An hour later, they were in Ethan's car. He'd been thinking, trying to remember a place where he thought Mr. Andrews might have hidden the flash drive to keep it safe. There were a few that came to mind, so that's where he was headed.

The first was a campground. Ethan could remember them talking about it and laughing at the experience. Honor had been young when they'd gone, but it was a good memory. He watched her out of the corner of his eye as he approached the wooded area. He was holding his breath, waiting for some sign of recognition.

Her face remained blank as she took in their surroundings.

Ethan parked in a clearing and shut off his car. "Feel like a walk in the woods?"

"What is this place?"

"You and your parents camped here a couple of times."

"Only a couple?"

"Yeah," he laughed softly. "From what I understand, it didn't go over very well with you and your mom. You guys never came back."

"If we stopped coming, why would you think this might be the place?"

"It was worth a shot. You never know who or what will be the trigger."

Just before he reached for the door handle, he noticed she was looking at him with an odd expression. He couldn't quite read what it was.

"What?"

Paige shook her head and turned away. "Nothing."

She obviously didn't want to talk about it, so Ethan let it drop.

They tromped around for about half an hour before Ethan conceded. No stunning revelations would be made here. Maybe the next stop.

But hours later they were no further ahead. Nowhere he'd tried had even caused a glimmer for her. Not their old high school, not the putt-putt course she and her dad used to visit most weekends, not even the bank where her dad had worked. Ethan hadn't allowed her out of the car for obvious reasons, but he'd parked so that she could see the building.

While he waited for any sign of familiarity, a thought occurred to him.

"Evan?"

"Yeah?" came a distracted reply.

"Did anyone ever look to see if Mr. Andrews left a safety deposit box?"

"As soon as Grier explained the situation, we ran all combinations of their names. No match."

"Okay, thanks. It was just a thought."

"Any luck with jogging her memory?"

"No. I'm not sure what else to try."

"What about the girls?"

"What about them?"

"Aria has visions and Anna reads emotions. One of them may be able to pick up on something buried in there."

Ethan glanced over at Paige. "I don't know if she'll go for that, but I can ask."

"Let me know what she decides."

"Sure will."

When Ethan turned his attention back to Paige, he knew by the disappointment he saw on her face that this stop hadn't garnered anything either. There was one more place, but he'd been holding off on it as a last resort. As much as he wanted to help her remember, he didn't want to cause her any unnecessary pain. Seeing where her mom and dad had died might be too much.

"I have one more place in mind. But if you don't think you want to go there, we don't have to."

"What is it?" She looked tired, dejected.

"Where you lived. The house is gone, but the property hasn't changed."

He waited while she thought it over, myriad emotions flickering in her eyes. When her mouth set in a firm line, he knew her answer.

She took a deep breath and then nodded. "Yeah. Okay. Let's try it."

Silence consumed them as he made the short drive. He glanced over at her to find her staring out the side window. He wished he knew what was going on in her mind. Her expression was somber—almost forlorn—and he wished so much that he could fix that for her. Seeing her struggle was killing him.

When he slowed and turned left into the concrete driveway, she brought her gaze around to see where they were. Ethan pulled up to where he knew the garage had been and stopped. He turned off the car, and all that could be heard was the clicking and pinging of the hot engine.

"Do you want to get out and look around?"

She only shook her head. Her face was a mask of sadness as she took in the scene before her.

The foundation of the house could still be seen through the grass, giving an indication of its size and shape. Beyond where the structure had stood was a tall, full oak tree. Its leaves had shaded the entire backyard and most of the house too.

Ethan could remember sitting underneath it with her more times than he could count. Her mom would bring them lemonade and snacks and smile at their young love.

It tore at his heart to recall that sweet time. When he looked back at her, there were tears streaming down her face.

"Paige, what is it?"

Shimmering grey eyes met his. She sat miserably for a moment and then knuckled away the moisture. "I hate this!" she suddenly yelled. "Why can't I remember them? They're my parents, for God's sake! Out of any memory," her hand flung out to indicate the property, "theirs should be the strongest. Theirs should be the ones that come back first."

He couldn't stand what this was doing to her. "It'll come, we just have to be patient."

"I've been patient for four fucking years!" She blew out a breath and slumped back into her seat. "I'm sorry. I didn't mean to take this out on you. This isn't going to work. Please, just take me back."

"There *is* one more thing we could try." He hated to even bring it up now, given how upset she was, but it was worth a shot.

Her head rolled to the side and she watched the world from the side window. "I don't want to take any more trips down memory lane, Ethan."

"That isn't what this would be."

"Then what would it be?" Her tone told him she was done with this whole experiment.

"My sisters."

Her head swung around and she sent him a quizzical look. "What?"

"Anna is an empath. She may be able to pick up on something that's tucked away in your mind. And Aria has visions. Maybe either of them could see something."

"I've tried psychics before, Ethan." The frustration was back in her voice. "No one could help me."

"You haven't worked with my sisters," he told her with no little pride. "Neither of them has ever been wrong."

Paige thought about that, and he saw a glimmer of something come into her smoky eyes. "You *really* think one of them can find what's locked away in my brain?"

"We won't know until we try. What do you say?"

She shrugged. "Sure. Why not." But he could tell she wasn't completely convinced.

Ethan felt hope swell inside of him. "I'll set it up."

They were almost back to her condo when Ethan got a mental call from his brother.

"Ethan. You need to come over to Beach Street right now. We've got a fire. It's in a strip mall, and it's jumping from store to store, fast. There are still people inside. Fire crews are here, but it's not looking good. We need you, bro."

He didn't hesitate. *"I'm on my way."*

Then he remembered who was seated next to him. *Shit.* There was no time to set up another guard for her. The situation sounded dire, and he needed to get there now.

"Paige, I'm about to ask you to do something you're not going to like. But I don't have any other option."

"Ethan, what's wrong?"

Her eyes went wide when he wheeled the car around, barely slowing.

"Where are we going?"

"Evan just called and needs my help."

"What? No, he didn't. I've been sitting here the whole time." One hand was on the door and the other was braced on the dash. "You didn't answer your phone."

"My siblings and I can communicate telepathically." Ethan couldn't look at her to see her reaction; he had to keep his eyes on the road so he didn't kill them, or anyone else. "There's a big fire, and people are in danger. The local fire departments are hitting it with all they have, but they can't handle it on their own. Evan needs me to take control of it and get it out before it hurts someone."

"A fire?" He didn't need to see her face to know it had lost all color. Her voice was just as washed out.

"I'm sorry to have to do this to you, but there's not enough time to get someone else out to keep watch over your place. You'll have to come with me."

She sat in silence as he sped onto Beach Street and skidded to a stop behind some police cruisers.

The sight before them was horrific. A structure of about five stores was three-quarters of the way engulfed. Flames had already burst through the roof and were dancing and licking at the sky. Ethan turned to Paige and saw that she was statue still, her eyes wide.

"We have to go, Paige."

She shook her head. "I can't."

"You have to. I can't leave you here unguarded. I can't risk you getting hurt or taken."

"I'll get hurt if I go out there." She had yet to take her eyes off the inferno. "It'll find me."

Did she think the flames were hunting her? Ethan would have to give that more thought later, but right now, there were innocent people that needed him.

He turned in his seat to face Paige. "Nothing will happen to you—I will be controlling the fire, and I won't let it get you." He gave her a second. "Paige?"

She'd come so far, and it tore Ethan's heart out to see her this scared. He wanted to wrap her up in his arms to offer some kind of comfort, but thought he was causing her enough stress as it was. Gradually, her head came around. Her eyes pleaded with him to let her stay in the car, but she just wasn't safe alone. Too much could go wrong. "I promise you, Paige. Everything's going to be all right."

Her troubled gaze held his, then slowly her hand inched over and opened the door so she could get out.

He hurried through his own door, rounded the hood, and gave her a small nod. "Okay. Here we go."

As he drew closer and closer to the fire, he could hear Paige beside him. "Oh God. Oh God." Fear was etched on her face when he glanced down at her. Her eyes were rounded in panic, but she was still moving forward with him.

Ethan turned his mind to formulating a plan when Paige suddenly spun around and darted towards the car.

He always tried to stay the need to touch her, knowing she didn't like it, but there was no choice now. Reaching out, he wrapped his long fingers around her upper arm and hauled her to a stop. If she ran off now, Noor or Cabot would probably have someone lying in wait nearby to snatch her up. And he couldn't let that happen. Ethan tightened his grip on her and she struggled.

"Let me go!" She frantically fought his hold on her, using her fingers to pry his off her. "I have to go. I can't stay here."

Ethan hated what this was doing to her, but leaving was too dangerous to allow.

"Paige. Listen to me." He reached out and took hold of her other arm, pulling her around to face him. "Stop! And hear me."

The terror in her gaze nearly undid him. "You're going to be okay. I swear it to you."

Her lids widened even further as she pulled back with all of her body weight. "We need to go. Now. We have to run or we'll die."

Ethan held firm. "You'll be far worse off if you run. You have too many men watching you. You're going to have to trust me on this. Can you do that?" He dipped his head until she met his gaze. "I promise you, on my life, I will not let anything happen to you."

She still wanted to flee. Her need to escape was stamped all over her face, and her body was poised to bolt. But at least she was listening.

The fire crackled loudly behind him. "I can stop this. But you're going to have to come with me. I can't leave you here alone, and there's no time to call anyone else."

"Wh...what do you mean I have to go with you?" Her gaze

flicked over his shoulder to the fire. "Over there?" Her hair swayed as she shook her head. "I can't. I can't go into that. You're crazy."

"Not *into* the fire, no. But I have to get closer." Ethan looked behind him and judged how much larger it had gotten. He just needed a few minutes, but unless Paige cooperated and stayed with him, the fire would only spread.

A pain-filled scream rent the air. It was closing in on the people trapped in there. "I can save them. Will you help me?"

"How…how can *I* help?"

"I just need you to stay close to me. I can't do what I need to do and worry about you running off and right into trouble. Can you trust me long enough for me to fix this?"

She peeked over at her worst nightmare. He thought she was going to refuse but she surprised him. "I can try." Her voice was barely a whisper.

"That's all I ask." Ethan needed to hurry. He turned around to face the burning buildings and then stopped. "Grab hold of my belt loop, and don't let go. I need to know you're still with me."

Once she had a good grip, Ethan crossed the road with Paige trailing behind him. He worked his way to the front of the gathering crowd. When he could feel the heat against his skin, he stopped. Taking a breath, he tapped into his element and felt the power build.

Behind him, Paige buried her face into his back. Her hot breath washing over him broke his concentration as nothing else could have. But as much as he'd like to bask in the feel of her against him, he steeled his resolve.

Narrowing his focus to only the task in front of him, Ethan bore down and delved deep into the heart of it.

It fought his intrusion at first, but Ethan quickly found and connected with the core of it. He became a part of it, and it of him. He guided the searching fingers away from the sections of the building that were still intact.

Ethan's heartbeat became one with the rhythm within the blaze. He became its thinking mind. He pulled it back farther and farther. With nowhere else to go, the energy of it flowed into him. Ethan absorbed it and let it burn itself out inside of him.

He worked steadily until the last ember was contained and extinguished.

Becoming aware again, Ethan searched out and found his brother. Evan nodded at him from across the parking lot.

"Thanks, man." Evan sounded tired.

Ethan caught sight of soot-covered shoppers milling around. Some were receiving oxygen from the EMS crews. *"Did everyone make it out?"*

"Yeah, the last two came out the far end just as you pulled the flames back."

"Do they know what caused it?"

"Noor did. Inadvertently."

He didn't like the sound of that. *"What do you mean?"*

"This started out as another mass hallucination. We've been getting calls from all over town. Someone here thought it would be a good idea to torch the spiders crawling all over everything."

No wonder Evan sounded tired. They were being run ragged. *"Fuck."*

"Yeah. That about sums it up. We're spreading the story that there's an odorless, tasteless gas responsible for the outbreaks of mass hysteria. But that won't fly for long. We need to find a way to stop him." There was a beat of silence. *"I forgot Paige was with you. How's she handling this?"*

"Not sure. She's burrowed into my back. I'd better get her out of here now that everything is under control."

"Okay. I'll see you later."

Ethan turned his attention to the woman behind him. Paige was still plastered against him. The top of her head was tucked right up against his spine and her hands were gripped onto his waistband tightly. Her panting breaths were blowing shiver-inducing puffs of air through the material of his shirt.

He hated to move—hated to lose this closeness—but he needed to assure her it was over. He reached back and dislodged her grasp from his jeans. With her hands still in his, he turned to face her.

"Paige?"

Her eyes were still clamped shut.

"Paige. You can open your eyes. The fire's out."

Reluctantly, her head came up and her lashes fluttered as she looked up at him.

He was afraid she was in shock. Her eyes looked glassy and unfocused. "Come on. Let's get you home."

He guided her back to his car and buckled her in. Neither said a word.

Back at her condo, Ethan followed her in and watched as she sat down on the couch. She still hadn't said anything at all.

Crossing into the kitchen, Ethan poured her a cup of coffee. Returning to the living room, he handed it to her.

"Thank you." She didn't drink it, but she wrapped her hands around it like they were cold and seeking the heat.

Ethan sat adjacent to her. "I am so sorry I had to put you through that." When she didn't answer, he took the opportunity to study her face closer. She was pale, and her eyes were cast downward to her cup. She didn't meet his eyes, and he started to worry that she really was in shock.

When she took a hesitant sip, Ethan noted that her hands seemed steady, and so he settled back into his chair to wait. She'd talk when she was ready.

18

Paige couldn't look at him. He was worried about her reaction to being so close to the fire, when in reality it wasn't the flames at all that had her mind reeling. The physical contact with him had her head boggling with an Ethan Burke overload, and she just couldn't handle even the simple banter of conversation.

She'd been scared out of her mind and ready to run for her life when they'd first arrived at the site. But somehow, and she still didn't know how he'd done it, Ethan had talked her into staying. Even going towards her mortal enemy.

In a desperate need to shut out the raging inferno and the oppressive heat, Paige had forgotten her no-touching rule and, without thinking, had buried her face in Ethan's muscular back. Shockingly, as she'd cowered behind him and inhaled his spicy, woodsy scent, her fear had loosened its hold.

Enough so, that the contact between them had inundated her with more of Honor's life.

As Ethan battled the blaze, she'd been lost in a past that was consumed with him—sitting in class as she tousled his hair from the desk behind him. A first kiss shared on the beach. Making love for the first time on a night when her parents had been out of town.

Before, they'd only been snapshots, pictures. Glimpses that spared her the emotions that had gone along with them. This time was different, though, and so much more profound. These had played out like a movie reel, and she could actually *feel* the total adoration she'd had for this man. The depths of Honor's feelings had been so intense, it had taken her breath away to experience those particular scenes. She didn't understand how something like love could be so all-encompassing...so overwhelming.

She'd always been a stranger to it and had never understood all the swooning from the women she knew. But this—what Ethan and Honor had shared—had hit her with the force of a Mack truck. And it terrified her.

She had never known anything like it.

So now here she was, with not only the visual images of kissing him and touching him and making love to him floating around in her head, but also the emotional and tactile memories.

Just thinking about it made the butterflies take flight again.

What the hell was she supposed to do with all of this? A relationship that powerful carried a lot of weight and would surely overshadow anything that she and Ethan could build together. Could she handle that? Him always comparing her to who she used to be? Did she want that on her shoulders? Always trying to live up to the Honor he remembered?

She wasn't the woman from those flashes any longer. Even if she just *told* him what was happening—the touching, the flashbacks, the memories—what then? It would only get his hopes up, and then he'd surely pressure her to remember more. He'd expect it all to come flooding back, so they could pick up where they'd left off.

Paige wasn't sure she could handle that kind of pressure. She didn't think she could ever equal the love and complete devotion that she'd felt in those memories. She was too changed. Too damaged. Too...*Paige.*

This whole situation was so disconcerting. She'd only experienced a small blip of what they'd shared before her accident, and look what it was doing to her. She was confused and scared and overcome to the point that she couldn't think at all. She couldn't help but imagine what recovering a lifetime's worth of memories loving him would feel like.

She didn't want to know.

Not until she could figure out her own mind. And deal with the crap-tastic turn her life had taken since coming to Daytona Beach. She had to protect herself and her heart. And in order to do that, there could be no more touching Ethan Burke. She couldn't take any more memories of him right now.

She had to think of her own sanity and well-being first.

Paige stiffened her spine and attempted to put a little mental distance between her and the man studying her so intently.

More to escape than because she needed it, she pushed herself up from the couch and took her coffee cup into the kitchen. As she did, she spoke to Ethan over her shoulder. She hoped it came off as casual.

"It certainly wasn't one of the more fun things I've ever done." She filled her cup the mere half inch it was missing. "I hope everyone made it out. That was why we had to go there, after all."

She had yet to look at him as she slowly returned the carafe to the hot plate. Paige lifted the mug to her lips and took a small sip. With nothing else to distract her, she looked over to where Ethan had been sitting.

Only he wasn't there. She jumped when she saw him standing behind her just outside the kitchen area. She hadn't heard him move.

And now, his attention was completely locked on her. He stared at her for so long, she became nervous. When she could take no more, she turned to face him fully and snapped with a huff, "What?"

"I'm just wondering when you decided to embrace fear, rather than meeting it head-on."

It didn't matter that his assessment of her echoed her own thoughts. It still pissed her off. So much that she forgot all about her resolve and her vow to maintain some distance between them.

"First off, the person you knew is dead, she's *gone*." Paige poked at her temple with her fingertip. "She's not in here anymore. No matter how much you want it otherwise, she's not coming back. And secondly, how dare you judge me. You don't know anything about me. You have no clue who I am now."

He took a step forward, his gaze scorching. Paige took one involuntary step back, but the galley-style setup of the kitchen prevented her retreat. She was utterly trapped by this giant of a man bearing down on her.

"She *is* still in there, and I *do* know you." Ethan's face could have been etched from stone, his dark features hard and unyielding. "I know who you are deep down where, no matter what's happened, nothing will ever change it." He stalked closer. "You're smart and compassionate. Generous and strong-willed. Gentle and thoughtful. But, most importantly, you are one of the strongest women I have ever known." Closer still. "I never thought I'd see the day when you'd be a coward."

Only about a foot separated them. Paige could feel the heat pumping off his chest. She had no choice but to tilt her head back to look up into his coal-black eyes. What she saw there drew a gasp. So many emotions were swirling around in their troubled depths she couldn't keep up with them all. But there was one that stood out more than the rest. And that was anger.

"I am not a coward," she denied, but her voice wavered.

"Really?" He glared down at her. "I can feel the wall you're trying to erect between us, Paige. Why? I know you were scared out there, but that's not what made you pull back just now. I've seen you face your fear of fire—and of me—more than once in the last few days. You're dealing with it. Successfully, I might add, so that can't be the cause."

His head cocked and that dark, fathomless gaze drilled into her. "No. I'm betting it's more about what happened this morning. And the feelings you're beginning to have for me."

Paige lied, because he was getting much too close to the truth. "I don't know what you're talking about."

Ethan braced his hands on the counter on either side of her hips and leaned in as she turned her face to the side. His mouth was so near her cheek. "Oh, I think you do," he whispered, his breath washing over her skin in ripples. "I felt those smoky gray eyes of yours on my body earlier, drinking up the sight of me. Did you like what you saw, Paige? Were you wondering how it would feel to touch me? Stroke me? Feel me on top of you?"

His lips tickled her ear as he spoke sensually against it. Touching her, yet not. Paige fought not to succumb, but her heart was pounding in her chest and her breaths were coming out in shallow pants.

"Were you picturing my mouth on you?" His face nuzzled into her hair, and her head tilted towards him despite her will to remain impassive. "My tongue trailing along your collar bone and down to your breasts? Did your nipples get hard imagining me licking and kissing my way down your body?" He inhaled deeply and hummed approvingly. "Were you wet, fantasizing about me sucking on your clit and dipping my tongue inside you?"

That husky, seductive voice sent shivers racing through her. If she hadn't been before, she was definitely wet now. He hadn't even really touched her, and yet, suddenly, she longed for that contact.

"When you had your hands on me at the fire, were you wondering what it would be like to fuck me? To have my cock deep inside of you? Is that what has you tucking your tail and running, Paige?"

At his blunt and offensive words, she snapped out of her

arousal-induced state like she'd been doused with icy water. Before she even realized her intent, she reared back and slapped him. Hard.

The force of her strike whipped his head to the side. It stayed there for a beat before he brought it back around. As he did, he stood to his full height, his face unreadable as he held her stare.

The imprint of her hand was bright and clearly visible on his cheek.

Oh, shit. What had she done?

She was still trying to figure out what to say when he spoke.

"I'm sorry. I was way out of line." Ethan pivoted on his heel and walked out of the kitchen.

Paige followed him as he swore under his breath and plowed his fingers through his long black hair, sending it into disarray. Stopping by the table, he scooped up his keys and went to the door. Was he leaving?

"Ethan..."

"Don't." He stared down to where his hand was grasping the knob. "I told myself I wouldn't *ever* put that kind of pressure on you. If you were going to find your way back to me, it had to be on your own terms."

He turned his head to look at her over his shoulder. Even from her position in the kitchen doorway, she could see the torment in his haunted gaze. "It's just so fucking impossible sometimes. Living without you was hell. But seeing you now, and knowing I'm nothing more than a stranger to you, has been so much harder. I look at you, and it's like you were never gone. I smell the floral scent of lilies you still favor, and it taunts me. Parts of me that have been shut down, essentially dead for four years, have come roaring back to life." He took a deep breath and shook his head. "You don't have to worry. Nothing like this will ever happen again."

Paige was left speechless as he pulled the door open and

stepped out. When he closed it behind him with a soft click, she felt it almost would have been easier to take if he'd slammed it. The note of defeat in the action nearly broke her heart.

She thought more about what he'd said. Was she to believe he hadn't had another woman since she'd supposedly died? Knowing what she did of him now, that seemed hard to believe. The few memories she'd had and his display only moments ago had shown her that he was an intensely sexual creature. Could he have abstained with a need like that inside of him for so long?

Slowly, crossing the room, she moved the heavy curtains aside enough to see where he was going.

Not far, it turned out. Ethan leaned against the opposite side of the very window where she stood. His hands were in his pockets as he looked out over the ocean.

Unbidden, Paige's hand came up to rest on the middle of his back. "I'm sorry too. For so much."

Confused and at a loss for what to do next, Paige shuffled into the bathroom. When she gazed into the mirror, she saw flecks of ash dotting her hair. Taking note of her clothes, she found that they smelled of smoke. Stripping out of them, she stepped into the shower with a heavy heart. As the water beat down on her, she was caught off guard by the sobs that suddenly racked her body.

Sliding to the floor of the tub, she cried for the mess her life had become and for the man who had lost so much.

Exhausted, Paige eventually turned the faucets off and stepped out. After wrapping herself in a towel, she walked out into the bedroom and sat on the side of her bed. Before she could talk herself out of it, she reached out, picked up her phone, and dialed.

"Hey, sweet girl."

Paige's breath hitched at the sound of Gail's loving voice.

Of course, she heard. "Tell me what's wrong, honey."

"Oh, Gail. It's so screwed up." Between bouts of tears and anger, Paige laid it all out for her friend. The lies that had been told to her and why. Matt's role in it. That she was still in danger because she had something they wanted. She explained who she'd been and her ties to Ethan. The memories she'd experienced and how much they scared her.

She left nothing out. Not who or what Ethan was, or Noor and his past.

Paige finished with, "It's all too much. I just don't know what to do."

"I am sorrier than I can express for what has happened to you, but you listen to me, Paige or Honor, or whatever you choose to go by." Gail's tone was sharp. "For as long as I've known you, you haven't ever been a quitter." Her words echoed Ethan's so closely. But Gail's didn't set her off the way Ethan's had. "So, you pull up them big girl panties, and you show those men what you're made of. Ain't no criminal, or witch, or ancient evil dirt-bag got big enough balls to get you down. Do you hear me? Or do you need me to come out there and kick your ass for you?"

"No, ma'am." She sniffled away the last of her tears. This was exactly what she'd needed. Paige felt a weight lift off her shoulders and she smiled.

"As far as the memories you're getting back, you take as long as you need to sort those out. No one knows what you need better than you do. And by the sounds of it, they're some real doozies."

"That's an understatement." Paige gave a soft laugh before taking a deep breath and straightening her spine. "Okay. Pulling on big girl panties right now."

"Good." Paige knew Gail well enough to know she'd given a quick, decisive nod as she'd said that.

"Now, tell me more about this Ethan." Gail's voice had changed to a more animated and inquisitive tone "He's cute, isn't he? I can hear it in your voice. Spill it. And don't leave out the details."

"Oh, you have no idea."

By the time Paige hung up, she felt so much better. She also knew what she had to do. And that was to take back control of her life. No more hiding out in her condo wringing her hands, waiting for the next bomb to drop. She was done. Done getting pushed around and used and threatened by assholes whose beefs had absolutely nothing to do with her.

Nick Cabot wants a piece of her? Great, let him come. In the end, she'll be the one to put him behind bars. Noor thinks he can use her against Ethan? Well, he'll just have a big surprise coming when he tries.

Feeling confident, Paige's mind moved on to her next problem.

Ethan Burke.

And that's where her grand plan to fight back and stand up for herself came to a screeching halt. What was she going to do about him? She had no clue. There were so many conflicting emotions there, she didn't even know where to begin figuring them out.

By the time she finished getting dressed, she still didn't have any answers about the tall, brawny witch. But she did know they couldn't avoid each other. Too much tied them together. They were going to have to make this work, whatever *this* was.

When she walked out of the bedroom, he hadn't returned. Going to the window, she grasped the plastic rod hidden within the slats and slid it back. Light washed over the room.

But Ethan was nowhere in sight.

Pulling open the door, she stepped out and looked around. His car was still parked across the lot, but the angle of the sun reflecting off the window prevented her from seeing if he was in it. Maybe he'd retreated there to watch over her as he'd done at first.

After making sure she had her keycard, Paige shut the door and started towards him as she'd done so many times before. About halfway across the asphalt, massive arms clamped around her waist and lifted her up off the ground. Her scream was cut short by the giant-sized palm that slapped over the lower half of her face.

She fought and kicked, but nothing she did loosened the hold he had on her. Struggling to keep her head, Paige scrambled for a way to get out of this.

But before she could make a move, her assailant grunted and dropped her unceremoniously to the hot pavement. The unmistakable sound of flesh striking flesh had her clambering to right herself.

When she finally had her feet underneath her, she turned to see Ethan thrashing the guy who'd grabbed her. Fists flew and Ethan took as many knocks as he gave. His lip was split and bleeding, and a bruise was forming next to his eye.

But he showed no signs he'd felt any of the injuries. He methodically beat her attacker down, landing blow after blow.

A part of her got lost in watching the way Ethan moved and fought. The ferocity with which he battled held her enthralled. But she was ripped back to the present when the guy he was beating went down and didn't move. When Ethan crouched over him and continued wailing away, she became frightened Ethan might kill him.

"Ethan! Stop!" she yelled. "That's enough!"

He didn't hear her.

Sirens split the air. Someone had evidently called the police. She had to stop him, or he'd be taken to jail as a murderer instead of hailed as a hero.

Not thinking of her own safety, Paige snagged his arm with both of hers before he could deliver the next swing. He tried to shake her off, but she held on. She could feel heat pouring off of him. His skin was hot to the touch and getting hotter.

The fire that was so much a part of him raged just as he did. Paige knew she'd have marks along her exposed flesh as his power rose further. But she couldn't let go, even as her fear pushed her to flee.

"Ethan, you have to stop. The police are coming." Tears clogged her throat. "Ethan. Stop. Please."

Her words must have finally gotten through, because all the fury drained right out of him. His arm went lax in her grip and cooled. She released him and wrapped her stinging arms close to her body.

He slumped to the side, exhausted, and sat staring up at her. Neither was able to say anything more as a car with lights flashing tore into the condo complex.

Paige turned and saw Evan and Seth jumping from their vehicle, and the relief she felt almost made her cry. She'd been worried about how to explain this to someone who didn't know what was going on.

Evan approached where she stood with a disheveled and bloody Ethan.

"You okay?" Evan directed at Paige.

She surreptitiously glanced down and saw that in the places where it stung, there were faint red patches dotting her limbs. No permanent damage, and the marks should fade soon. "I'm fine," she assured him.

He took her at her word and sent a scathing glare to the unconscious man.

"Noor's or Cabot's?"

Paige waited for Ethan to answer, but when he remained mute, she filled his brother in. "I don't know. He didn't say anything; he just grabbed me from behind. Ethan…he, ah…"

"Beat him to a bloody pulp," Seth supplied dryly. He looked from the downed man to Ethan sitting near him. "That's a lot of pent-up rage there, Skippy."

Ethan grimaced in pain as he slowly got to his feet and shot

Seth a scathing glower. "Fuck off."

"Aww, that's so sweet, but no thanks."

Evan shook his head. "Are you two about done?"

"Why are you even here?" Ethan braced his right arm around his middle as he glared at his twin.

"Call came in about a disturbance," Evan told him. "I recognized the address and thought it might be something like this, so I told them I'd take it. You're welcome." He glanced down at the heap again. "Is he alive?"

Ethan and Seth followed his gaze. "Don't know." Ethan shrugged as if unconcerned.

Paige stared incredulously at him. "Yes," she shot out. "He's still alive."

"Bonus." Seth smirked. "We get to question him."

"We should probably call an ambulance." Evan was reaching for his phone when the man groaned to indicate he was coming around.

"Naw. Put that away. He's good." Seth leaned over him just as his eyes flittered open. The thug took in the large form looming over him. "You don't need an ambulance. Do you?"

The detective got a scowl for his trouble.

"See?" Seth grinned and then bent to haul the man to his feet. He made it look easy. Like he wasn't lifting over two hundred pounds of uncooperative scumbag.

Seth was a very large man. His shoulders and chest were so wide, Paige was surprised he could fit through doorways. He had dark brown hair and eyes that reminded her of her favorite milk chocolate. Tattoos covered his forearms from shirt sleeve to wrist, and he looked like he could rumble with the best of them. She definitely wouldn't want to get on his bad side.

As he walked away with his prize, she swung her attention back to Ethan. And instantly those damned butterflies she'd always been so jealous of took wing. Why did he affect her this way? Fear and lust all wrapped up into one angst-inducing package.

Self-preservation had her switching her focus to Evan. Thankfully, the confusing and disconcerting emotions she felt every time she was near Ethan seemed to settle into the background again.

So she concentrated on the problem she could see might arise. Evan may be Ethan's brother, but he was also a cop. She didn't know him. She didn't know how by-the-book he was. Even understanding the circumstances, would he arrest Ethan along with the other guy until he got it all sorted out? No matter how he made her feel, Paige didn't want Ethan to suffer for saving her.

"Ethan was only protecting me. He shouldn't get into any trouble for this."

"He won't," Evan assured her. "But the next time, he may not be so lucky."

Paige's brows dipped to the middle. "What do you mean?"

"Just that there're too many players in this game. We need to clear the board a little. I know you and Ethan were working on getting Cabot and his goons off your ass... Did any of your memories resurface?"

Paige suffered a moment of awkwardness at his question. Other than Gail, she'd not told anyone she'd begun to have small memory flashes. Up to now, they'd all centered around her and Ethan, but what was to say if she delved further, more of her past wouldn't be revealed?

If she weren't so afraid she'd have to wade through her entire history with Ethan first, she would have done it already. But until she had the guts to face those and what they might mean for her future, she was keeping tight-lipped.

"No. Ethan drove me around this morning, but nothing came of it. He mentioned maybe working with your sisters to see if they could sense anything."

"Yeah, we talked about that. Just let me know if anything

comes of it." Evan turned to leave but stopped. "Oh. And we'll need you to come down to the station to press charges when you get a chance."

"I will. As soon as possible," Paige nodded.

The stinging in her arms had diminished quite a lot. She chanced another peek down and saw that some of the redness had gone too. It wasn't as noticeable as before, but keeping them out of sight was still the best option for all concerned.

Moving them to behind her back, Paige slid her fingers into her back pockets. She looked over at a silent and slightly battered Ethan. "Come on. We'll get you cleaned up."

He didn't move. He just stood staring down to where the man had fallen.

"Ethan?"

"You should go in."

She'd had enough. This day had been an emotional rollercoaster since she had rolled out of bed that morning. And now his brooding was more than she could take. Paige rounded on him and pinned him with a hard glare.

"Get your ass into that condo so I can fix you up, or I'll kick it myself." She spun and stomped back to her room. She didn't bother to look and see if he followed. If he knew what was good for him, he'd better.

When he begrudgingly walked in shortly after her, she pointed to the couch. "Have a seat. I'll be right back."

19

Ethan was still pissed off. Mostly at himself.

His actions earlier had been beyond inappropriate. He'd all but attacked her in her own goddamned kitchen. She'd had every right to slap him. She still didn't know him from Adam, and he'd moved in on her like it had somehow been his place.

He could take her phobias and skittishness. Those could be worked through and overcome. But that damned wall she'd tried to put between them had pushed him over the edge. He'd felt it the moment she'd erected it. He'd seen it in her eyes. The distance, the wariness.

Realizing what she was doing had pissed him off.

It hadn't helped matters that he'd been sporting a hard-on since that morning when she'd first seen him as a man instead of imminent death. And to have her hands on him and her breath heating his back…four years was a long fucking time.

They'd always had a very passionate relationship. He loved her with everything he was and wanted her to know that through his words, as well as his actions. Making love with her could get fierce at times, but that had only made their bond deeper and stronger.

When he'd thought Honor had died, he'd locked that part of himself down. Now that it was coming alive again, he was having a difficult time controlling it. It had taken everything Ethan had to concentrate on putting out the fire while his blood flowed so heatedly through his veins.

He'd been primed to blow for hours, and the spark that set him off was her unwarranted full-on retreat from him. It had ignited all that loose powder that had been building up all day long.

And then, to top off his fuck-up, he'd gone and left her alone. He'd stood watch outside her condo for what seemed like forever while he collected himself, and had only stepped around the corner for a second. But that's all it had taken for her to walk right into the waiting arms of danger.

Ethan hadn't cared whose henchman the dickhead had been. He was going to be sorry for laying a hand on her. Using every ounce of the frustration and anger coursing through his body, Ethan had taken on a guy who had at least fifty pounds of muscle on him.

And he'd beat him into the ground with his bare hands. If not for Paige stopping him, he would have kept going. He'd been completely out of control, both with her assailant, but especially with her. And now here she was, insisting on doctoring him up.

His gaze shot to her when she came back into the room with a washcloth and a small first-aid kit. It continued to bother him that she was being so nice after everything he'd said and done.

"I'm fine. Just a busted lip that'll heal in no time and a bruised rib. You don't have to do this."

She sat next to him on the couch and set the kit in her lap. "Yes, I do. You were hurt because of me."

"That's where you're wrong." Ethan stood, despite the stab of pain in his side, and stalked to the window to stare out at nothing.

"And what part of you saving me *again* is incorrect?"

"You wouldn't have been out there at all if I had kept my head and not assaulted you."

"Ethan," she gasped. "You did no such thing."

He swung around to face her, his dark gaze heated. "Didn't I? I backed you into a corner, forced myself into your personal space, and I was deliberately crude in what I said and did. I made you uncomfortable and scared, to the point you had to resort to violence to stop me. How is that *not* an assault?"

Her gaze dropped to the box still in her lap. She fiddled with the latch for a second before taking a breath and looking up at him again.

"I wasn't scared. Or uncomfortable. Not in the way you think."

Ethan assumed she was only telling him what he wanted to hear. He pushed his hands up through his hair. "Paige—"

She set the small white box on the seat next to her. "Will you please just sit down and listen to me?"

He huffed at her but reluctantly walked over and dropped down into the chair.

Now she stood to pace the confines of the condo. He watched her move around the room and gather her thoughts.

"This isn't going to be easy. But you deserve the truth after the mess that resulted."

Finally, she stopped and turned to face him. She wrapped her arms around her middle, a new habit she hadn't had before.

She looked him right in the eye. "I didn't slap you because you frightened me. Or because I thought you were going to hurt me. Or even because your nearness bothered me. I'm pretty sure it stemmed from the fact that..." she paused, drew oxygen in, and on an expulsion of air said, "everything you were saying was true."

Her gaze slid away from his and she looked at anything but him. "*That's* what upset me. *That's* what had me striking out at you. You were so damned right, and I didn't want you to be."

Her face was tinged pink with embarrassment when she brought her head around to meet his eyes again. "I'm sorry I hit you. I didn't know it was going to happen until it did. It was as much a surprise to me as it was to you."

Ethan was a little taken aback at her admission. It should have made him feel good; she was starting to have feelings for him again. But it didn't change what he'd done, and that dampened any pleasure he could have taken from it.

"It still doesn't excuse the fact that I pushed myself on you. And what I said..." Ethan shook his head, remembering. "It was wildly inappropriate. I apologize for not taking better care with you."

"It may not seem like it at times, but I'm really not going to break. I'm stronger than you've seen."

"I know exactly how strong you are." As much as he wanted to avert his gaze from hers, he held it. And confessed. "It's me who hasn't been strong enough. I've let you down in so many ways over the last four years. That very first day I saw you walking down the sidewalk, I'd just come from visiting your grave to apologize for screwing up so badly."

"I have a grave?" That seemed to surprise her for a moment. "Well, I guess it would only make sense. But that's quite disconcerting to think about. To know there's a headstone out there that has my name on it. Even if the body in there isn't mine."

Ethan frowned and then nodded. "We'll have to make sure that FBI agent gets to her proper resting place—back to her family."

"I wonder what they told her parents." Sorrow dulled the gray of her eyes. "She died in my place. They probably never got to mourn, *if* they even know she's dead. Matt and his cohorts have lied to so many people to keep this farce going all these years."

"We'll get it all straightened out, and we'll put everything to rights. I promise."

Ethan glanced at the time. It had gotten late and they'd had an eventful day. "I'd better go and let you get some rest."

He rose.

"Don't go," Paige surprised him by saying.

"You've had a long day, and I haven't helped it any. I'll just be outside." He turned away and headed for the door.

"I sleep better when I know you're here. Please."

Ethan closed his eyes and dropped his head forward. She wasn't making this easy. Being this close to her day in and day out was taking its toll on him. He should let someone else watch over her, but he just couldn't pry himself away from her.

She was his, dammit. He'd failed her before, and he wasn't going to let that happen again. So, if she felt safer with him near, he'd just have to suck it up and deal.

Releasing the door knob, he turned back to face her. "If you're sure."

Paige bobbed her head. "I am. I'm also hungry. Since you know what's good around here, you can call an order in. I'm going to change." She turned and headed for the bedroom.

Ethan had just slid his phone from his pocket when she stopped at the doorway. "Ethan. I can't even begin to imagine what you've gone through, thinking I was dead all this time. As far as letting me down, I don't think that could ever happen. You were trying to survive. You may have made some mistakes, but then again, who hasn't? If there's one thing I've learned about you through this, it's that you are a good, honorable man."

She smiled softly at him before turning around and disappearing into the other room, leaving him on his own, speechless.

<p style="text-align:center">~~~</p>

Hours later, Paige lay in bed staring at the ceiling. Her mind wouldn't shut off. It was hard to believe that only a month ago she'd been living easy with only a sketchy past to deal with.

Now, here she was, a mere few weeks later, and her life

was in constant turmoil. So much had happened to shake her foundation in that short amount of time. The most shocking was learning she wasn't who she thought she was. And that those closest to her had been lying to her for years. The people she thought of as friends were actually undercover government agents getting paid to act that way.

She wished someone would have trusted her enough to explain what had happened to her. And why. If she'd known the danger that was awaiting her, she probably wouldn't have gone blundering in to put herself back in the crosshairs of a murderer.

But since they'd lied, and she'd done exactly that, Paige now found herself in more danger. As if one whack-job wasn't bad enough, she'd landed herself in the middle of a supernatural war. One with an enemy who could strike at her at any moment, and she wouldn't see it coming.

Evan was right. She needed to take some of the players off the game board. One threat at a time was plenty to deal with. Since she couldn't do anything about Noor, Cabot would be the one she needed to stop.

But how could she hope to find the evidence against him when she had no memories? Either of her father or places he might consider significant?

The memory angle clearly wasn't going to work. She needed to come at this from a different direction—use her God-given brain power instead of relying on what she'd once known and then lost.

She reached over to the bedside table and picked up the photo of her family.

Okay. If she were a parent and she was leaving something to her child to find sometime down the road, where would she hide it? It would have to be a safe place that no one would just stumble upon it by accident. Yet, in a spot that would remain the same, no matter how long it might have to stay there.

Since she was looking for a computer flash-drive, she could rule out any location where the elements might have affected its contents.

Considering her dad's profession, a safety deposit box would have been the most likely choice. But if he'd put it under his own name, or even hers, it probably would have been found already, as that would be the first place someone looking for it would search.

She tried to think of anywhere else, but nothing was coming to her. Her mind kept going back to the bank. It was the most logical answer.

Could he have secretly opened an account under someone else's name? Working there, he'd probably known how to do it without drawing unnecessary attention to himself. It sounded feasible, but the question still remained. Whose name would he have used? Who would he have trusted to protect her and the evidence?

There was only one reasonable conclusion. Paige kicked the covers off and went out to the living room.

"Ethan?"

He sat up instantly. "What's wrong?" His quick response told her he hadn't been sleeping either.

"I had a thought." She sat down in the chair. "I was trying to think of where my father could have hidden that USB drive. And I keep going back to where he worked. Banks have the highest security, and it would make perfect sense. I'm assuming everyone checked for safety deposit boxes in our names?"

"Yeah. There weren't any."

"What about *your* name? Or maybe a combination of both our names?"

He swung his legs around and off the couch. "I can't speak for the FBI, but I don't think Evan would have thought to check on that. You think that's what your dad did—that he hid it in plain sight."

"Since he couldn't use our names, I tried to think of someone else he would trust with the evidence, and with me. I can't imagine that would be anyone but you." She nodded. "I think it would be worth looking into."

"I do too." Ethan's gaze scanned the dim room. "But it's too late to do that tonight. It'll have to wait until morning. I'll call Evan first thing, and he can do a search. If it's there, you can bet your ass I'll be on the bank's doorstep the minute it opens."

"And I'll be right there with you."

Ethan shook his head. "I don't want you anywhere near Cabot if we can help it. I'd rather you hang back and stay with my brother while I go in. Once I've confirmed it's the drive, we'll figure out what to do next."

Paige hated to be left behind, but she could see his point. She'd be walking straight into hostile territory.

"Okay, I get it. But when this is done, I want to see him. I want to look him in the face and let him know *I* put him away. He destroyed my life and killed my parents for no other reason than to protect himself."

Ethan grinned. "I'll hold your hat."

A hitch to their plan popped into her head. "Oh, crap. Do you remember what Matt said when we talked to him? He said my dad told him that I was the key. What if we need a key to get into the box, and I had it but it's gone now?"

Ethan thought that over. "Hopefully they have a contingency plan in place for when a client loses theirs. Either way, we'll get into that box. Don't worry."

It was closer to ten the next morning when Paige found herself tucked into the back seat of Evan's car. He and Seth were in the front, watching as Ethan parked and strolled up to the doors of the bank. A quick computer search that morning had confirmed that there was indeed an account in the name of Ethan Burke.

As she sat staring at the entrance, Paige discovered that

patience wasn't her strong suit. Time was moving so slow. One minute became ten, and ten minutes became hours.

She was jumping out of her skin when Evan finally relayed information he'd gotten from his telepathic link to Ethan.

"He's in, but he says we could have a problem."

"What kind of problem?" Seth asked before she could.

Evan turned in his seat. "The key question is moot. He said there are signs all over touting the fact that they were one of the first banks to implement biometric security on all their safety deposit boxes. It's going to take a fingerprint to gain access."

Paige felt her stomach drop. How would her dad have gotten Ethan's print without him knowing? But then something else occurred to her.

"He doesn't think it's going to be his, does he?" she guessed.

"That's a possibility." Evan told her. "He's going to test it out and we'll go from there."

"If it's not his, it has to be mine." Paige glanced at both men. "I could have been with my father when he set this up. I just don't remember." She glanced at the building again, wishing she could see what was going on in there.

A short while later, Evan sighed. "No go."

"What do we do now? Is he coming back out to regroup?"

Evan gave her a grin. "Nope. You're going in."

"But, he said—"

"You're not going in through the lobby. You're going the direct route to the room where Ethan is. No one will even know you're there."

"What? How?"

Evan winked and wiggled his fingers at her. "Magic."

"Oh." It stunned her just how powerful this family was. "You can do that?"

"Just relax. Jacob loves this." Evan's face was calm and at ease. "Ready?"

At her tentative nod, he took a breath and closed his eyes.

The next thing Paige knew, she was standing beside Ethan.

"Holy shit." She gasped and wobbled, trying to catch her balance.

"You okay?"

"I think so. That's a hell of a way to travel."

She looked around. Three of the four walls were covered top to bottom in a grid of little metal doors. The fourth was a wall of black steel bars with a locking gate at the doorway. She brought her gaze back around to the wall nearest her. Each rectangular flap had a small oval-shaped print reader right in the middle.

This is how her dad had ensured she'd be the only one able to open it.

"Which one?"

"One twenty-four. Right there," Ethan pointed.

Paige glanced at him one more time before raising her hand and placing her right thumb against the reader.

There were a few beeps, it flashed green, and then with a click, the door swung open. She was just about to reach for the handle on the end of the container inside, when a voice sounded from the gated front wall.

20

"I don't know how you got in here without my knowledge, Ms. Andrews, but that's far enough. I'll take it from here."

Nick Cabot stood with two other hulking men just outside the doorway. The men had guns trained on her and Ethan through the bars. Paige recognized them instantly. They were the same ones who'd been watching her, and the assholes who'd driven her off the road.

Her gaze tracked to the guns and then up to the camera in the corner.

Cabot's eyes followed and he smirked. "Isn't it fortuitous that we're having a system-wide scan at the moment? All surveillance for this area is down."

"You think you've won, but there's no way you're getting your hands on this." She glared at the man who'd killed her parents.

"Oh, but I am. What's in there can destroy me, and I just can't have that. I thought I had taken care of any threat your father posed when all of you mysteriously died."

"By your hand," Paige shot back.

He shrugged. "I didn't learn of what he'd done here," he gestured around at the boxes, "until later. Even as manager of this establishment, I was stymied. This system is state-of-the-art and can only be accessed by the person programmed in. I thought about having Mr. Burke here taken out, but he never came for the prize that was left for him. My associates had him watched for a while, but he gave no indication that he even knew about it. For all these years, I was home free. And then suddenly, a few weeks ago, I find out that someone is digging into me. Lo and behold, I find out it's little Honor. That was a shock, believe me."

"So, you sent your goons to tail me."

"I needed to know what you knew."

"And putting me in the hospital was going to get that for you?" she demanded. "How was killing me going to get you what you wanted?"

"If you couldn't tell Mr. Burke what your father had done, the better for me."

Paige couldn't believe her ears. This jackass was insane.

"Now, enough talking. If you will step away, I'll take that." He came farther into the room, leaving his protection on the outside.

"Do you trust me?" Ethan whispered, his voice low and barely audible.

She felt his hand on her back and stepped into it, closing the distance between them.

Paige nodded but only slightly, not at all surprised to realize it was the honest truth.

His dark eyes hardened and heated. They slid to Cabot and then past him to the doorway. The heavy metal gate suddenly slammed shut. Paige jumped a little at the sound but made no other movement.

Cabot started also, spinning around at the loud clanging behind him. Before he or his men could make a move though, a wall of flames erupted between them, engulfing the whole end of the room, and blocking the henchmen out while trapping Cabot inside with them.

He quickly backed away from the heat of the fire. As he did, he dug in his pocket. When his hand emerged, he was holding his cell phone. But it tore from his grasp before he could call for help.

Cabot ripped his focus off the fire to watch his phone snap into Ethan's hand across the room. "What the hell is happening? Someone call 911, for God's sake."

Paige looked up at Ethan and he winked at her. She found herself grinning helplessly. With fire raging only a few feet away, she was actually smiling. Ethan gave her a nod towards Cabot.

Ethan's eyes softened as he spoke to her. "You have a captive audience. This is your chance. Say what you need to say."

She swallowed, suddenly overcome with emotion. He was allowing her the opportunity to close this chapter of her life by delivering the final blow. "You'll have to make it quick though—the cavalry is on their way in."

"Thank you," she said, before turning to the man cowering away from Ethan's blaze. Every time he tried to move, fingers of the inferno would follow and reach out for him. He had no choice but to remain absolutely still.

"Hey!" she shouted to draw his attention to her. She waited for him to finally look at her. "You're going down, Cabot. Not only for embezzlement, but for the murder of my parents. You took my life away from me, and now I'm taking yours. You're going to spend the rest of your pathetic life behind bars, you worthless piece of shit."

Commotion past the fire told her that reinforcements had arrived. The flames slowly disappeared and the door swung open. Standing on the other side were Ethan's brother and his partner. They'd cuffed the two men and had them off to the side sitting on the floor.

Evan glanced from Ethan to her. "You good?"

Paige threw a defiant look in Cabot's direction. "I'm better than good."

Wanting this finished, she reached up and pulled the inner

box out of the slot. Ethan held out his hands to rest it on as she opened it.

Inside lay a small black plastic rectangle. Picking it up, she showed it to Cabot as Seth snapped the cuffs around his wrists behind his back.

"See this? This is *your* death. Once this is given to the FBI, you'll be buried in the deepest, darkest pit to rot. Which is just where you deserve to be."

Paige handed it to Evan and stalked out of the room. She wasn't surprised to discover that Ethan was right behind her. When she stopped a few yards away, he stepped up next to her, his dark shining gaze boring into hers.

"I'm sorry I had to do it like that," Ethan told her. "It was the best I could come up with. I didn't want those men taking any shots at us once I locked them out. It was the only way I could hold them off *and* obstruct their view."

"It's fine. Other than being a little startled, the fire didn't seem to bother me." She was somewhat amazed by that fact. "No panic attacks in sight."

Had she overcome her paralyzing fear? Had Ethan, just by being who and what he was, healed the part of her that had been broken for so long?

Could she attribute more to him than just saving her life? Could she also credit him with saving her mind? There was something about him that soothed her, drew her, despite the terror that had gripped her when she'd first met him. Before Paige could think on that further, more people started to file in.

She was shocked when Matt Grier, followed by three others in suits, stepped into the hallway. Ethan must have felt her shock at the new arrival.

"I had Evan call him this morning." Her eyes flew back to his. "We had a feeling things might go down this way. We told him if he wanted to be in on the bust, he needed to get his ass down here."

Paige returned her gaze to Matt and saw concern etched across his face. He came to where she and Ethan stood, his face wary and uncertain.

"Are you okay? Are you hurt?"

"No, I'm fine. I'm just glad it's over."

"We'll need to talk," Matt told her. "There's a lot to sort out."

"We will," she promised.

Matt's hand softly touched her arm before he went to deal with the fugitive he'd been hunting for years. He and the rest of the agents would take custody of him and the USB drive, while the Daytona Beach PD handled his thugs.

As the police and agents busied themselves with the tasks at hand, Paige turned to Ethan. "Can we go?"

"Yeah. Let me just tell Evan." He was back in moments, and as they exited the bank and out onto the sidewalk, Ethan asked, "Are you hungry?"

Paige didn't even have to think about it. "I am, actually. I was so nervous this morning, I didn't dare eat anything, but now my stomach is demanding food."

"We'll get some lunch. I know a great place."

As part of the morning's ruse, he'd driven separately from the rest of them, so they didn't have to wait around afterwards for a ride. A few minutes later, they were pulling into the parking lot of a building that looked more log cabin than restaurant. The sign read Charlie Horse.

Walking in, Paige was met with aromas that made her mouth water. She was still taking it in as Ethan led her to a booth. A waitress came with menus, and once they ordered their drinks, she excused herself to give them some time.

"It smells amazing in here. What do you recommend?"

"Do you still like seafood?"

"Love it." Louisiana was known for their fresh-out-of-the-sea catches.

"We always used to get the crab legs and shrimp. It was a

favorite of ours."

"That sounds amazing." Paige set the menu down and breathed out a sigh.

Ethan studied her for a moment. "How are you feeling about all of this?"

Paige contemplated that briefly. She found that Cabot's arrest—and knowing he would be punished for stealing her family from her—eased her heart considerably.

"On one hand, I'm relieved. Justice will finally be served. But at the same time, his capture doesn't change the fact that my parents are still dead. Because of him, I'll never know what my mom's perfume smells like, or how it feels when my dad hugs me."

"I'm sorry, Paige. I really wish I could help you get back all that you've lost."

Little did he know, but he seemed to be the one person who could. If only she wasn't the coward he'd called her. "Me too."

Ethan sat silent for a bit. "So... Now that Cabot is going away and you know who you truly are, were you planning to return to Louisiana?"

Paige saw the carefully held-in-check hopefulness in his eyes and knew he was hanging on her answer. She hadn't really thought that far ahead yet, but she was surprised to discover she wasn't as anxious to get home as she thought she'd be.

She *should* go. There wasn't anything keeping her here anymore. She may have been raised here and grown up with the people, but without the memory of it, Daytona Beach was no different than any other random place she went.

And leaving would eliminate the other threat still after her. Noor.

Paige dropped her eyes and ran her finger around a knot in the wood of the table. "I think that's probably for the best."

She could finally get back to the only life she'd known. Doing the volunteer work she loved and hanging out with her small group of good friends. Her thoughts halted there, and she frowned. Except how many of those so-called *friends* had really been agents charged with guarding her? How many of them had kept the truth from her? How many had reported her every move to Matt?

And what exactly did she have in that life? Spending most of her time alone. Not dating. Not feeling a fraction of what she'd felt since coming to Florida. Yeah, a lot of it had been beyond bad, but she'd dealt with it. Hadn't she stood by, calmly she might add, while Ethan used his fire to protect them and hold Cabot prisoner until the authorities came? A week ago, that would have crippled her.

And what about the rest? The time she'd spent with the Burkes. They'd made her feel welcomed and included and valued. Like *family*. She could easily see herself loving every single one of them.

And then there was Ethan. He'd caused in her a range of emotions she'd never thought possible. From gut-wrenching fear to stomach-fluttering desire. A need she'd never experienced for anyone else. Not to mention, at this point, he knew her better than she knew herself.

And…he was the only catalyst she'd found that broke open that locked door in her mind where her memories were kept. Not that she'd pursued that in any way, but still. Was she really going to throw all that away because she was too afraid to take a chance?

"Paige?"

"Hmm?" She looked up, distracted.

"Are you going back? Do you have someone waiting for you at home?"

His features and body were rigid as if expecting a blow, and her insides twisted when she realized what he meant. He obviously thought she had someone she loved back in Louisiana, and it was clear the idea wrenched at him. But unbeknownst to him, even though *she* didn't remember him, her *body* evidently did. And that had been enough to deter her from any other man she'd met.

She could lie, and make her escape that much easier. But she found she wanted him to know the truth. And besides, he'd already admitted as much to her.

"No." She held his gaze. "No significant other. There never has been. I couldn't."

Heat flared in the dark depths of his eyes, and it had nothing to do with his inner fire. "Would you consider staying?"

As much as her mind was telling her to go, her heart was insisting that she stay. And she knew what Gail would tell her.

"I would consider it."

~~~

The next few days were busy for both of them. Paige and her attorney were closeted away, trying to untangle the legalities of her coming back from the dead. In the meantime, Ethan had his own problems to deal with. And all of them went by one name.

Noor.

He was still wreaking havoc all over town. Every time they turned around, a new outbreak was making the news. The police force was stretched thin trying to contain the mass hysteria. Most had no clue what was really going on—only the Burkes and those closest to them knew the truth.

Ethan and his family were doing what they could, but it was getting out of hand.

On top of that, his parents were back from their trip. They'd received some new information and had called for a meeting. He sat with Paige at his parents' home, surrounded by the rest of his family.

"The news isn't good," his mom said as soon as everyone
~~~

was settled. "From what the researcher was able to decipher, the deal Noor made with this Bringer didn't end with him completing the trials and gaining his power."

"What do you mean it didn't end?" Aria's question echoed Ethan's own thoughts.

"It means that, according to what he read, the arrangement between Noor and the Bringer was ongoing. In exchange for his powers, Noor would have to keep making acceptable payments, so to speak, in order to satisfy the Bringer's demands.

"The trials were only meant to be the beginning," Mary explained, "to prepare him for the life that he had chosen. Noor would have had to continue his murdering rampage indefinitely. Because the only thing that would appease the Bringer, the only method of payment that he would accept, were the souls of innocent people. He, or it, feeds on those souls."

Shocked gasps punctuated the silent room.

Seth cleared his throat. "But Noor's been locked away for centuries. He couldn't have been keeping up with his end of the bargain. What's going to happen when his cage door opens?"

"We don't know." Paul looked from his wife to everyone else. "I can't imagine Noor was the only one to ever make this pact, so odds are this creature has been getting fed. But for all intents and purposes, Noor is in breach of contract, and because of that, I would think his master plans to dish out some hefty payback. But how that manifests is anyone's best guess. Will it come for him once he's free? Will it demand payment? Who knows?"

Kyra posed the question, "What are our chances it'll take Noor out for us?"

Evan shot down his fiancés hopes. "Slim to none."

Kyra stuck her tongue out at him. "Spoilsport."

They spoke more of what this news could mean for them, but in the end, no one really knew. They would just have to be ready for anything when the time came. With that in mind, the four of them gathered once again to attempt to merge their elements.

But no matter what they tried, their goal still remained out of reach. Time was beginning to run short, but they had to believe that the knowledge would come when they needed it.

Ethan's thoughts were interrupted by a sound they were all growing tired of hearing—Evan and Seth's phones going off. Noor was at it again, sending throngs of innocent people into full-on panic. Spreading suffering and pain all over town just to amuse himself.

As the two detectives left, Ethan was thinking that they couldn't just kick back and continue to let this happen.

"We have to do something," he told the group. "This can't go on."

"How do we help, though?" Aria questioned. "He's choosing highly populated areas to play his games. It's not like we can wage a magical war with him in the middle of Main Street."

"What if we just drain his power?" Kyra looked around thoughtfully. "Send him back to his cell. It wouldn't be a permanent fix, but it'll put him down for a little while."

"Beatrice's letter said it only worked for a few seconds," Anna reminded Kyra. "He'd be back and more pissed off than ever as soon as he figured out what we'd done."

Kyra's face fell briefly before, apparently, another idea struck. "Could you guys come up with a spell that could…I don't know… amplify the effect? Keep him human longer?"

"I don't know of any spell," Mary said. "But there are some crystals with that ability. For it to work though, it would have to be on his person."

"I can get close enough," Kyra stated. "I'll just slip it into his pocket."

"What we see here in this world isn't tangible. It's only a projection. It may be becoming more corporeal, but it's still just an image," Anna interrupted. "If we did somehow manage to get the crystal into his pocket, we don't have any way of knowing for sure if it would make the return trip back to his body."

"His injuries do." Aria glanced at each of them. "When we hurt him here, it has to affect his body, because it takes him time to heal and come back."

Ethan felt he needed to bring up one thing. "You do realize Evan is the one we'll have to worry about when he finds out we're even talking about this." He scanned the group.

"You let me handle Evan." Kyra didn't take shit from anyone, his brother included. When she decided she was going to do something, she didn't let anyone talk her out of it. And it was evident by the glint in her eye that she'd set her mind on going forward.

"So are we doing it?" Kyra's determination was contagious, and the others finally agreed.

Once the decision was made, they had to move fast. There was no telling how long Noor would stick around to witness his handiwork. To save time, they did a glamour spell on Kyra instead of taking the long route and doing her up to look like Isabel by hand.

Within half an hour, Ethan, his sisters, Joe, and a very well-disguised Kyra were headed downtown. It wasn't hard to find out where Noor was—every news station in town was covering the incident. It just so happened that he actually *was* on Main Street this time.

Even coming in the back way, they had to park several blocks away, as the police had it cordoned off.

Before anyone could jump from the vehicle and rush off, Anna turned to Kyra. "You have to remember that you're Isabel now. She's a terrorized and abused woman. According to the journals, Noor was brutal to her."

"Yeah, I got that part firsthand." Pain flashed in Kyra's eyes, and Ethan knew she was recalling her time as Noor's prisoner.

"I can handle it. I've got this," she assured them all, and then quickly got out and started up the street.

The rest of them followed, spreading out to cover her better. She'd be on her own facing off against Noor, but everyone else would be close by.

As they neared, Ethan could see that Noor had gone all out for this one. There was blood and gore coating every building, every bench, every street lamp and planter. People running to make their escape had to wade through muck about six inches deep in the street.

The man himself stood dead center of the road. His back was to them as he laughed gleefully, reveling in the chaos he'd made. At the opposite end were the police, ushering people out and trying to calm them down.

Ethan saw the exact moment that Evan noticed them.

21

"What the fuck are you guys doing here?" he demanded. His gaze shifted and landed on Kyra. *"Oh, hell no! You get her ass out of here right now! Do you hear me?"*

Kyra suddenly appeared beside Ethan. "He's glaring at you. Is he yelling?"

"You could say that," Ethan summarized.

"You tell him I said to pipe down. This was *my* idea, and he can holler at me all he wants later, *after* I save the day."

Ethan so did not want to be in the middle of this right now. But he forwarded her message. And the blast of anger he got back from his twin nearly knocked him off his feet.

"Girl, I sure hope you know what you're doing."

Kyra grinned. "Always."

She sobered and spun to face Noor. "All right. Let's do this."

She started forward slowly, her steps halting, unsure. If Ethan didn't know better, he'd never have guessed this was the same woman who had just scoffed in the face of his brother's anger.

"Husband?" Kyra spoke softly, her voice trembling. "Husband? What's happening?"

Ethan never took his gaze off of Noor, so he saw the flash of recognition when he heard Kyra's voice. His laugher evaporated and his posture became tense. He pivoted around and came face-to-face with his wife.

"Edrick?" Kyra looked around, scared.

Noor paused and looked confused. "What game is this?" he shouted.

Kyra curled into herself as if she'd received a blow. "I apologize, husband. I meant you no disrespect by my question. I came looking for you, is all. I only want to do as you please, so I don't require punishment."

Noor took a stride towards her, studying her closely. He walked around her as she stood absolutely still, recoiling.

He leaned in. "You will take whatever punishment I decide is appropriate."

She had him. Ethan let out a breath.

Kyra bowed her head, hunched her shoulders, and cowered. "Yes, husband." She paused for a moment, and Ethan saw Kyra's arms move. She was rubbing her hands over her own swelling bump. "Would it please you to know I think this babe will be a boy also?" Her head slowly came back up. "Another son to carry your noble name."

From his concealed vantage point, Ethan couldn't see that anything was changing yet. The blood Noor had created still clung to every surface. His powers weren't waning.

He turned his head to find his sisters. *"It's not working."*

"Give her a chance," Aria returned.

Ethan resumed keeping watch over his brother's fiancé. Kyra stroked Noor's ego and played her part to perfection. When Noor grabbed her by the arm, Ethan felt the earth rumble and thought Evan was going to come unglued.

Ethan tried to soothe his twin. *"Easy, bro. We've got her covered. He won't hurt her."*

Evan sent him a savage glare. *"She shouldn't even fucking be here at all! If anything happens..."* He let the words trail off.

"She's strong, Evan. She'll handle him."

Ethan could feel his frustration. *"I'm not angry at you guys—I know how she thinks. I also know she didn't give you guys a shot at talking her out of it. Just keep her safe."*

"*We will.*"

Out of the corner of his eye, Ethan saw something flicker. Shifting his gaze, he looked for what had caught his attention.

The nastiness on the building nearest to his position was gradually receding. Ethan swung his head around to study the rest of the storefronts. It seemed Noor's reach was lessening. Those farthest away from him were going back to normal.

"*Told ya so,*" Aria's voice whispered triumphantly in his head, and he grinned.

He turned his focus back to Kyra. *Keep it up, hon.*

Inch by inch, Noor lost control of the magic. The longer Kyra played the part of Isabel, the more it drained him. She would have to get that crystal in his pocket soon, before he vanished back to his cell. If she failed and didn't get it in place, he would only return when his powers did, and take his fury out on them and everyone else.

The mess was pulling back, and more of the downtown area was revealed. Ethan and the others watched carefully, waiting for Kyra to make her move. As the crimson stains faded and withdrew, the Burkes held their breaths.

Thankfully, Noor seemed to be oblivious of her effect on him. Kyra was playing her part perfectly, keeping all focus on her. But they all knew it couldn't last forever. She only had a few more minutes.

When only the street around Noor's feet was still red with blood, Ethan watched and waited for her to slip the stone into his coat pocket. As the last of his magic fell away and Noor disappeared, Ethan thought they'd failed.

Until Kyra spun around and did some kind of happy dance, which with her pregnant belly, looked quite comical.

They all rushed her.

"You did it?" Ethan was amazed. "I didn't see a thing, and I was looking for it."

"Sleight of hand, Skippy." Kyra waggled her fingers in front of his face. "You forget I was once a juvenile delinquent."

Ethan chuckled. "Yes, I did."

"How long will it last?" Kyra asked.

"Until he finds it and destroys it," Mary supplied.

"Well, let's hope that day doesn't come any time soon." Ethan was ready for a break from the threat of Noor hanging over their heads.

And he planned on using that time to spend with Paige, getting to know each other all over again.

~~~

Noor stayed down, life went on, and before Ethan knew it, the new year was upon them.

He'd made plans to take Paige out to dinner. Then afterward, they'd head over to Anna and Joe's house where they'd ring in the new year with family and friends.

Standing in front of the bathroom mirror, Ethan adjusted his tie. The dark smoky gray exactly matched Paige's eyes. Reaching up, he tamed an errant lock before smoothing the steel blue dress shirt down across his chest. Straightening the cuffs, he gave himself a final once-over.

He cleaned up pretty well, if he did say so himself. All that was left was to put on the charcoal-colored suitcoat and he was ready.

Driving to pick up Paige, he found himself a little nervous. They'd been slowly finding their way back, and he didn't want to do anything to jeopardize that. He had to keep cautioning himself to give her time. To respect whatever speed she needed to go.

But when she opened the door to him, his good intentions took a direct hit. She was stunning.

Her long, fiery hair was loosely piled on top of her head.
~~~

It looked like it would tumble past her shoulders with the slightest touch. It was sexy as hell, and he wanted his fingers in it, dislodging whatever she'd used to hold it.

The makeup she'd applied made her eyes look even more sooty and mysterious. Her lips. Oh, Lord, her lips. Ethan had to swallow the tightness strangling him. Those full, pouty lips were the color of a deep red wine he wanted to sip from.

The dress she wore clung to her like a second skin and was a dusky pink, the thin shoulder straps giving way to a deep neckline that gave him glimpses of her rounded breasts. The material just kissed her flat stomach as it flowed down her body. It hung in a straight line down her thighs, the hem hitting her gorgeously tanned legs just above the knee. He finished his perusal at her feet which were adorned with sexy, strappy high heels that perfectly matched her dress.

As his gaze made the return trip up her body, Ethan's blood blazed a scorching trail through his veins.

Maybe this wasn't such a good idea, he thought. How was he going to get through the entire evening without making a fool of himself? His body was already drawn tight, his erection straining against his pants, fighting the need to haul her up and carry her back to the bedroom.

This was going to be a very long night.

"You look beautiful," he finally choked out.

"Thank you." She smiled up at him, and his heart was equally as affected.

He gathered what little sense he had left, took a half-step back, and pivoted. Sweeping out a hand towards his car with a wide flourish, he bowed. "Your chariot awaits, Miss."

Ethan would have preferred to take her arm in his, but it hadn't been lost on him that she didn't touch him. Ever. Other than accidental brushes, there'd been no contact between them. He didn't know if it was related to any lingering fears, or if there was another reason. Whatever it was, he'd try to keep his head and follow her lead.

Opening the car door for Paige, he waved off the guard on duty who'd been keeping watch over her, dismissing him for the night. Running around to his side of the car, Ethan climbed in and started the engine.

Dinner was incredible. They talked and laughed, and time had passed much too quickly. Before he knew it, the check had arrived. He would have loved to linger over coffee or drinks, but he didn't feel right about holding up the table for anyone else looking for a great night.

When they arrived at Anna's, cars already lined the driveway and street. It was a nice night, so Ethan didn't mind when he found a spot down the block. As he guided Paige up the walk, he could hear music and laughter pouring out of the house. It was only ten in the evening. but the party was already going strong.

They were instantly swallowed up in the merriment. Drinks and food were plentiful, and Paige seemed to be having a good time. Because some of the people there had been friends from high school, Ethan kept a careful eye on her to make sure she wasn't feeling overwhelmed by their questions. News had gotten out about what had happened, and they were curious. He just felt the need to protect her.

They'd been there about an hour when he made his way back to her, carrying a glass of wine and his own bottle of beer.

She smiled when he handed her the glass. "Thank you." Paige sipped and looked around at all the guests before returning her gaze to his. "This is fun. I'm happy I came."

"I'm glad you're enjoying it." Ethan stared down into eyes alight with joy and got lost. The need he'd been fighting for weeks took advantage of his distraction and gave him a hard kick. Right in the gut.

Without any command from his brain, his body edged in closer to hers. Mere inches separated them, and he caught the scent of her glowing skin. He breathed deep, pulling it down into the center of his being where it could never escape.

Paige didn't move. She only held his gaze, heat flaring in the silvery pools of her eyes. When her tongue slid out to moisten her lips, Ethan's focus dropped to her mouth to follow its path.

The compulsion to trace those lips with his own tongue bore down on him with savage intent. His head was descending toward hers before he knew what was happening. He had to taste her, reacquaint himself with her uniquely spicy flavor. He could remember the feel of her skin against his, and he wanted that again. So badly.

He was so close now. Her warm breath rushing from her lungs brushed across his lips and tempted him beyond control.

Ethan's free hand snaked around her waist, found the small of her back, and pulled her body flush against his. Her gasp offered him the opening he needed, and his mouth came down over hers. His tongue dipped in to sample and savor and tease.

When hers answered in kind, just as it always had, Ethan's heart soared. He sank into her softness and let himself go.

Until screaming and shouting yanked him from his own personal bliss. Mind still muddled, Ethan didn't immediately pick up on what was happening. When he finally did, he knew they were in trouble.

Four armed men poured into Anna and Joe's house, herding the twenty-or-so people there all into the living room. Ethan and his siblings had no choice but to follow their instructions; they couldn't risk innocent lives.

They would have to bide their time.

He glanced around to see where his twin and their sisters were. He felt better when each, with their mate, was accounted for.

"What's the plan here, guys?" Ethan sent to his family. *"General douchebags or Noor?"*

"My guess would be Noor. He had to have found the crystal,"

Anna replied. *"We have to get everyone out of here. They're all in danger because of us."*

"I don't think that's an option right now," Evan countered. *"He orchestrated this attack with a specific purpose in mind."* He paused. *"He's pissed off we bested him. I think our safest bet is to wait and watch to see what he'll do. He'll show his hand eventually, and then we'll shut him down. Again."*

Ethan felt Paige's hand on his arm and looked down at her. Large frightened eyes met his. "What's going on?"

He only had to say one word. "Noor."

Remembering what had happened the last time she'd encountered him, the color drained from her face.

"I won't let him hurt you." Ethan laid his hand over hers.

Anything else he would have said to her was lost as scared voices rose again. Ethan scanned the room for the source and found Noor's men pushing in on the group. Containing them to a smaller area.

When one came their way, Ethan thrust Paige behind him. "Back the fuck off." His voice, aimed at the intruder, was cold and deadly. He let some of his fire show in his stare.

The henchman didn't seem to notice, or maybe he just didn't care. Instead, to press his point, the dumbass lifted his gun to aim it straight into Ethan's face. Ethan felt Paige's grip tighten on him, but he sent their assailant a look that said *"Seriously?"* before he sent him flying across the room with only a thought.

More shouts and cries filled the space at the sudden commotion.

"Easy, Ethan," Evan warned. *"We have to be careful using our powers here."*

Evan was right. With this many of the uninformed close at hand, throwing power around would be a mistake.

Ethan turned his attention back to the man he'd tossed. He was getting to his feet and glaring over at him, but he didn't try to come near him again. Smart man.

Motion in the doorway caught Ethan's eye. He looked over to see Edrick Noor strolling in as if he owned the place. Coming to a stop in the middle of the room, he took in the scene before him and nodded as if pleased.

One of their old classmates, Tiffany, found her nerve and stepped forward. "What do you want? Why are you doing this?"

Ethan's gaze jerked to find his siblings all wearing the same astonished expressions. He glanced down to Paige to see her stare focused on Noor.

They could see him.

22

He sneered at her. "Because I can, my dear. Because I can."

Tiffany suddenly shrieked, "No, no, no! Get 'em off! Get 'em off! Oh, God! Make them stop!"

Ethan spun to see cockroaches crawling all over her. She was jumping around and swiping at herself frantically, trying to dislodge the infestation Noor had used against her. Ethan opened his mouth to demand he stop, but Anna was faster.

"Stop this! These people mean nothing to you."

"You're right." He sneered viciously. "They don't." He nodded to one of his men, who in turn shot a male guest in the leg.

Horrified cries erupted, nearly drowning out Aria's shout. "You bastard!"

She started to go to the downed man, but Noor stopped her with a look.

"Stay where you are, or I will kill every last one of these humans." Hatred blasted from his crazed eyes as he slowly reached into the pocket of his coat. Ethan went on full alert, not knowing what Noor had planned.

But when his hand emerged, he held nothing but the shards of the destroyed crystal.

"I'm sure you all recognize this." His glare shifted to Kyra. "I will enjoy making you pay for what you have done, you traitorous whore."

"Aww, Eddie." Kyra dramatically brought her clasped hands

to her chest. "That's the nicest thing you've ever said to me."

Ethan nearly choked as Kyra antagonized the psycho further.

"You will not be so flippant when I'm finished with you, wench!" Noor promised her. "You will be begging me for death."

Kyra dropped the sarcasm and met his glare with one of her own. "Bring it, motherfucker."

Such was his rage at her defiance, he actually took a step towards her. Until all the Burkes shifted towards her, closing ranks on one of their own.

Seeing the move, Noor fought to bank the burning rage. When he had it more under control, he turned his attention to the four of them.

"You thought you could hold me with this paltry magic?" He held his hand out. The remnants of glass rose off his palm to hover about eight inches in the air. Without any warning, Noor blasted the shards at them. Jagged spears of crystal shot around the room, searching out their targets.

Ethan had only a split-second to react. With his own telekinetic gift, he took control of the serrated missiles before they could hurt anyone. And just because he could, Ethan directed the crystal to reassemble itself as it floated in mid-air.

Only a beat later, it dropped whole and perfect into his hand. He slipped it into his own pocket while he held Noor's fuming stare.

"I will see you all cowed and bowing before me."

"The way you bow to *your* master?" Evan goaded.

"I have no master!" Noor shouted.

"Oh, but you do." Evan sent him a deadly smile. "And I can bet he's one pissed off bitch with you right now." He moved forward, putting himself between Noor and the group of innocents. "We know all about the Bringer. And how your payments are severely past due."

Evan cocked his head to the side and considered. "Exactly

how many have you missed since you've been locked up?" He snapped his fingers as if remembering. "Oh, that's right. *All of them.*" He strolled a few more steps. "From what we've been told, he doesn't seem like he'd be the forgiving type. Just how do you think he's going to enact his revenge?"

Ethan sent Paige a look that said to stay put before he eased forward to align himself with his brother. Out of the corner of his eye, he saw his sisters do the same. Seth, Joe, and Kyra were slowly herding the others back, putting two lines of defense between Noor, his men, and the party-goers.

Evan continued to hold Noor's attention. "But look on the bright side. At least we'll put you out of your misery before he has a chance to get his hands on you. Because I have to admit," Evan gave an exaggerated wince, "that is one performance review I would *not* be looking forward to."

Noor's neck and face turned red with fury. His fevered eyes were focused directly on Evan.

"Watch it, bro," Ethan warned. *"He looks like he's getting ready to blow."*

"Better at me than the others."

"Link up. That way if he goes, he's taking on both of us."

Ethan sent his mind to his twin. They both opened and became one. Now the earth and fire they wielded became shared, just as the conjuring and telekinesis did. Everything they were and everything they had were now joined.

They felt a shift in the air around them and knew Anna and Aria had followed suit.

"He will have his due," Noor vowed. "And I'll start with the four of you. From there, I'll take your parents, and then all who are close to you." Seth came under his scrutiny. "You could have led by my side. But like my worthless wife, you chose to consort against me—your own flesh and blood—with these abominations."

He turned his attention to Joe. "You are nothing but a weak, insignificant human, and I'll squash you like the bug you are beneath my boot."

When that deranged gaze focused on Paige, Ethan tensed.

Venom spewed and spittle flew as Noor pointed a finger at her. "Did he tell you how he begged me to give you back to him? For just one more day with his precious Honor, he willingly subjugated himself to me. He was so pathetic in his grief over you."

No one provoked him. They all remained silent and let him rant. Noor eventually lost interest in Paige and returned to Kyra. He stared at her for a long moment, letting his eyes travel up and down the length of her. "You, I'll save for last, just so I can take my time and enjoy your punishment." He sneered at her and an evil delight lit his eyes. "Do you remember the feel of my whip across your back? The way it tore at your flesh and muscle? You will carry my mark until I decide to end you. And every time I see it, it will bring me such pleasure to know I put it there."

Ethan knew how hard it was for Kyra not to blast him back. But she stayed mute, and when Noor realized she wasn't going to respond, he finished off his threats.

"And once you are all destroyed, I'll move on to everyone who carries your tainted and filthy blood. No one will stand in my way."

His voice had risen with each of his final words. On the last one, the atmosphere in the room changed. Heated wind thrashed around them as the lights flickered on and off. Noor was gathering energy and would strike out at any minute. Because no one knew the true extent of his power now that he was visible, Ethan and Evan prepared themselves for the worst.

As a prisoner of Burke magic, Noor had been bound, unable to use any of his ill-gotten rewards. But now that time was winding down and they were drawing nearer and nearer to their twenty-fifth birthdays, those abilities were returning. And they grew stronger with every passing day.

"We have to protect our friends." Aria and Anna's voices had blended into one with their link. *"This monster will not be allowed to hurt anyone else here tonight."*

"Can we shield them somehow?" Ethan and Evan asked. *"Build an energy field between him and them?"*

Each of them were well-versed at building fortifications. Anna and Aria each had mental abilities that required them to close off the outside world or risk becoming overwhelmed. Ethan and Evan too, had been trained to shield their minds, both to lessen the burdens on their sisters, as well as keep the girls out of their own heads.

Drawing upon that knowledge and training, the Burke quads—using every bit of magic in their possession—wove an invisible yet unyielding barrier and erected it directly behind them. As Noor raged in front of them, they did what they could to ensure that nothing got past them to those they loved.

Noor's men raised their guns, taking aim at any who made a move to run. Their threats worked in the Burkes' favor, however, guaranteeing that everyone stayed within the confines of their protective shield.

Noor let loose the force of his power, but the four of them took the brunt of his anger. He hit them with everything he had. Which was considerably more than the last time they'd faced off against each other last Halloween.

Back then, he'd taken their minds into a hell-realm. He'd kept them separate—alone and unable to find the others. While they'd been unaware, their physical bodies had been under attack by his men.

What he hadn't counted on was their family. They'd fought and protected them until they'd been able to defeat Noor and send him back to his pit.

This time, though, he didn't bother with mind games. He

demonstrated his abilities by using brute force.

His mistake. He wasn't the only one who'd advanced in strength.

To even up the odds, Evan and Ethan ripped the weapons from his goons' hands. They caught a glimpse of Seth, Joe, and some of the other men taking them on, now that the threat was equalized.

But Noor—he was all theirs.

The four of them matched him blow for blow. For every wound he caused, they delivered one much worse to him. The ground beneath their feet rumbled. The very air around them shook with power and energy.

They each came forward, forming an arc around him. They were a united front against that which would harm. Noor screamed his wrath when his feral mind finally realized the futility of his attack.

He was out-numbered and out-classed. He fled, leaving those who had pledged their loyalty to him to fend for themselves. He only thought of himself and his own revenge—not of those who'd sworn their allegiance. Once it became apparent that this too would result in failure, they were quick to flee as well.

They released their bond and turned to the assembled guests to see expressions that ranged from scared to awe-struck at what they had just witnessed.

It took quite a while to calm their friends, but none of them left as they all talked over what had happened. They, of course, had a lot of questions. Aria inspected the injured man's leg and saw that the bullet had only grazed his outer thigh. With a quick burst of healing power, the laceration closed completely, leaving only a scab that could have been any random scratch.

As his brother and sisters talked and distracted their friends, Ethan walked to the outskirts of the room. Muttering quietly under his breath, he cast his spell.

"The unenlightened, may they unsee
A truth for them that's not to be
Words spoken, be they undone
Only an evening full of fun
A party as was meant to be
As I will, so mote it be."

Ethan met the eyes of his siblings and gave a subtle nod as he joined the rest of the group. The cadence of steady conversation cut off as the party-goers blinked and looked around in bewilderment.

The clock on the wall chimed midnight, and their previous state of confusion was forgotten amidst cheers for the new year and a brand new start. Ethan and Paige followed along as hugs were shared among their friends, kisses were planted, and handshakes spread throughout the crowd. An excited tone of merriment filled the space, and the quads relaxed, knowing their friends were none the wiser about the evening's most recent events.

The last guest left several minutes later, and Ethan collapsed next to Paige on Anna's couch. She reclined back into his embrace, and he reveled in the easy familiarity of holding her.

"Well, that wasn't how I pictured spending the evening." Paige leaned her head back and looked up at him. There was weariness in her eyes.

"I'm sorry." He pulled her in closer to his side. She didn't seem to have the same issue with touching him, so he'd enjoy it while it lasted.

The others joined them, sitting or standing around the living room.

"That's a New Year's Eve party we won't soon forget." Aria dropped down onto the floor, and Seth settled in next to her.

Joe took the chair and tugged Anna into his lap. "Being a part of this family is always an adventure."

Evan flopped onto the other end of the couch. "Hey, we tried to warn you off."

"Is that what that was?" Joe laughed. "I could have sworn you and Ethan were trying to *scare* me off."

"Same difference." Evan shrugged and grinned.

"Yeah. Not so much, buddy," Joe quipped. "I *will* say it's a hell of a lot easier to fight things I can see. Too bad Noor's beast is gone. I would have liked to get a look at that thing."

"No, you really wouldn't have." Ethan shook his head. "I got an up-close-and-personal view of that bastard, and it was fucking *ugly*."

"I can agree with that," Kyra added as she emerged from the hall, presumably coming from the bathroom. "Even in my dreams, that thing scared the shit out of me. I, personally, am glad it's gone."

Evan got up and motioned for her to take his seat. Before she sat, Kyra smiled up at him and dropped a kiss on his mouth. "Pretty hot there, ace."

Ethan caught the steamy look that passed between his brother and his fiancé when she wiggled her nose at him. It was a not-so-inside joke between them, referring to a classic TV show about witches. Kyra had teased him about it since the day she'd found out the truth.

"I know I'm still new to all of this," Paige pulled his thoughts back, "but you all seem so calm about what just happened."

"It's not the first time," Anna told her. "And it won't be the last before the end of February. He'll make every effort he can between now and then to ensure we don't send him on a one-way trip to hell."

23

Paige had so much whirling around in her head on the drive back to her place, she took no notice when Ethan pulled into the lot and parked. The incident with Noor worried her, naturally, but nowhere near as much as what she was thinking of doing.

Was she nuts for even contemplating this? Her body was telling her no, but her mind was still hesitant.

When Ethan had grabbed her and kissed her before all hell had broken loose, she'd been lost in the intensity of his gaze. But that had quickly shifted to pleasure. Pleasure like she'd never known. His lips, that mouth, that hard body pressed to hers.

She flushed just thinking about it.

For once, she hadn't been dropped into the past when they'd touched. She'd stayed blessedly in the present, able to enjoy him in the here-and-now without the reminder of what they'd once been.

That need he'd caused in her was still fluttering through her system. A nagging ache that she knew only he could salve. She felt warm all over and her center was throbbing. For him. Only him. Always him.

"Paige?" His tone told her he'd said her name more than once.

"I'm sorry," she started. "What did you say?"

"We're here."

She looked around, surprised. "Yeah, I guess we are."

Paige grasped the handle but didn't open the door. She turned back to Ethan, sitting tall and oh-so-sexy in the shadowed interior of the car.

"Do you want to come in?" She held her breath.

In the glow from the dash, she saw his gaze drop to her mouth. Was he remembering that kiss as vividly as she was?

"More than you know." His voice was whisper-soft and gave away the urgency pushing him too. He shifted in his seat. "But I don't think that would be a good idea."

"Probably not." Her eyes stayed steady on his. "But why don't you come in anyway?" She jumped out before he could answer.

Paige thought he might hold to his guns. But by the time she'd rounded the rear of the car, he was out and locking it up. They walked in silence to her door. He waited until she had it unlocked and then opened it for her.

She couldn't take her eyes off him as he shut it behind them and turned the deadbolt. When he came around to face her, she stepped in close to him as he'd done at the party. Her breasts just grazed his chest. Her hand rose and slid up his stomach. Paige waited for flashes to come, but her mind was pleasantly filled with only the man in front of her.

Her hand looked so small compared to the expanse of his chest. And he was so much harder than she. Long and lean and over six feet tall, Ethan had the build of a runner. Muscle in all the right places, as she so clearly recalled in vivid detail from that morning when he'd stayed over the first time.

Hiding beneath his blue dress shirt were ropey muscles that bulged and rippled down both arms. A six-pack of abs, well-defined pecs, and firm, taut shoulders.

She ran her hand up and over one of those gorgeous shoulders and continued up his strong neck and around to the back. The shaggy hair brushing over her fingers sent quivers throughout her body. His skin was hot under her palm, scorching her nerve endings and igniting a raging fire within her.

He let her pull his head down. When only inches separated them, Paige saw herself reflected in his black eyes. What she saw there emboldened her. She stretched up and closed her mouth over his.

Instantly, his strong arms surrounded her.

They remained there for millennia, both of her hands tunneling through his silky hair. When his teeth took her bottom lip between them, her hands fisted tightly, holding him against her mouth.

Her breathing became ragged as the kiss changed angles and began anew. By the time Ethan finally lifted his head, they were both gasping, and Paige was burning up. Desire had taken control of her.

She needed him in a way she'd never known before.

Taking one step back, she reached up her own body and slid one spaghetti strap off her shoulder. Ethan's eyes tracked the thin piece of material as it drooped to her elbow. The other side soon followed, leaving only her aching breasts to hold the front of the dress in place.

The slightest shrug had it skimming down her body to puddle on the floor at her feet. She stood before him now in nothing but tiny nude-colored panties and high heels.

Ethan bent towards her, his teeth grazing the top of her shoulder. His lips blazed a trail upward to behind her ear and she shuddered. He knew her body, he knew what would make her weak, what would drive her crazy, and what would make her want him beyond life itself.

Long before she'd recovered from that assault, he kissed a path down the valley between her breasts. As his mouth lowered, so too did he until he was kneeling before her. His large hands came to rest on her hips as he licked and nipped his way across her torso.

He left no inch of skin neglected.

Seeing this self-assured and powerful man kneeling to her caused Paige's heart to fly. This was a man who loved her deeply and wholly. He would never put his own needs before his mate's. He would cherish the woman he'd chosen for the rest of his days.

Was it past knowledge that revealed this to Paige, or was it what she knew of the man himself? And the way, in the brief time she'd known him, he'd been nothing but respectful and patient with her.

She didn't know, and right now, it didn't matter.

"Ethan."

She heard the demand in her voice. She felt his hands tighten at her waist as he rose, picking her up to carry her further into the condo, back to the bed where she knew her world would change.

He laid her down gently and then stepped back. As she watched, he slowly removed his tie and let it fall to the floor. Hands, that had not so long ago had been on her, unbuttoned and parted the shirt he'd worn.

The glimpse of his chest was tantalizing. The sculpted planes of his abs more defined in the moon-lit room. She wanted to see more, but he was working on the cuffs, denying her the full view of him.

Finally, finally, he stripped out of it and tossed it away.

She couldn't look away as his fingers found the button and zipper of his dress pants. How could she have ever been afraid of this man? Each new inch of skin brought more heat and fire to her center. It filled her and branded her from the inside out. Marked her as his. She knew once he was buried inside her, she would ignite and go up in flames.

Placing one knee on the bed, Ethan glided his hands up her thighs to her hips. He found the narrow strips of her panties and slowly backtracked. Left in only her shoes, Ethan stretched out on his stomach, making room for himself between her legs.

His hot breath seared her most sensitive skin. Her lower body undulated, searching for more.

To hold her still, he placed his hand on her belly. He splayed his fingers wide, encompassing her entire abdomen. Paige lifted heavy lids to track down the length of her body to watch him. His black-as-pitch eyes never wavered from hers. He locked her complete attention to him as his tongue reached out to taste her.

The bedspread bunched in her grip as a long, low groan ripped from her throat. She tried to keep that connection with him, but her eyes rolled back in her head and her lids closed as her world disintegrated.

His lips closed over her, sucking her further into his mouth. Her first orgasm ripped through her before her next breath, but he didn't ease up. Ethan pushed her up that peak again, not relenting until she'd fallen for a second time. It should have been impossible to take any more, but as he kissed and licked his way up her body, the inferno blazed again.

Paige scored his back with her nails, trying to get him to hurry, to fill her, to make this burning ache go away.

"Ethan." Now, instead of a demand, she was begging.

But he wasn't having it. He tormented her further by drifting his mouth over to one nipple, biting and tugging before circling and laving the hardened nub with his tongue. Sucking gently, he pulled off of it, blowing over her sensitized flesh, his breath both hot and cold at the same time. He gave the same attention to her other breast, and she was out of her mind with need. She was drowning in a sea of sensation, her whole world narrowed to this one man. This unbelievably sensual, power-wielding witch.

He'd woven a spell around her this night that she would never recover from.

Taking her mouth with his, Ethan settled himself into the juncture of her thighs. As he melted her brain with his deep, languid kisses, he rocked his hips against hers, the length of his shaft gliding up and over her folds, hitting the over-sensitized nerves and then slipping back down. The tease of him sliding against her was agonizing, and her channel clenched, waiting—pleading—to be filled.

"Ethan, please," she gasped against his lips.

He rose onto his elbows and gazed down at her. His hair dropped forward to hang on either side of his handsome face. He was cast in shadow, but Paige could see enough to know he was holding on to the last shreds of his control.

Never taking his eyes from hers, he reached between their bodies and guided himself into her. As her lids tried to close, he stopped.

"Keep them open. I want to see you. I want to watch those beautiful eyes when you shatter."

If he'd take her, she'd do whatever he asked.

He thrust forward just enough to bury the head, and her breath flew in sharply. Ethan pulled back, flexed his hips, and pushed into her again. Not nearly deep enough, but the stretch was glorious.

"Oh, God," she moaned, but she kept her focus completely on him.

He retreated again and this time, drove all the way in.

Paige cried out at the same time he swore.

"Fuck," he ground out through gritted teeth.

It took them a moment to recover after so many long years without, but in only a few heartbeats, Ethan began to move. Slowly at first as they found their rhythm, but Paige knew she wouldn't last. He'd held her at the precipice for so long, she was a grenade with the pin already pulled.

Ethan knew exactly how and where to hit deep inside of her. When he thrust as far as he could go and ground his hips against hers, the fire engulfed her and she was lost.

Another orgasm seared through her as her eyes burned into

his. Finally giving in and burying his face into her neck, Ethan drove once, twice more, and found his own release with hers.

Paige couldn't move. Even when she started to shiver as the sweat dried on her skin, she couldn't make her limbs work to get under the covers.

Ethan took the matter out of her hands. He stood and pulled the covers back, lifting her and laying her on the soft white sheets. He crawled in beside her, and after he covered them both, she snuggled into his side and promptly fell asleep.

Where she dreamed.

She was on the beach, looking out over the water as she'd done a dozen times since coming to Daytona Beach. As she stood there, she became aware of a presence. Turning slowly to the right, she saw two people.

She knew who they were. She recognized them from pictures. They were her parents.

"Hello, Mom," she greeted.

"Hi, baby." The woman smiled with tears in her pretty blue eyes.

Paige swung her gaze up to the man. "Hi, Dad."

Smoky gray eyes stared back at her. "Hey, princess." His smile was a little sad too.

"We...ah...we got the man who hurt you," she told them.

"We know," her mother nodded. "And we're so very proud of you."

Paige felt the burn of tears, and her throat tightened at the love that washed over her. It broke her heart that there were still no memories. "I'm sorry," she choked back a sob. "I'm so sorry I don't remember you. I want to. I really do, it's just that..."

"You're scared." Her dad reached out and cupped her face. "We know."

Paige closed her eyes and pressed her cheek into his palm, soaking in this moment.

"It's a lot to go through, sweetheart." Her mom laced her hand through her husband's arm and held on to him. "You've had trauma after trauma. And most of that was our fault."

"How can you say that?" Paige stepped back away from her dad. "None of what happened was your doing."

"If I had only listened to the authorities," her dad countered, "we wouldn't have even been there that night."

"That's not true." Paige remembered what Matt had told her of the incident. "You're dead because of *me*. I fought them. I'm the reason we didn't get out in time. I wouldn't go without telling Ethan we were leaving." Tears blinded her and she cried, "It's all my fault."

"Oh, honey." Her mom took her into her loving embrace. "We don't think that at all, and you shouldn't either. You and Ethan love each other. Of course you would want to explain it all." She grasped Paige's upper arms and set her back away from her. Determined blue eyes drilled into hers. "No one blames you for anything, darling. And if anyone says differently, I'll just set their asses straight."

Paige smiled through the tears trailing down her face.

"Who we all need to blame is that bastard, Cabot." Rage filled her father's voice. "That greedy son of a bitch is the one who did this to us."

Paige wiped away the remaining moisture. "Well, he'll have a long time to think about all he's lost. I found the USB drive you hid. He's going to be locked in a cell for the rest of his life."

Her dad leaned in and kissed her forehead, stroking her hair. "I knew you'd figure it out."

Her parents glanced at each other and then at her. "We have to go, honey." Sadness rang clear in her mother's tone. "Just know that we love you, and we couldn't be more proud of you."

Paige hugged her tight. Breathed in the scent of her. "I love you, Mom."

It was her father's turn to say goodbye. He brushed her

cheek with his finger before wrapping her in his strong arms. "You're going to be okay. Trust in your heart. It'll never lead you wrong." He kissed her forehead again. "It's all out there, just waiting for you to accept it."

She nodded with a weak smile and sniffed. "I love you, Dad."

With that, they disappeared.

When she woke, the sun was shining and Ethan was asleep beside her. She watched him, thinking about her life and what to do with it now. She hadn't had any new memories in a while and began to wonder why.

Had her fear of discovering her past shut the door that had opened at Ethan's touch? From what her dad had said, it sounded like simply *wanting* it would be enough to restore her memories. Did she want Ethan? Did she want her old life back?

Paige studied his darkly handsome features and knew in her core that this was where she belonged. Was it her past connection with him? Maybe. Possibly. But who really cared? And why did it even matter? As Honor or as Paige, they fit. They worked.

Could she be content if her life as Honor never returned?

She searched deep for the answer, and then let out a sigh of relief. Yes, she could.

Paige rolled into Ethan's warmth. Sliding her hand below the covers, she cupped him gently. He, and his body, began to stir under her fingers.

Sleepy, sexy eyes opened and focused on her. "Good morning."

"Hi," she grinned. "Did I wake you?"

"Only in the best way." He leaned in to kiss her, but she pulled back.

She shook her head. "Sorry, haven't brushed my teeth yet."

"That's right," Ethan laughed. "But I have the cure for that, and we won't even have to get out of bed."

She heard him whisper a few words and suddenly, her mouth tasted fresh and clean.

Paige tipped her head back and ran her tongue over her teeth. "What did you do?"

Ethan tucked her back into his arms and nibbled at her chin. "A little spell my brother and I worked out a long time ago."

She continued to fondle him as she cocked an eyebrow. "What other kinds of spells do you have up your sleeve?"

The gleam in his eyes was wicked. "Oh, the possibilities are endless."

Paige laughed when he rolled to his back, taking her with him. She sat astride his hips and gazed down at him. His expression was adoring, and she found that she was drinking him in too. When his hands came up to rest on her upper thighs, they stared at each other for several more moments before she spoke.

"I have something I need to ask you."

He searched her face, his eyes quizzical. "Ask away."

She hesitated, not sure if she wanted to know the answer.

"If my memories never come back—if *Honor* never comes back—will I be enough for you?" She kept her face relaxed but watched him closely, waiting.

His features softened, and his voice was strained with emotion. "Baby, it doesn't matter if you don't remember me or what we had. I love the person you *are*, regardless of what name you go by or what you call yourself. You're strong, beautiful, fierce, and passionate, and I consider myself lucky to be here, in this moment, with you—*my Paige*."

He smiled softly as his fingers came up to brush over her cheek and down her jawline. "We have time. We can build a lifetime of new memories. The only thing I care about is spending the rest of my life loving you."

The remaining heaviness in her heart let go, and she sighed as the weight of Honor's burden lifted and disappeared. A smile broke over her face as joy and hope for their new future together filled her to bursting. Her eyes pooled with happy tears, and she laughed as she leaned down. "Thank you for that. I love you, too." She grinned as her lips met his.

And gasped as it all came flooding back.

She was assailed with images, flashes, movie reels, and emotions so strong, she could only squeeze her eyes shut as she watched the incoming torrent. She sat up, only vaguely aware of Ethan following her upright, calling to her.

But she couldn't answer him. She was lost in the maelstrom of memories. Being four or five and riding on her dad's shoulders. Dinner around the dining table with her parents. Shopping trips and pedicures with her mom. The first day of seventh grade, and the boy who'd stolen her heart. Her and Ethan lying together in bed when he'd stolen something else. All leading up to the very last time she'd seen him before her life had gone up in flames, and she'd woken up in a hospital with nothing.

By the time the surge of nostalgia had filtered back in and clicked into place, she was dizzy and panting. It felt like a whirlwind had been let loose inside her head.

"Paige, honey? What's happening? Are you okay?"

The urgency and worry and love in his voice tipped her over the edge. Tears fell freely down her cheeks.

"Baby, you're killing me." The large hands that framed the sides of her face trembled. "Tell me what's wrong."

She laid her hands over his and smiled through the tears. "Nothing is wrong. Everything's going to be all right now." She leaned forward and kissed him tenderly. "I love you, E."

That was something that only Honor had ever called him. It took a split second for what she'd said to register, and when it did, Ethan jerked his head back from her. His dark gaze searched her face, his expression a mix of confusion and disbelief.

"Honor?"

She laughed through a sob and nodded. Her eyes devoured

him as her hands ran through his hair before trailing down his shoulders and back up to cup his cheeks. It was like seeing him through new eyes. She laughed again as the tears continued to fall, taking in the subtle changes that time had left on his face. "Yeah, it's me. It's all back. The memories. Everything."

~~~

Ethan sat, stunned. "How? Why? Just now?"

Honor told him of the dream she'd had and how, ever since the conversation with Matt Grier, she'd felt responsible for her parents' deaths. His heart broke for her, never realizing that she'd blamed herself. But once her mom and dad had convinced her that it could have only been Cabot's fault, she'd finally been able to let go of that guilt.

His chest tightened, wishing he would have known, so he could have tried to help—could have made it easier for her somehow.

"And then afterwards, when you said you'd love me no matter what, there was nothing else left to be afraid of."

"Afraid?" His head tilted in confusion. "What do you mean? You're not saying you were still scared of me, are you?"

She was quick to shake her head. "No, that's not what I meant." She sighed and then shifted off of his lap to sit at his hip. "I have a confession to make."

Ethan tensed, not sure of what to expect. Honor looked so contrite, her eyes pleading and her hands wringing, that he knew it must be serious.

She pulled the quilt up to her chest. "I've been having flashes of memories."

His gut clenched, her words landing like a physical blow. Ethan pushed himself up to sit back against the headboard, taking the sheet with him. How could she not tell him something so important? Why wouldn't she have confided in him? Didn't
~~~

she trust him?

"You've been recalling things from before your accident? For how long?"

"It only happened a few times, but when we'd touch, I'd see a quick blip of our past together."

Ethan's jaw flexed, but he drew in a deep breath, trying to keep the hurt and anger at bay. "And that was enough to scare you? I thought you *wanted* to remember."

"I did." She looked over at him, her eyes silently begging him to understand. "But these memories weren't just images or pictures—I could actually feel the emotions that went along with them. The intensity and depth of the love you and Honor had for each other was overwhelming. I'd never felt anything like it before, and I didn't know how to handle it. Up until recently, I wasn't even sure I was capable of having those kinds of feelings for a man. They just didn't exist for me, and getting hit with it all at once was terrifying."

His insides relaxed a little as what she was saying sunk in. What he and Honor had shared *was* intense and overwhelming. The force of his love for her had knocked the air from his lungs, even when she'd still been alive. He could only imagine what that must have been like—the strength of those emotions slamming into her when she'd least expected it.

Honor closed her eyes for a moment and seemed to gather herself. He was watching her when she gazed back up at him

"But most of all, I was afraid that, as Paige, I wouldn't ever measure up to the Honor you'd loved. That when you'd look at me, you'd always compare us—and I was terrified that I'd come up lacking. That I'd lose to the memory you had of her, because I was too different. Too damaged. Too *me*."

Ethan's heart broke, and his disappointment fell away. "Hey." His voice was soft but firm as he sat forward and reached out to loosen her fists in her lap. "You were never damaged, and I don't *ever* want to hear you say that again."

Her eyes teared up again as she looked at him. "But I *was* different from the woman in those flashes. It was like looking at someone else entirely, and I didn't think I could risk putting myself out there. The old Honor was vibrant and full of life, and I've always just felt like I was wandering around, lost in my own skin."

Honor looked down at their clasped hands. "I'd wanted my memories to come back for so long. But then when they did, they were all-consuming, and I didn't know how to handle them. I couldn't say anything, because I didn't want to get your hopes up before I figured it out."

Realization dawned, and he brushed a strand of hair away from her face. "That's why you made sure we never touched."

Honor nodded. "They crushed me, Ethan, and I couldn't bear to see how the two of you had been before."

She took a deep breath and swallowed. "But then last night, when you held me and kissed me, there was nothing. No more glimpses of the past. They'd stopped. I thought that, maybe by pushing them away, I'd locked that door again. And I was relieved. I could forget about them and live my life as just me— Paige."

Ethan wrapped his arms around her, trying to absorb everything she'd told him. His heart ached to know she'd been suffering like this. He'd always just assumed that the troubled looks he'd seen on her face had stemmed from her lack of memories. Not *actual* memories that taunted her with who she might never be. Or that she might never be enough for him.

Her very carefully-kept distance. The wall she'd tried to erect between them that day in the kitchen.

And a new wave of shame crashed over him at how he'd treated her. That had been just after the fire. Just after she'd been buried into his back for only God knows how long. *Touching him.* So many things clicked into place, and now he finally understood.

He spoke softly into her hair as he stroked his hand slowly up and down her back. "I'm so sorry for what you've been going through. And for the times I've made it harder on you. I wish you would have told me about the memories, just so you wouldn't have to shoulder them alone. But I get why you didn't. I know firsthand how deep our love was, and still is. And it *is* intense, you're right about that. I can see how that would scare or intimidate you if you were dropped into the middle of it unprepared."

He pulled back and put a finger to her chin to tilt her face up to his. "But all of that is behind us now." He brushed his thumb over her full bottom lip as he gazed adoringly into soft, smoky eyes. "Your memories are back, and you're whole again. *We're* whole again. I love *all* of you, and that's never going to change."

He pulled her back into his lap and wound his arms around her, hugging her tightly to him, so thankful to have this amazing woman back in his life. Paige, Honor—it didn't matter. She was the girl he'd always loved.

Honor melted into his embrace, whispering at his ear, "I love you so much, Ethan Burke."

He pulled back to look into her beautiful face. He took in her wild, fiery locks that were always so silky. And the storm of love that had always raged and thundered in his chest once again broke free, consuming and engulfing him. He lowered his lips to hers softly, gently, the warmth building as the kiss deepened.

Their souls entwined as lost lovers finally, blessedly, reunited.

24

January flew by in a blur. Ethan's life had finally gotten back on stable ground again. He was happy and in love, and he and Honor spent as much time together as they could, trying to make up for all the years they'd lost. As February rolled through however, the mood shifted.

He and his siblings worked every possible minute, trying to bring their magic together. But as again and again they failed, an air of desperation fell over the group. The prophecy clearly stated that four into one would defeat the devil unearthed.

So how the hell did they do that? They just couldn't solve the riddle.

It was February twenty-fifth. They had three days left to find the answer that had so far eluded them.

They were all gathered at the family home to go over everything once more. They spent hours re-reading every journal in their possession, looking for anything that might give them a clue.

But found none.

Moving on to the prophecy, they took it apart and pieced it back together in countless ways to see if any new meaning could be given to the cryptic lines.

It stubbornly held on to its secrets.

As they sat and tried to figure out what to attempt next, Aria cleared her throat before glancing at each of them in turn.

"There's something else we need to address. The part of the prophecy we've all kept glossing over."

Anna blew out a breath, deflated. "The personal sacrifice."

"Yeah. I don't know about the rest of you, but that line has scared me from the very beginning," Aria admitted.

"You're not the only one," Evan agreed. "We can all agree that Noor is strong. But how much will we have to give up to beat him?" His dark eyes were filled with disquiet when he gazed down at Kyra and the baby they'd made through their love. "Personally, I don't even want to think about that."

"None of us do." Ethan looked at Honor and thought of all he had to lose now too. "But we have to. There are only two parts to defeating that bastard. Four into one, and the sacrifice. We'll have to accept whatever the terms are to stop him once that door opens."

"What if it's *us* it wants?" Aria held Seth's hand in hers. "Would this prophecy demand our lives to stop Noor once and for all?"

"I pray to whatever higher power is out there that Fate wouldn't be so cruel." Ethan sighed in resignation. "But no matter what it is, we have to be prepared to accept it. This sacrifice isn't going to be easy. But it's one that *has* to be made."

Everyone took a moment to reflect on what they'd be willing to forfeit to fulfill the prophecy. It was a daunting task, but they couldn't afford to take it lightly.

Joe broke the silence. "Speaking of the battle... Does anyone know where or when it's supposed to go down? Is a bell going to go off at midnight signaling the final round? Is it when the girls were born, or the guys? Or is it just some arbitrary time The-Powers-That-Be have chosen and kept to themselves?"

"Those are all good questions." Evan pondered it for a minute. "It would make more sense that it would be when Ethan and I were born. 'Four witches born—two light, two dark.' All four of us were here by that point, so I'd say just after sunset on the twenty-eighth. Where though, I have no clue."

"Hopefully, we'll figure that out beforehand," Anna offered. "As well as everything else we need to know."

Through the rest of the afternoon, they refined strategies and discussed the multitude of ways this could go. In the end, all they could do was hope that when the time came, they would know exactly what to do.

Ethan and Honor left and headed for his place. Since her memories had returned, there was no longer any question about whether she'd stay in Daytona Beach. She was home for good and had moved into his apartment. They were making do in the small space until they could look into getting something a little bigger.

The next two days passed quietly. Everyone was subdued and reflective, sticking close to their homes and loved ones, and reveling in these last moments. Ethan and the others kept in close contact in case something happened. But nothing did.

Even Noor was bedded down, which didn't bode well. That could only mean he was storing up his own power in preparation.

As the hours wore on and night descended on their last unspoiled day, Ethan held Honor close. They lay in bed that night, trying not to think about what tomorrow would bring. When he kissed her, it wasn't rushed or hurried. They made love softly, gently. Ethan moved in and out of her in long, slow strokes, savoring every sensation, every emotion. Mere words could not convey what he felt for this incredible woman, so he showed her how much he loved her in every way he could.

She seemed to understand his need to cherish her, returning his tenderness and veneration. Languid, undemanding, they shared everything they were and expressed beyond words what they meant to each other.

At some point as they lay after, Ethan dozed off. And found himself on a stretch of beach with Evan, Aria, and Anna.

"Noor?" Evan scanned the area in all directions, looking for any sign of trouble.

"I don't think so." Aria watched something in the distance.

They all turned and saw an elderly, bent woman walking towards them. She was dressed in old-world clothing and carried a cane to assist her movements. Her silvery-gray hair was set in an intricate braid that wrapped around her head.

She smiled fondly when she drew near. "My children." Her voice was strong and sure, even though her body was withered and frail. "The time has come."

"Who are you?" Anna asked.

"I am Iris Burke. I was one of the thirteen who first imprisoned the evil."

Ethan's voice was reverent. "You were there?"

"I was, along with the strongest of our line. We fought to end him, but it was not for us to do. That duty falls to the four of you, the children of my children down through time."

"Is there anything you can tell us that will help us?" Aria questioned of her.

"Only that you have what you will need to see this through. What is going to be asked of you will be difficult. You will have to decide if it is a price you can afford to pay. When the time comes for you to make your choice, know that the entire coven is standing behind you. Even if, for whatever reason, you feel the cost is too great, know that we understand and thank you for bearing this burden that was placed on you so many years ago."

Iris's words left them speechless. And afraid.

She went on before they'd fully recovered. "As the hour of your births draws near, gather in a safe place and be ready, for this war you'll wage won't take place in your time. The final battle will be fought in the realm where his prison lies. At the very moment the last of you entered this world, your consciousness will be taken to another."

Iris gazed at each of them in turn. "I love you, my children.

Stay true to yourselves, and Blessed Be."

She faded away, leaving the four of them in stunned silence.

Evan spoke first. "Well, we got some of the answers we were wondering about."

"And even more questions about the sacrifice we'll be asked to make." Fear loomed large in Anna's icy blue eyes as Ethan was sure it did in all of them.

Ethan felt the pull back to his own body. "Looks like our time here is done."

He opened his eyes to see Honor watching him. There was worry on her face, and he pulled her close. "Come here."

She turned to him in the soft dawn light of February twenty-eighth, and they made love again. Savoring what could possibly be their last time together.

Honor's head was pillowed on his chest as he ran his hand over her silky hair.

"I love you, Ethan Burke," she whispered.

He wrapped his arms tightly around her. "I love you too, Honor Andrews." Those were words that, not too long ago, Ethan hadn't thought he'd ever say again. Now that he could, he had so much more to lose.

They showered and dressed and headed to his parents' house. They had already decided to gather there today to wait, and Iris's words only reinforced that need.

His mom had a table full of breakfast food ready when they all arrived. And as they ate, their time in the dream world and Iris's words were shared with everyone. For once, Jacob wasn't pleading to play the video games he loved. He was quiet and thoughtful, his manner reflective of the somber and weighted mood lingering over them all. Burkes the world over understood the significance and meaning of this day.

The day the clock ran out.

The phone rang steadily throughout the morning and afternoon, relatives both near and far calling to offer their words of support and encouragement. Mary answered the calls, passing along the messages of love and gratitude to her children, who would soon meet their destinies.

The hours wore on and the time of their births drew closer. When the sun started its descent into the horizon, Ethan glanced at the clock—six fifty-nine. He'd been born at seven eighteen, six minutes after Evan.

He gazed down at the woman in his arms. "I love you."

Honor smiled softly up at him, her fingers brushing his face. "I love you too. I'll be waiting when you get back."

As soon as the clock clicked to seven o'clock, Ethan knew it was time. He glanced at each of his quad-mates and got acknowledgements that they felt it too.

"It's time," Evan said to the room in general.

They moved as a group to where they would be safest and where their powers were most centered. Jacob had once dubbed it the magic room, and the name had stuck, given how fitting it was. The familiar scent of drying herbs and old books greeted them as they filed into the space. Chairs had been set up for their comfort, and the others would stand guard for however long it took. Noor still had an army out there, and they could have been ordered to strike when the quads were set to be their most vulnerable.

As Ethan picked his chair and took his seat, he grabbed hold of Honor's hands and kissed them tenderly. Looking up into her face, he winked. "We've got this."

She gave him a saucy grin. "I know you do. Now go torch his ass."

Next to him, Evan sat down and hugged Kyra to him, his face buried in her belly. He kissed it before saying softly, "Daddy will be right back." He looked up into his fiancé's eyes, and she bent to plant a kiss on his mouth.

With a smirk, she held his chin. "Bury that asshole, ace."

"Count on it." Evan looked around to the rest of his quad-mates. "All right. Let's do this."

Anna nodded before looking to both Joe and Jacob, one of their hands clasped in each of her own. She bent to Jacob and hugged him tightly, whispering against his ear. "I love you so much. You listen to your dad and Nana and Papa and do anything they tell you, okay? I'll be back before you know it." She kissed him on the cheek before turning to Joe, who pulled her in for a crushing hug.

"You can do this. Remember your training and watch your back. He's never fought fairly, and now's the time to fight dirty. Beat him to it." His face softening and pep talk over, he leaned in for a heated kiss before taking Jacob's hand and backing away to let her take her seat.

Aria and Seth were locked in a tight embrace, murmured *I love you's* passing back and forth. Seth kissed her on the forehead and then met her gaze. "Blow that bastard straight to hell, pixie." Dropping a quick kiss on her lips, he squeezed her hand before turning to join the rest of the family.

Then it was their parents' turns. There were tears in their mom's eyes as she went down the line and kissed each of them, her hands cupping their faces as she looked lovingly on her sons and daughters. Backing away, she addressed them all.

"Twenty-five years ago, the four of you were born into this prophecy, and you've lived every day since in preparation for this moment. You each have a special gift, so given for the sole purpose of putting this beast down once and for all. No matter what is required of you, know that your father and I couldn't be more proud of the amazing adults you've grown to become."

Sniffing softly as the tears spilled over, she took a step back, met the eyes of each of her children, and spread her arms out in a wide arc.

*"A mother's love, a witch's grace
Hear me now in this time and space*

I cast this spell for the war ahead
That those I love know not harm, nor dread
Send protection from our family line
To end this evil one last time
Eternal love to them from me
As I will, so mote it be."

A soft light glowed around them and then extinguished, and Mary went to join the rest of the family as their father stepped forward.

"I don't think there's a dry eye in here, but then again, your mother always has been the best at saying exactly what needs to be said. And she's right. I admire so much the strength and fortitude each of you has shown in facing this challenge head-on. And although I don't possess any magical abilities of my own, it doesn't take a witch to see how far you've all come. Whether you feel it or not, you are ready for this, and when the time comes, you will know what to do. I love you all very much. Kick his ass and then hurry home, because I can't wait to celebrate this victory with all of you."

Paul went to each of his children, doling out hugs and kisses, before returning to the rest of the family and wrapping Mary up in a supportive embrace.

Ethan glanced among his siblings and checked his phone. "T-minus three minutes."

He took a deep breath and relaxed into his chair, keeping his gaze on Honor until he felt his consciousness slipping away.

And just like the dream they'd shared before, he and his siblings all appeared together in the dark and shadowed world Noor had been trapped in for centuries.

25

Barren and desolate, nothing thrived here. The air was filled with dense, dank fog, the ground beneath their feet hard and unyielding.

The only thing visible was directly in front of them. It was an enormous box-like structure with etchings covering the entire surface. Ethan guessed they must be the spells that had held Noor prisoner for these many years. As they stood there absorbing this strange reality, the carvings flared and blazed.

"Is everyone seeing this?" Ethan didn't take his eyes from the glowing runes, his gaze traveling the expanse of the designs to reveal the exact size and shape of Noor's prison.

"Oh, yeah." Evan too watched carefully.

The markings continued to shine brighter, and when they became so intense it hurt their eyes, grinding sounds emitted from somewhere inside the giant cube.

"Here we go," Aria muttered.

Just then, the corner where two walls came together cracked open. A deep crimson glare shot outward from the split. As the gap grew wider, Ethan could begin to see a silhouette.

"Heads up, guys. I can see him."

Ethan instantly began to feel a little unsettled. He assumed it was just a natural reaction to seeing his nemesis for the first time in the flesh. But as the edgy feelings grew, morphing from a subtle disquiet to an insistent urge, he felt a tug on his element. Like it was restless inside of him. Like it knew what was happening. And wanted out.

He wondered if the others were feeling the same thing. *"Are your elements acting weird all of a sudden?"*

Nods and murmurs of agreement echoed in his mind, and he tamped down on his magic, amassing it close to be ready to strike. He could sense his siblings doing the same.

When the opening was wide enough, Edrick Noor strolled out.

Immediately, the air around them crackled and snapped with energy. Thunder and lightning pounded overhead, and the wind whipped and lashed out at them, as though picking a fight on Noor's behalf.

"Well, well, well. Look who came to welcome me back." Noor stood tall and sure of himself, his visage one of pure arrogance and conceit. "It's a pity only I will make it out of here alive."

"Don't count on it," Evan taunted. "The only place *you'll* be going is Hell."

Ethan felt Evan's mind in his and opened to link with him. Beside them, they felt their sisters unite as well. They waited, but no divine enlightenment came as to how to combine their earth and fire with Aria and Anna's air and water. They were still missing that last, crucial piece to the puzzle, and here they were at ground zero.

Without that final merge, they had no hope of finishing Noor and protecting those of their line. Or anyone else, for that matter.

Noor must have noticed their powers gathering and threw his hands to the sky. The lightning that had been flashing across the expanse of black above only moments before suddenly bolted down to his waiting palms, infusing him with its energy as his body took on a maniacal, eerie glow.

In response to the imposing display, Evan and Ethan struggled to hold on to their combined elements, their magic warring against them and demanding to be set free.

"Why is it fighting us?"

As one, they bore down and held it with a tighter grip. They'd been taught never to make demands of their gifts—to always have respect for that which had been given to them. But here and now, Evan and Ethan had to command with all their might to bend it to their will.

Their sisters' unified voices reverberated in their minds. *"Um, guys? Our magic is resisting."*

"Ours too," Evan and Ethan sent back.

"Is it this plane that's affecting our power?"

"We're not sure. But we'll have to be careful and make sure we keep control of it."

After that, there was no time for talking. Noor bellowed and let loose his centuries of anger, vengeance, and frustration upon them.

His first wild strike nearly took them all to their knees, it had so much pent-up rage behind it. But Ethan and his quadmates battled back, hitting Noor with all of their combined elements. Anna and Aria's water and air whipped and tore at him. The funnel of wind and water they brought forth rivaled any hurricane Mother Nature had ever made.

The breath was ripped from Noor's lungs, and the rush of water flooding the ground beneath his feet made it so he couldn't catch his footing. Their Burke gifts aided their attack, their shared empathy and clairvoyance allowing them to know both what was effective, as well as what he'd try next.

While the girls kept him busy, Evan and Ethan added every bit of earth and fire power they possessed to try and end him quickly. They conjured great chunks of rock, but when they went to set them aflame, the power that had always answered readily now faltered and fought their hold.

Ethan and Evan bore down on the element and got it back under control.

They hovered the enormous fireballs above them briefly before they drew back their magic and hurled the massive spheres. Left, right, left, right, they bombarded Noor as they advanced on him.

And it was working. He couldn't withstand the force of the four of them working together. They were backing him down. He was withdrawing. Running.

Maybe that was all the prophecy had intended—that the combined powers of the four of them at once could finally defeat him for good. Their spirits lifted, lending them strength, and they pushed forward, dealing blow after magical blow.

They banded together, following Noor's retreat, and continued to hammer at him from all sides. Their gifts, both elemental and Burke, overwhelmed him and beat him down.

Intent on their final goal, none of them saw the bolt of lightning until it was too late. It struck the girls and blew them completely off their feet, hitting them with such force, it threw them twenty feet backward before they landed and skidded over the brutal, unforgiving ground. So hard was their impact, it robbed them of their breath and weakened their mental link.

"Ari! Anna!" the guys yelled.

"We're all right." There was strain in their voices and blood dripping from their noses, their clothes ripped and torn where red stains seeped through the shredded fabric. They weren't as all right as they tried to let on.

Aria and Anna got back to their feet. *"Our powers. They pulled away. They wavered for only a second, but it was enough that Noor must have sensed the moment of vulnerability."*

They were able to get their magic in check quickly, but the damage had been done, and Noor crowed with delight as he rose to his full height and returned fire on them with renewed determination. Anna and Aria tried to regain the upper hand, but the hit they'd taken had weakened them considerably.

In addition to the injuries they'd sustained, the fight to

maintain control of their own abilities was also taking its toll. The internal struggle was using up precious energy. Energy they needed to wage this battle. But the longer it went on, the more their powers pulled harder for release.

And just that quickly, the scales tipped in Noor's favor. No matter how hard they fought now, they couldn't seem to gain back their advantage. Noor pounded them mercilessly, taking great pleasure in each and every blow he landed.

They were all suffering, both body and mind. Morale plummeted as loss was looking more and more like a real possibility in this battle. It seemed they would fail and Noor would go free.

NO! They could not allow that to happen. This is what they'd been born to do.

Ethan and his twin redoubled their efforts to strike their enemy down. Together they fought—conjuring knives, spears, fireballs, boulders, anything they could think of in the hopes that it would be enough.

But everything they threw at him, he turned back on them ten-fold. They felt the pain as one of their own spears came hurtling back towards them, glancing off a thigh and taking skin and tissue with it. Not knowing which of them had been hit through their shared link, they pushed on, neither willing to admit that the battle was nearing its end.

They were weakening. The girls had never fully recovered from the lightning, and now Evan and Ethan too were losing ground.

How could this happen? Had they not prepared all their lives for this very moment? It had taken everything they had and everything they were, and still it wasn't enough. Countless people were depending on them to set this right, and they were about to let them all down.

Why hadn't that final step ever been revealed to them? Had they not proven themselves? What else could they do to ensure they fulfilled the prophecy? Had Aria been right about the sacrifice? Were the four of them going to pay the ultimate price with their lives?

Ethan and Evan looked up to see Noor gathering more power from the skies. They glanced toward their sisters and met their gaze, the same questions echoing in their eyes. As though sensing that this may be the last thing they ever did, the four of them formed a line, clasping hands.

The Burkes united. One final time.

If the cost was their lives, then they'd pay it. Together.

As Noor once again lit with an unholy glow, the quads braced for the impact.

Time stilled. All motion stopped. The thunder and lightning that had boomed and slashed across the sky only seconds before went quiet. The gusting, howling wind that ripped at their clothes and hair ceased, and a deafening silence reigned.

It was almost as if someone had hit the pause button. Even Noor was held frozen.

Not trusting their luck, they watched for a new threat. When none was found, they looked to each other.

"What's going on?" the girls asked through telepathy. *"Who did this?"*

"We don't know." Evan and Ethan spun in a circle, looking for whatever was coming. *"But stay alert."*

Suddenly a familiar voice whispered to them out of the gloom. "You have fought admirably. But it's time to let go."

"Let go?" Evan and Ethan demanded. "Let go of what?"

"Then we *do* have to die here?" Anna and Aria asked, their combined voices a tone of outrage.

"That choice is yours. Fulfill your destiny and release that which you possess, so it may do as was foretold. Or refuse and perish."

Evan and Ethan felt the restlessness of their magic again. Stronger this time. They were shocked when realization struck.

"Are you saying that giving up our powers is the only way to defeat Noor?"

"The choice must be made. All or none," the omnipotent voice stated unequivocally.

"Give them up?" Aria and Anna gasped.

"The sacrifice must be willingly made for the prophecy to be fulfilled."

Their moment of truth had come. *This* was the choice they'd have to make. Not that they would pay with their lives. But that they would go on living without the very essence of who they were.

"Can we at least have a moment?" Ethan and Evan requested.

"You shall have it. But no longer, as the time for decisions is now."

To better discuss the shocking turn of events, Ethan and Evan released the link between them, just as their sisters returned to themselves.

No one said anything for a few heartbeats, and then Anna asked, "Why would they do that to us? We're Burkes. We're witches. It's who we *are*."

"Iris warned us that the sacrifice we'd have to make wouldn't be easy," Aria reminded them.

"But to give up our powers?" There were tears in Anna's eyes. "To not *be* who we are anymore? What about my students? Without my empathic gifts, I won't be able to help them."

Ethan tried to think of what it would be like not to have his fire. Not to have his telekinesis. An innate part of him would be gone. Could he live like that? Could he go through the rest of his life with a huge part of himself missing?

Ethan turned to his brother, who'd been quiet. "Evan. What are your thoughts?"

His brother's worried gaze met his. "A few months ago, I wouldn't have batted an eye. I would have said yes before the question had even been uttered. We've been jerked around all our lives because of who we are. Having abilities was never anything I was interested in. That's why I refused to allow any part of my witch side into my work. I wanted something for myself, separate and apart from all of that. I wanted to be normal."

"We all did." Aria reached out and laid her hand on his. "I ran for six years because I wanted normal. But in the end, we all had to accept what we are—what we had to do."

"I know that," Evan agreed. "And I have...with Kyra's help. She's made me see the good in it. She's taken something I've tried to ignore most of my life and made it silly and fun." Evan gave an embarrassed laugh. "Shit, she's even made it sexy as hell." He sobered again. "Without her, I wouldn't have had a problem giving them up. Now, I don't know."

"Being witches—having magic—has shaped every aspect of our lives, whether we wanted it to or not." Anna gazed at each of them. "All of us have found our soulmates in large part because of that. How can they ask us to give that up? How will I teach my son? And what about our future children? Will they have power? Or will our decision here affect generations to come?"

"Weren't we all willing to give up our lives just a few minutes ago?" Ethan countered.

"Yes." Aria wiped at the moisture on her cheeks. "But that was before we knew that our lives weren't the sacrifice they meant. We were losing the battle and were left with no other alternative."

"So you'd all rather be dead *with* your powers, than alive without them?" Ethan studied their faces.

"No! We're not saying that," Anna cried. "It's just—"

"What about the thousands or even millions of people out there who will die if we don't do this? Us included, because if Noor is allowed into our world, he won't stop until every last one of the Burkes is dead." Ethan rubbed his forehead. "Aren't we being selfish by even discussing this? Considering our own happiness instead of the welfare of many?"

Evan rounded on him. "And you can give up *your* powers that easily?"

He'd made the wrong decision so many times in the past. In his heart, Ethan knew this was the right one. He wanted to be the type of man Honor could be proud of. He never wanted her to look at him and not see an honorable man. By doing this, by sacrificing himself for the good of so many others, he'd always know he'd done all he could to make their world a better place.

Ethan didn't hesitate. "Yes, I can, if it means the world is safe and I can live out the rest of my days, happy and healthy, with the woman I love." He held each of their gazes. "I've made a lot of mistakes. But this isn't one of them. This is a choice I'll be proud to have made."

Before the others could respond, the voice was back. "The time has come. What is your decision?"

Four sets of eyes met and held. They stayed on Ethan's longest. Then, taking a breath, Ethan turned his face to the sky and raised his voice. "We have. We'll give up our powers to put an end to Edrick Noor."

"Do all of you concur?"

"Yes," Aria said.

Anna's eyes swam with tears. "Yes."

It was Evan's turn. "Yes."

26

The words had no sooner left his mouth than Ethan felt his gifts stir. His first instinct was to grab hold of them, but he made himself let go. His chest burned for a moment, and then he watched as his birthmark lifted from his skin to hover high in the night sky, the red of his fire burning bright.

It was joined by Evan's brown, Aria's green, and Anna's blue. Along with their elemental powers, their Burke gifts each shone like a twinkling star as they swirled and wove around the colors. They spun and danced as one after another, they melded and blended together.

As this new power grew, so too did the energy surrounding them until the hair on Ethan's neck and arms stood on end. Looking around, he saw that each of his siblings were feeling just as apprehensive.

When all but his fire had been assimilated, Ethan wondered what would happen next. He braced himself as it slowly flowed into the mass above their heads.

A resounding crash echoed across the land, and it was done. All their magic was now merged into one massive, undulating force.

That seemed to be all that time was waiting for. Once the feat was completed, the world resumed at normal speed.

Noor, mid-attack, noticed the roiling, churning, flashing object hovering over him, and stared upward in shock.

"What have you done?" His gaze jerked from them to the rolling orb that continued to build and grow as it shown in the inky black of night. "What is that?"

"That," Ethan grinned at him, "is what the end of your reign of terror looks like. 'Four into one to defeat the devil unearthed.' Isn't that what the prophecy says?" Ethan looked up at the beauty that was their magic. He lost himself in the magnificence of it before bringing his gaze back to Noor. He shook his head and laughed. "You are so fucked."

Ethan gave a good show of it, but none of them really knew exactly what would happen now. They didn't have any control over what they'd made, and they were sitting ducks with no other ways to defend themselves. They'd voluntarily given up that privilege, leaving The-Powers-That-Be to do with it as they wished.

Just then, a potent surge swept outward from the churning core. The wave of it washed over them. Where he and his siblings felt nothing but a warm caress, Noor screamed as it rolled over him.

"I won't let you do this! I will have my revenge!" Noor bellowed, before striking back with all the magic in his possession. He raged, roaring like someone crazed while he battled to keep it at bay. But no matter how hard he fought, nothing could quell the strength of their combined Burke magic.

Desperate, Noor screamed to the heavens. "Master! Aid me in defeating my enemies, and I will provide whatever lives you need! I know I have been negligent in my duties, but it was at the hands of these witches that I have failed you. Aid me now, and I shall be your most faithful servant!"

Ethan and his siblings knew exactly who Noor was beseeching. The Bringer. Would he help his charge, or allow him to meet his doom? Suddenly, the mass of their conjoined magic shot out on one side like an arm, dealing an immense blow and knocking Noor to his knees.

A black, shadowy form like a cape billowing in the wind came into being opposite them. The four Burkes looked at one another in alarm, because they knew what this meant. He had answered Noor's call. The Bringer was here.

Noor saw their expressions and, with a smirk, shifted around to face his master. "I knew you would not abandon me." Noor bowed his head briefly. "I can kill them. I only require more power."

The Bringer said nothing, nor did he move for several heavy beats of Ethan's heart. Would he help Noor to end them all? They were defenseless—there would be no way of fighting back.

As The Bringer raised his arm, Ethan's breath stopped in his lungs. He knew his brother and sisters were equally anxious, fearful of what might happen next.

Noor turned to face them again, taking his master's action as agreement. "You will know true pain now. And when I am released from this hell, your families will know it too."

He closed his eyes and puffed himself up, waiting for even more power to fill him. And in his moment of inattention and arrogance, he missed it as The Bringer simply bowed his head and drifted backwards away from him.

Expecting to be bestowed with a new gift from his master, his eyes popped open wide with shock and dread when what he got instead was another attack from the combined magics of the Burkes.

It spit out a violent stream of water that overtook him and swallowed him up, cutting off his shouts and leaving only silence as they watched him wrestle and flail from within. He tumbled and thrashed through the churning waves that appeared to lance into him from every direction.

The huge bubble burst, spilling Noor back out onto the parched ground, just in time to see a whirling cyclone funnel out from the surging ball of power. It swirled around him, lifting him and tearing at his clothes and body, each swirl of wind sucking and pulling at him, rendering him weaker as the onslaught continued to drain him. When the cyclone abruptly disappeared, Noor fell from the air to land hard on his knees.

The Bringer only watched.

Realizing that each of their powers were taking a turn at him, the quads looked on as Evan's gift speared into the ground around Noor. The solid rock beneath their feet rumbled and began to shift and crack. Noor, at the epicenter of the quake, tried to flee from what was coming for him.

But before he could gain his footing, a spire shot straight up from below him, impaling him and driving him ten feet into the air. Run through from bottom to top and exiting out behind his neck, Noor screamed in agony as he dangled from the barbed tip, an oily black sludge gushing from the entry and exit points.

When the jagged stalk began its downward descent back to the ground, it squelched obscenely as it withdrew from Noor's body to disappear back into the bedrock, leaving him a quivering heap at their feet.

Ethan knew what was coming next. Fire erupted around a broken and battered Noor in a furious, blazing circle. And within that sphere, just as it had in Ethan's birthmark, flames leapt and raged. It obscured their view of Noor, but they heard his final shriek until only the sound of sizzling pops and cracks remained.

When the pyre finally died down, there was nothing left in the center but a pile of ash that blew away in the fretful wind.

Ethan tore his gaze from the scorched ground to focus on the threat still looming a few feet away from them. But instead of attacking them, The Bringer slowly inclined his hooded head towards them and disappeared.

Stunned silence fell for several minutes until Evan spoke. "Do you think that means he's happy with how that turned out?"

"That would be my guess," Aria said. "Otherwise, I think

we'd all be dead."

They were still in shock when the storm of their power drew closer, bobbing and undulating gently in front of them. It hovered there for a moment, almost as though saying goodbye.

It lit up from the inside and glowed infinitely brighter before shooting high up into the air to then blast outward in a shower of glittering sparks.

Their magic, returning to the universe.

Ethan and his siblings stood in the eerie quiet and resulting darkness.

In the next moment, they were opening their eyes to find their loved ones watching protectively over them.

A flurry of questions erupted, but their mom shushed them all. She went to each of her children and hugged them tight and kissed their cheeks.

Ethan felt the tremors that still rocked her as her arms wrapped around him. To assure her he was okay, he squeezed her a little tighter.

Regaining their senses, the quads rose and went to their respective partners.

Ethan scooped Honor into his arms and held her close, whispering in her ear, "It's over."

Kyra was the first to speak aloud. "Well? Is he toast?"

With Honor still held tight to his side, Ethan announced to the group. "He's gone. Forever."

Evan turned and kissed his fiancé, glancing down to Kyra's baby bump. Running his hand over it, he said, "Our daughter will never have to hide again. She'll thrive and learn and live out her life, free of any dark threats."

Anna had her little family wrapped up in her arms. "Just as Jacob will." She kissed him on the head before looking down at her son. "You're the first of the next generation of Burkes, Jake. It'll be up to you to show the rest of them the ropes."

Jacob grinned and nodded eagerly.

Seth turned to Aria. "That normal life you've always wanted is yours. Now we can finally get on with our lives and start making a family of our own."

Aria laughed and leaned into him, her face coloring to a delicate shade of pink.

Ethan looked down at Honor. "And we can get back to the lives we were always meant to have."

His eyes swept the assembled group. "For the first time in our lives, we are free."

A hum of excited chatter broke out around them, and Paul whooped heartily as he ushered his family out of the magic room and back towards the family meeting space.

Back in the living room, the quads recounted everything that had happened during the final showdown, and as they approached the part where Iris had once again intervened, they grew quiet and somber. A glance traveled between the siblings, and when they all came to rest on Ethan, he nodded and told the rest.

A stunned stillness engulfed the room as the weight of what they had done—what they had just sacrificed—settled over the family. When Ethan looked at their mom, she had tears spilling in rivulets down her anguished face. Her hands were clutched tightly under her chin, as if holding back a tirade of emotion that was threatening to break loose.

Looking to his father, he saw an equal though opposite reaction. Ethan could tell by his clenched fists and grinding jaw that Paul was only barely containing his anger, obviously outraged at the hefty price they'd had to pay. His control finally slipped, and through gritted teeth, he swore. "How dare they! You're *Burkes*, for fuck's sake! Magic is part of who you are, and the reason you four were specifically chosen for this task!"

Mary's broken voice countered her husband's fury. "Why would they do that?" Her hands shook as she gestured towards her children. "Why would they demand such a thing of you?

Haven't you all given enough in the past twenty-five years? Your childhoods, your freedoms, the innocence of youth? You've done *everything* they've asked."

Anna rose and went to their parents, wrapping an arm around each of them. "We were given a choice," Anna said softly. "We didn't *have* to do this. But knowing what he's become, upon truly understanding his hatred and depravity and the depths he'd go to for power, we all agreed that Noor could not be allowed out into the world. The cost of losing our magic—though high—was still nothing in comparison to the destruction that would result if we hadn't. As hard as it was to give up our gifts, the alternative would have been unthinkable, and we made the right choice."

In the end, their parents understood. It wouldn't be easy for any of them, but together, they'd learn how to live with their decision.

Ethan was driving Honor back home a short while later. She'd been quiet since they'd come back from fighting Noor. Her silence was starting to worry him.

She was staring out the side window as the scenery sped by. It shocked him to see tears trailing down her face.

He reached across the seat and ran a hand up and down her arm. "Baby, what is it? What's wrong?"

"I still can't believe what they made you give up." Her words were aimed at the door.

Ethan cast her a quick look. "And I'd do it again if I had to."

Turmoil dimmed her usually bright eyes when she turned to face him. "And I am so proud of you for that. For the choice you made. What you did was truly selfless. You lost a part of yourself to make sure the world stayed safe for the rest of us. That's incredible, Ethan. But I also know how big a piece of you your magic was. I know what being a Burke meant to you. I'm just sad it had to come to that."

He reached out and took her hand in his. "I did give it up

to save everyone else. But there was another reason. A bigger one." Ethan pulled off to the shoulder of the road. He didn't want any distractions when they had this conversation.

"When we were asked to make that sacrifice, I knew there wasn't anything I wouldn't do to spend the rest of my life with you. I'd made so many bad decisions since the night of the fire that took you away from me—ones I'd made for all the wrong reasons. Well this one, I made for most right reason of all. *Love.* And as long as you're willing to have me, I refuse to live without you again. With Noor gone for good and Cabot out of the picture, I know you're safe, and I don't regret for one minute what I did."

The anxiety he'd seen in her lessened. "I just hope one day you don't look back and wish you'd done it differently."

"How could I, when the decision I made was the right one?"

She took a deep breath, and her shoulders relaxed. When she looked up at him with a new hope in her eyes, Ethan leaned across the seat and kissed her beautiful mouth.

And for the first time in a long time, was completely and totally happy.

<div align="center">~~~</div>

In the weeks that followed their battle with Noor, Ethan learned to live without his magic. Just as his brother and sisters were doing. It wasn't easy, but that was the choice they'd made.

So here they were, just regular humans.

Anna seemed to be having the most trouble making the adjustment, as she'd used her gifts on a daily basis to help the children she taught. What got her through it, though, was that she knew enough about them already to know what their struggles were. She was able to balance that with her skill as a teacher and continue to give them exactly what they needed.

Every time it got to be too much for Ethan, he'd remind himself that he would get to live out a normal life with the woman of his dreams. It made the situation infinitely more bearable.

He turned his mind back to what needed to get done today. Ethan still had a little left to finish on a client's deck, and Honor was interviewing with local shelters. She'd told him how much she loved the work she'd been doing in Louisiana and wanted to continue it here. She was out this morning meeting with the heads of those shelters to see about volunteering.

But later, he'd have his love all to himself.

Their life together was finally beginning, and Ethan couldn't be happier. They'd even begun to look for a house. He was almost giddy to be starting the rest of his life with the woman he loved more than life itself.

By afternoon, he was back home and walking into his bathroom to get cleaned up. He stripped out of his clothes and started the shower. Catching sight of his reflection in the mirror, he saw the bare spot on his chest where his mark used to be. He still remembered its exact shape and traced where the outer circle would have been with a single fingertip.

It was hard not possessing active magic any longer. He hadn't used it much in his everyday life, but he'd known it was there when he'd needed it. Another drawback of their decision was that he and his siblings could no longer speak telepathically. They'd only had that ability for a short time, but it was one they'd relied on to always keep in close contact.

But despite it all, Ethan was still proud of the choice they'd made. Given the chance to do it all over again, he wouldn't change a thing.

Ten minutes later, he was stepping out, wet and naked. He'd just reached for a towel to dry himself off when he found himself gathered on the same stretch of beach with his siblings. Suddenly worried about his state of undress, he glanced down quickly and saw that he was wearing clothes.

Thank God. That could have been embarrassing.

Ethan idly wondered what everyone had been doing when they'd suddenly fallen asleep. "I hope no one was driving when we got pulled here."

"I was at my desk," Evan filled in. "I'll probably get razzed for sleeping on the job."

"I'm in my studio," Aria said.

Anna was last. "In my classroom. Hopefully my kids don't take advantage of my inattention."

"Your students are great." Aria grinned. "I'm sure they'll entertain themselves for however long we'll be here."

"Fear not, my children," Iris said as she appeared with them. "Only a blink of time will have passed when you return."

"Why were we brought here, Iris?" Anna stepped forward. "Is there more we need to do?"

"No, my dears. We wanted to give our thanks for what you've already done. The sacrifice you've made will benefit generations to come. And as a token of our gratitude, we wanted to bestow a gift."

"That's not necessary, Iris." Aria's blue eyes were sincere. "He was a threat to all of us. We did what had to be done."

"We don't need anything." Anna backed up her twin. "Knowing everyone is safe is enough for us."

"And still more reason why all of you are so worthy. Please take our thanks, and know that you are loved and appreciated. Blessed be, my children."

With that, she was gone. But where she'd stood now hovered the same ball of energy that had finished Noor all those weeks before.

"No way," Evan said in awe.

The colors split into four, reforming into their individual elemental marks, and moved to float just in front of their hosts. A white star followed each one.

Not sure of what to do, Ethan went with instinct and held his arms out to his sides, opening himself up. After a brief moment, the fire that had been a part of him for so long returned home, and he felt a warmth on his chest where his mark had now appeared. Out of the corner of his eye, he saw the rest of his quad-mates accept their magic back.

"I can't believe this." Anna called her water and let it flow and ribbon around her fingers. Aria summoned the air and had it lifting and tugging at her hair. Evan had pieces of the earth dancing in his palm.

Ethan took a moment to bask in the power that filled him. His fire and his telekinesis—old friends dearly missed. He opened his hand and with only a thought, had a ball of fire rolling and blazing over his palm.

Whole and complete, Ethan knew the rest of their lives, and the lives of their children, would be forever blessed.

~~~

He was waiting for Honor when she came home. He could see by the light in her eyes that her interviews had gone well.

"They loved you, didn't they?" He grinned as he took her into his arms as soon as the door closed behind her.

She beamed up into his face. "Pretty much."

"When do you start?" Ethan kissed the end of her nose, barely containing his own good news.

"Next week." Honor drew back a little and really looked at him. She narrowed her eyes. "You have a look on your face I can't quite figure out. What did you do?"

Ethan chuckled. "I didn't do anything." He paused to drag it out. "We had another visit from Iris today."

"Oh, God. What did she want?"

He distracted himself with her long, slender neck, bending to lick from her shoulder to her ear. She shuddered in his arms.
~~~

"Ethan, stop. This is serious. What did she want?"

"Loving you is *always* serious." He nibbled on her lobe. "She wanted to thank us for a job well done." Honor's breathing hitched and stuttered, and Ethan smiled against her silky skin.

"Oh…ah…was that all?" Her head lolled to the side, giving him better access.

Who was he to not take advantage when she offered? He feasted on her, sucking lightly and nipping at her with his teeth.

"No," he said when he lifted his lips away from her. "That's not all." He switched sides and dedicated himself to giving equal attention to the other side of her neck.

"What…mmm," she hummed deep in her throat. "What… what else?"

Ethan stepped away from her and felt love swell when she swayed on her feet. He slowly reached up and began to unbutton his shirt. Her eyes were glued to every move he made. Completely open, he slid it off his right shoulder and down his arm. She greedily took in the exposed skin.

Next was the left side. As it revealed the upper part of his chest, she gasped and darted forward.

"Oh, my God." She reverently touched the birthmark which had been missing since that fateful day. "Your powers." Gray eyes speared into his. "She returned your magic."

Ethan lit a small flame in his palm as his mark flared to life. "Yeah, she did."

"Oh, Ethan." Honor leaned forward and placed a soft kiss in the center of the glowing symbol. Ethan's heart did a flip in his chest, and he groaned with need.

Reaching down, he grabbed her behind the knees and lifted her so her legs could wrap around his waist. He stared into her face a moment before lowering his head to seal her pouty lips to his.

Honor's arms went around his neck and her fingers threaded

through his hair at the back of his neck. She gripped it in a tight fist and held him there. The kiss was scorching, and a fine layer of sweat broke out over Ethan's body.

His need for her was so strong and so immediate, he didn't think he'd last very long. He needed her here. Now.

Turning with her still in his arms, Ethan bent and laid her on the couch. Following, he settled his larger and harder body over hers.

Her hands slid to his face, and she rubbed his whiskers with her palms just as she'd always done. Ethan's heart faltered. It was a little thing, but he'd missed it so dearly.

"I need you, E. No one's ever stirred me the way you do. I couldn't understand why I wasn't interested in any of the men around me. I do now. I may not have known about you during my amnesia, but my body remembered, and it knew there was no one else for me but you."

"I was dead inside until you came back to me. You were, and are, my one and only love."

Ethan leaned in and kissed her tenderly. All the love he was feeling poured out of him through the kiss. Her hands stayed on his face, her thumbs resting at the corners of his mouth.

Honor shifted underneath him, making room so he could rest against her core. The intense heat of her radiated through the pants she wore to brand him through his own.

Bracing himself, Ethan rose to his knees. Grasping the hem of her shirt, he lifted it up and off. Her blue lace bra was next. When she was bared to him, he zeroed straight in on her high round breasts. Taking one in hand, he took the other into his mouth to roll her pebbled nipple with his tongue.

Her back arched up, offering more of herself to him.

At the same time, her hand found its way down his abdomen. She made quick work of the fly and had her fingers closed so tightly around him, his breath caught in his chest.

Ethan had to raise his head to drag air into his lungs. "Jesus, baby."

Honor grinned up at him and squeezed again.

"Fuck," he panted. "You keep doing that, and it'll be over before it begins."

"Then finish getting us naked, because I can't take much more either."

Ethan didn't waste any time. Naked and ready, he came back to her, grasping his shaft and guiding it into her hot, wet core. Sliding in was always the sweetest torture. Muscles gave way reluctantly, clutching him firmly and driving him to the edge.

He fought to control his urges when all he wanted was to slam into her and fill her up. He pushed forward another inch, and she mewled softly.

"Ethan. Please. You're killing me."

Retreating a little, he flexed his hips and surged into her until he was buried to the hilt. He swore and she gasped.

As much as it pained him, he stilled, giving her a moment to adjust to the size of him, while he concentrated on not exploding into her.

When he felt her hips begin to swivel and raise, searching for more of him, he began to move.

The trip out was just as mind-blowing as the inward thrust had been. The walls of her sex pulled at him, fighting his retreat, before he once again pushed back inside. Long, slow strokes. In and out. In and out. Ethan was lost in her.

And she him. Honor's gray eyes were closed, and her white teeth bit into her full lower lip. She moaned with every move he made.

Ethan knew exactly what drove her crazy. Reaching down between them, he rubbed over the swollen nub between her legs.

And as he loved her, he knew she was nearing orgasm. Her eyes flew open, and her legs shook around him. When her body clamped down on his cock, Ethan let go. Her channel spasmed, sucking and clenching at him until he had nothing left.

Spent and winded, Ethan collapsed. Rolling to the side, he pulled her into his body and held her close.

"We're both whole again," he murmured. "And exactly where we were always meant to be."

Epilogue

Ethan had chosen his weapons. He gripped them tightly in his hands, waiting for the moment to strike his nemesis. He was ducked down behind a table, eyes scanning. There. His target was sneaking around the end of the house. Trying to get the drop on him.

When his unsuspecting victim was within range, Ethan let fly his bomb.

Jacob shouted as the water balloon hit and exploded dead center of his chest. He acted out an exaggerated death scene before falling to the ground in a fit of giggles.

Ethan was so tickled by his nephew's antics, he didn't see the missile coming for him until it soaked him from the shoulder down.

He turned to see Honor doubled over laughing. They'd tricked him, using Jake as a distraction while the sneaky woman lay in wait for him to break cover. He couldn't let this pass. He stalked slowly towards his wife.

"Uh-oh," she muttered, the smile faltering from her sexy mouth as she jumped to her feet to run.

Using his telekinesis, Ethan lifted her right off the ground. She dangled and kicked but hung there, trapped.

"Hey. No fair," she shouted at him, but he only grinned.

"All's fair in love and war, baby."

"A little help here, guys?" Honor pleaded with the rest of her teammates.

Before Ethan could take another step, he was bombarded with water balloons from all sides. Evan, Anna, and their dad pelted him mercilessly. Until his own crew of Aria, Seth, Joe, and Mom came to his rescue.

It was a pitched battle that waged until all ammunition had been exhausted. Only then did they call a truce to eat and grab something to drink. Soaked and laughing, they descended on the table where Kyra sat with her and Evan's one-month-old daughter, Sabrina Iris Burke.

Aria and Seth were giggling at the end of the table as they took in each other's battle scars. Aria was drenched from head to toe, her just-blossoming baby bump accentuated by her wet t-shirt. Seth only sported evidence of a single water bomb. His shorts were soggy from the waist down, making him appear to have wet himself.

Finding seats, they dug into the food his mom and sisters had prepared for this Fourth of July celebration. As everyone joked and ate and laughed, Ethan took a moment to bask in how lucky they all were. They had all found their soulmates to grow old with, and the next line of Burke witches was well on its way, both of his sisters expecting within just a few weeks of each other. He and Honor had decided to wait while she got her degree in psychology.

Whatever children came, they would never know the evil that had once plagued and stalked them for so long. They would grow and thrive and continue on for generations to come.

Ethan couldn't wait to see what the world had in store for them. But no matter what it was, they'd take it on, because they were Burkes and would always have each other.

He caught the eye of each of his siblings. They all shared a knowing smile, as if they too understood what he was thinking. Sentimental grins and adoring gazes passed over all the members of their now-extended family.

And four elemental marks glowed softly in the peace and love of a prophecy finally laid to rest.

Misha McKenzie has been an avid reader since learning how at four years old. Countless books later, she still loves to immerse herself into the lives of the people within those pages. After graduating high school, she went on to earn a degree in Business Administration, married her high school sweetheart, and had two beautiful boys. At thirty years old, while working as an office manager for a construction company, a family of witches began to brew, and The Magic of the Heart Series was born.

www.ingramcontent.com/pod-product-compliance
Lightning Source LLC
Chambersburg PA
CBHW051645180726
48284CB00006B/1865